ALL SHE WANTED WAS HER
FREEDOM—TILL HE
CAPTURED HER
HEART.

P9-DYD-233

OUTLAW'S BRIDE

"Intrigue and passion, combined with a tender love story, make this one delicious, and the subplots promise us closer looks at her riveting characters in future books."—*Rendezvous*

"ONE OF THE FINEST WESTERN ROMANCE NOVELISTS."—*Rave Reviews*

KID CALHOUN

"4+ Hearts! Powerful and moving . . . Joan Johnston has cleverly merged the aura of the Americana-style romance with the grittier westerns she has written in the past, making *KID CALHOUN* into a feast for all her fans. This irresistible love story once again ensures Ms. Johnston a place in readers' hearts and on their 'keeper' shelves."—*Romantic Times*

"UNFORGETTABLE . . . A TOUCHING TAPESTRY."
—*Affaire de Coeur*

"This most enjoyable western is packed with spunky women, tough men, rotten bad guys and ornery kids . . . just the ingredients for a fine read."
—*Heartland Critiques*

*Available from Dell Publishing

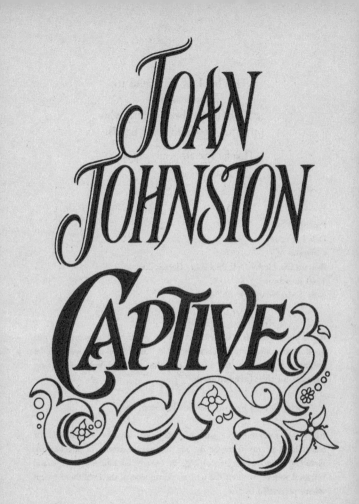

JOAN JOHNSTON

CAPTIVE

A Dell Book

This book is dedicated to
my readers,
and to all the booksellers who
put my books in their hands.

Thanks for all your support.

Published by
Dell Publishing
a division of
Bantam Doubleday Dell Publishing Group, Inc.
1540 Broadway
New York, New York 10036

ISBN: 0-440-22200-1

Printed in the United States of America

Published simultaneously in Canada

May 1996

10 9 8 7 6 5 4 3 2

Prologue

THE BRIDE WAS LATE. THE GUESTS WERE starting to whisper. Lionel Morgan, Earl of Denbigh, stood waiting near the altar of St. George's in London with his best friend and groomsman, Percival Porter, Viscount Burton, who also happened to be the bride's elder brother.

"Where is she, Percy?" Denbigh asked. "What do you suppose is causing the delay?"

"You know the ladies, Lion. It takes them an eternity to dress themselves. Alice hasn't been on time for anything in her entire life. She was even born two weeks late. You cannot expect a rare bird like Alice to change her feathers simply because she is getting married." Percy smiled and gave Denbigh a friendly cuff on the shoulder. "Be patient. It cannot be long now."

"I hope not," Denbigh muttered. He resisted the urge to stick his finger between his cravat and his throat and yank. The starched, intricately tied neck cloth seemed to have tightened in the hour he had been waiting for Lady Alice to arrive.

A commotion in the vestry attracted Denbigh's attention. Heads swiveled in the congregation to see what was amiss. It took Denbigh only a moment to recognize the Marquis of Peterborough, Percy and Alice's father, and another moment to see that the marchioness was hanging on his sleeve, trying vainly to stop him.

"She's bolted!" Peterborough said, his voice echoing off the church's high ceiling as he marched down the aisle toward Denbigh. He shook a piece of crumpled parchment—apparently a note from Alice—in Denbigh's face. "The foolish chit has run away. She says she will not marry you."

The wedding guests gave a collective gasp and began to whisper in earnest, creating a buzzing sound not unlike a nest of hornets.

Denbigh felt his skin prickle. His heart pounded in his chest as adrenaline laced his blood. He was having difficulty grasping the enormity of the catastrophe that had befallen him. The woman he loved—the woman he had believed loved him—had run away rather than marry him.

He turned to Percy in disbelief. "Percy? How . . . ? Why . . . ? Did Alice say anything to you, give any clue that she was unhappy with the match?"

Percy stared back at him. "I am as shocked as you are, Lion. There must be some good explanation for Alice's behavior, but I cannot imagine what it is." He turned with a confused look to his parents. "What does her note say, Father?"

"Please, may we go somewhere private?" Lady Peterborough begged. "There has already been scandal enough to keep tongues wagging for three lifetimes."

Denbigh glanced up, square into the gawking face of Lady Hornby, a notorious gossip. That flustered lady quickly hid her face behind an ivory fan, but as Denbigh's narrowed eyes scoured the pews, he found as many smirks as he did expressions of sympathy. He had never considered himself a proud man, but he was a private one. Today his pain and humiliation had been laid bare for the *ton*.

He felt cold, as though his warm, pulsating heart had ceased pumping blood to his extremities. He hardly noticed Percy ushering all of them into a nearby room used by the clergy. He saw, as from a distance, Percy retrieve the crumpled note from his father and spread it out to read what it contained.

"She does not say where she is going, precisely," Percy announced. "Only that she is going somewhere she cannot be found. And that she is sorry for any pain she has caused."

"I have to find her," Denbigh said. "I must speak with her."

"I would not advise it, my friend," Percy said gently. "Nothing good can come of such an interview."

"I don't care!" Denbigh said in an agonized voice. "I have to know why she ran away." He fought the lump in his throat as he met Percy's pitying gaze. "I love her, Percy. I'd have her even now."

Percy hesitated another moment before he said, "Very well, Lion. We shall go after her."

"I'll go alone," Denbigh said.

"I cannot let you do that," Percy said, shaking his blond head. "The gel may be in disgrace, but she is my sister and still an unmarried lady. If you're going to meet with her, she should have family nearby to protect her."

"I mean her no harm," Denbigh said.

"I believe you," Percy said. "But I shall come with you, all the same."

Percy made his farewell to his parents and promised to bring Alice home if—when—they found her.

"No," the marchioness said. "Not back to London, Percy. Take her to the summer house near Brighton."

"Very well, Mother," Percy said. "I will take

her to the manor in Sussex. But I can tell you Alice won't like being sent off to molder in the country."

"I don't much care what Alice wants at this point," the marquis retorted. "Do as your mother says."

"Yes, Father."

Denbigh's face felt stiff as he said his formal adieus to the marquis and his wife, who both avoided his stormy gray eyes.

"Is there some way out of here that does not require going back through the church?" Denbigh asked the clergyman who had hovered in the background.

"There is a back way out, my lord. Follow me, if you please."

Once Lion and Percy began the search, it wasn't difficult to trace Alice's movements. She had borrowed one of her father's town coaches that bore his coat of arms and taken her maid with her. The coach had headed south, toward Peterborough Manor in Sussex near Brighton. It was as though she expected to be followed. As though she wanted to be found.

Denbigh wanted to follow immediately, without taking time to change out of his wedding clothes, but Percy and reason prevailed.

"You will be a spectacle tooling along the road in velvet and satin. And I refuse to muddy this perfectly fitted Weston. I had the devil of a time convincing him to make a coat for me in precisely this shade of yellow.''

"Very well,'' Denbigh conceded. "I will meet you at the Boar and Hound in an hour.''

"An hour? Impossible!'' Percy protested.

"An hour.''

Denbigh reached the tavern that sat at the cross-roads of the New Road leading south out of London—the shortest route to Brighton and the one in the best condition—long before the hour was up. Dressed in a bottle-green riding coat and buckskins, he paced restlessly in one of the private dining rooms, his Wellingtons drumming on the floor-boards as he waited for Percy to appear. At five minutes after the appointed time, he left the tavern and stepped into his curricle.

"Tell Lord Burton I had to leave,'' he told the hostler who had been walking his prize pair of chest-nuts. "He can catch up to me on the road.''

Along the New Road, Denbigh made stops to inquire whether a carriage with the Peterborough coat of arms had passed that way before him. At each change of horses, he asked the hostler to point Lord Burton in his direction.

He had followed Alice's trail south from London for four hours when he came to the Duck and Goose, a small inn at a crossroad running east and west. He stopped to ask if anyone had seen Lady

Alice, unwilling to take the chance that he might lose her at such a turning point.

"Why, the lady's upstairs as we speak, milord," the innkeeper said. "Broke a wheel on that fancy carriage of hers a few miles farther down the road. Came back here to wait. Smithy's fixin' it now."

"Which is her room?"

The innkeeper rubbed his hand across his chin. "Who might you be? Maybe the lady won't be wantin' to be seeing the likes of you."

Denbigh could have offered the man money. That was obviously what the innkeeper was after in exchange for his information. Lion hadn't the patience for subtleties. He grabbed a handful of the man's linsey-woolsey shirt, lifted him to his toes, and demanded, "What room?"

"First one at the top of the stairs, milord," the innkeeper bleated.

Lion took the stairs two at a time, raised his fist to pound on the door and hesitated, uncertain of what he would say—more afraid of what he might do—when she opened the door. He had not previously acknowledged his anger, but it simmered under the cool surface expected of a pink of the *ton*.

He wasn't entirely sure whether, when he saw Alice standing before him, her guinea-gold curls stacked high atop her head to add inches to her petite stature, her dewy blue eyes glancing shyly up at him from beneath long black lashes, his first inclination would be to kiss her——or to throttle her.

He should have waited for Percy.

He could not wait another moment.

He gave the door two soft raps, and it opened instantly, revealing the frantic features of Alice's maid.

"Oh, thank the good lord you've come." The young woman's face was streaked with tears, her brown eyes dark with distress. She reached out as though to grab him, then seemed to realize who he was, and that she couldn't very well drag a lord of the realm inside by his lapels. "Come, quickly," she said, then backed away toward the bed, leaving him standing in the open doorway.

Lion stepped inside the tiny room, with its sloping ceiling and sparse, cheap furnishings, and closed the door behind him. He had endured quite enough of airing his dirty linen in public. Whatever he and Alice had to say to each other would be said without an audience.

It didn't take more than one look to realize that Alice was in no condition to say anything to anyone. She was lying fully dressed atop the bed in what he could only guess from the elaborate layers of pale blue satin and French lace was her wedding dress. Her eyes were closed, her hands folded across her chest. Her face was nearly white, her lips as pale as death.

For a moment he thought she was dead. He crossed to her side with a feeling of horror that this could not possibly be happening. Then he saw the sheen of perspiration on her forehead and above her bowed lip. Not dead, thank God. But very close to it.

"What's wrong with her?" he demanded.

"She's taken too much," the maid sobbed, wringing her hands. "I tried to stop her, but she swallowed it all."

"All of what?"

"The laudanum, milord. An entire bottle." The maid pointed to an empty glass bottle on the nightstand.

Lion picked it up and sniffed. The sickly sweet odor of laudanum assailed his nostrils. He hurled the bottle against the brick fireplace at the foot of the bed, where it shattered. "Damn her!"

The maid cowered against the wall, acting more like an accomplice, than an innocent witness.

"What is it you aren't telling me?" he demanded.

"Nothing, milord! I know nothing."

He was certain she knew more than she was saying, but he could not spare the time to question her further.

He lifted Alice by her shoulders and tried to get her to her feet. She was as limp as a child's rag doll. "Come on, Alice. Wake up." He slapped her cheeks, but her eyes remained closed. As she slumped against him, nearly lifeless, he felt an uncontrollable rage.

Because he was afraid she was going to die.

Because he could not live his life without her.

He shook her hard to wake her up, but her head flopped on her shoulders. She made no sound. "Please, Alice," he begged in her ear. "Please try to live."

He turned to look for the maid and found her staring back at him in terror. "What is your name?" he asked.

"S-Sally, milord."

"Go find a doctor, Sally."

She stood frozen, apparently too frightened to move.

"Go!" he bellowed.

The young woman fled as though the hounds of hell were chasing her.

Lion slid an arm around Alice's waist and pulled her upright and walked her—hauled her—around the room, trying to get her blood moving. Because she was unconscious, he was afraid to make her vomit up the drug, for fear she would choke to death. He did not know what else to do.

"I love you, Alice. I don't understand what went wrong, but we can fix it together. Please don't leave me." He repeated the words endlessly, because they were all he could think to say.

He wasn't sure when her spirit left her, but eventually her body lost its warmth. Finally, he had to acknowledge she was dead.

A sob broke free, and he choked back another that threatened to follow it.

He lifted her into his arms and laid her out on the bed, once again placing her arms across her chest. She looked as though she were sleeping peacefully. As he stared down at her, a knot grew in his throat, making it painful to swallow.

He was furious with her for wasting her life like this. Angry enough to kill her.

But she was already dead.

The door opened, and the maid appeared. "The doctor is on his way, milord."

"He's too late," Lion rasped. "She's dead."

"Oh, no," the maid cried, throwing herself across the lifeless body of her mistress. "Oh, milady, no! No!"

Lion leaned his head back against the wall of the dingy inn and let the woman weep the tears he had refused to shed.

Why had Alice killed herself? What had he done to disappoint her? If she had not loved him, why had she not said something to him? Why, Alice? Why?

That was the question that went round and round in his head. The worst of it was, he would never know why, because she had ended her life without giving him a chance to ask. The answers he sought would go with her to the grave.

Unless she left a note.

The idea came into his mind unbidden, and he tried to squelch it because he was afraid to let himself hope. But he had to know. He asked the maid, "Did she leave a note for me?"

"She wrote one, milord," the maid said. "But then . . ." She broke into sobs. "But then . . ."

Denbigh grabbed Sally by the shoulders and shook her. "Where is it?"

"She burned it."

Denbigh gave a cry of anguish and let her go. It was too much to bear. Not to know. Never to know. Glass crunched underfoot as he crossed to the fireplace and stared into the licking flames that had stolen the explanation for this tragedy.

The fire felt hot against his buckskins, but he stood rooted to the spot. He could not bear to turn and look at Alice's body. He wanted to pretend for a little while longer that none of this was really happening.

Lion did not believe his eyes at first, when he spied the piece of half-burned parchment lying at the back of the grate. He knew there was very little possibility it was the letter Alice had written to him. If Alice had intended to burn the note, she would have made certain the fire consumed it. But the longer he stared at the remnant of charred paper, the more irresistible became the urge to reach into the fireplace and pluck it out.

What if that fragment of paper actually is Alice's note? What if it holds the answers to all my questions?

He reached out, unconscious of the fire searing his wrist as he plucked the scrap of paper from where it had fallen behind the grate. It crackled as he unfolded it, and ashes blackened his hands as portions of the burned parchment disintegrated.

His heart began thumping wildly as he recognized Alice's handwriting. *"My dearest darling Lion,"* the letter began.

Tears stung his nose. He closed his eyes, afraid to read farther. How could she have started a letter with those words, if she had not loved him? If she had loved him, why had she taken her own life?

Behind his closed eyelids, a picture rose of Alice's face the last time she had said those words to him. When he had left her at the front door of her parents' London town house the previous evening, he had kissed her hand, and then, emboldened by the adoring look in her eyes, touched her lips with his.

She had lowered her eyelids and blushed at the intimacy she had allowed him and said in a voice so soft he had needed to bend down to hear her, "My dearest darling Lion, I do love you. Always remember that."

He had wondered at the time why she had

added those last few words. It had not made much sense at the time. Now it did. She must have contemplated abandoning him at the altar even as she pledged her love. She must have been considering the drastic step she had taken even then.

But why?

He opened his eyes and forced himself to read on. He clenched his teeth to keep himself from crying out in anguish as her letter revealed the truth. Part of the note was gone. Some of her reasons he would never know. But he knew enough.

He knew too much.

He made an animal sound in his throat as he crushed the letter in his fist. It was no accident she had overdosed on laudanum. She had purposely killed herself.

He thrust his clenched fist toward the maid, who recoiled as though he had threatened her with a handful of snakes. "Do you know what this says?" he demanded.

The maid's eyes went wide with fear at the violence in his voice. "I cannot read, milord."

Lion stared at her a moment longer before he threw the crumpled parchment into the fire. "Tell Lord Burton when he arrives that I have returned to London."

He turned on his booted heel and left the room, his tears dried in streaks upon his cheeks, his heart no longer a thing of flesh and blood, but cast forever in stone.

1

"Is that your sister I see riding neck-or-nothing over the fields like some hoyden?" Lady Frockman asked. "I thought you said she was crippled."

"She is." The Earl of Denbigh peered out the window of his town coach to identify the rider Lady Frockman had pointed out on a distant grassy hill. "Evidently Olivia has learned to ride again since last I saw her."

"When was that?" Lady Frockman asked.

The earl frowned. "Six months, at least." He would not be going home now if it were not for the series of indignant letters he had received from his neighbor, Mrs. Killington, the squire's wife, begging him to come take charge of his new American ward, Lady Charlotte Edgerton. It seemed the chit refused to be bound by convention and was upsetting the entire neighborhood with her outlandish activities.

He had come to Denbigh Castle to admonish his ward and ensure that any bizarre behavior she engaged in would cease. Not that he put much credence in the unbelievable tales Mrs. Killington's letters had told. No seventeen-year-old girl could possibly have done all the things Mrs. Killington had accused her of doing—driving a cow up the steps into church, dressing up in a sheet like a ghost and scaring the squire half to death, inviting the crofters' children to pick flowers in the earl's rose garden, and, to add insult to injury, using the squire's pumpkins for target practice with her bow and arrow.

He had decided that the best course of action was to marry the girl off as quickly as possible. Then she would become some other man's problem.

"Who is that with your sister?" Lady Frockman asked.

"It appears to be a country gentleman," the earl said in a cool voice.

Lady Frockman *tsk*ed. "And nary a chaperon in sight. Who knows what might happen to your sister under such unseemly circumstances?"

The earl arched a brow. "That's the pot calling the kettle black, Claudia."

Lady Frockman smiled in amusement. "But, Lion, *I* have no reputation to be ruined."

"True," the earl agreed. Claudia had been his mistress for the past four months, and it had been a satisfying relationship for both of them. It was a month longer than he had stayed with either of his two previous mistresses over the past year. Denbigh had employed the fair sex for only one use since his catastrophic wedding barely a year past. When a woman ceased to please him—or began to importune him—he parted company with her.

Although Lady Frockman was a widow and could expect to marry again, she had been careful not to press him for any future commitment, or to make demands of any sort, for that matter. She had been content with the expensive jewelry he lavished on her and the notoriety of being seen in his company.

Denbigh's silvery gray eyes narrowed as he watched the two riders racing toward the house which, thanks to a long-ago generation of forebears who had added crenels along the top and turrets at each of the four corners, looked a great deal like a castle. The hollowed-out square, a three-story stone structure, featured a central courtyard with a magnificent rose garden.

Ivy climbed the walls, softening the harsh look of the place. But perched high on a cliff overlooking the sea, Denbigh Castle was always cold and drafty. When the wind whistled through the windows at night, the old house sounded as though it were filled with ghostly spirits.

Denbigh's gaze skipped from the house back to the riders. The young man riding with Olivia had excellent taste in horseflesh, Denbigh would grant him that. The gentleman's black stallion was a powerful animal and fast as the wind. His sister's Thoroughbred was having difficulty keeping up with the beast. Nevertheless, he intended to give the young buck a stern warning for daring to seek out the company of the Earl of Denbigh's only sister without the earl's consent.

The earl's carriage reached the front door to Denbigh Castle a few moments before the riders. The earl had barely stepped down from the carriage, and had not yet helped Lady Frockman out, when the black brute nearly ran him down. The young man hauled back so hard on the reins the stallion reared, and Denbigh lurched backward to avoid being trampled. A moment later the rider was off the stallion and standing before him begging his pardon.

"I'm very sorry, sir. Mephistopheles doesn't like to lose. Sometimes it's difficult to make him realize when the race is over."

Denbigh didn't believe his ears. Or his eyes. What stood before him was not a young man, but a young lady. Her voice was husky, and it rasped over him, making his neck hairs stand on end. The hips—revealed by a pair of tight-fitting breeches—

and breasts—outlined by a thin lawn shirt whipped tight against her bosom by the sharp wind off the sea—were definitely female.

But she acted like no lady he had ever known.

She had been riding astride that huge brute of a stallion. She stood before him now with her hands on her hips, her legs widespread like a man, and looked him directly in the eye without a trace of embarrassment at her woefully indiscreet attire.

Her small nose was freckled. No wonder, riding in the sun without a hat. Her hair was golden and tied back in a queue that had hidden its length from him at first. Wispy blond tendrils framed a feminine, heart-shaped face. Green cat's eyes stared at him with open, honest curiosity, and a square chin dared him to . . . to what? Say something? Anything?

He could not have spoken to save his life. He still could not quite believe his eyes. This had to be his ward. Maybe Mrs. Killington was not so crazy, after all.

His sister joined them, but she remained mounted sidesaddle on her mare, wearing a perfectly respectable frog-trimmed velvet riding habit. At least she had not been corrupted by this imp of Satan.

"Lion! We didn't expect you," Olivia said.

"Obviously not," he replied. "I didn't know you had taken up riding again, Olivia."

She flushed. "Oh. Well. Charlie said she didn't see any reason why I couldn't. She said I shouldn't let my fears keep me earthbound, so to speak. So I tried it, and I can," she said, shrugging as though to make light of what she had accomplished.

Lion raised a disdainful brow. "Charlie?"

"Lady Charlotte," Olivia quickly amended. "I sent you a letter when she arrived here, Lion. You must have gotten it."

"I did." *Four months ago.* He had been appointed as guardian for the girl until she married or reached the age of one and twenty, whichever came first. He had ignored this unwelcome responsibility as long as possible. Obviously, it—she—could no longer be ignored.

Lion stared down at the pixielike urchin standing across from him who had convinced his sister— who had taken such a terrible spill during a hunt eight years ago that it had left her with an awkward limp—to get back on a horse. Not only to get back on, but to gallop neck-or-nothing as she had when she was a carefree girl. It was nothing short of a miracle.

"As happy as I am for you, Olivia, I must ask what you two ladies were doing out riding without a chaperon."

"We only went to the village and back," Olivia said.

"Good lord," Denbigh said.

"It appears things are every bit as bad as Mrs. Killington suggested," Lady Frockman interjected with a laugh.

"A few changes will be necessary," Denbigh agreed. "Olivia, take your horse to the stable, then go to your room."

"Yes, Lion," she said dutifully.

His new ward started to follow her, but Denbigh said, "Not you. I have a few more things to say to you first."

The girl's head cocked like a small bird's as she eyed him speculatively. "Since you're Livy's brother, I suppose you must be my guardian," she said. "You don't look as old as I thought you would, sir. I mean, for a man of your age. Twenty-nine is practically ancient."

Denbigh's jaw tightened at her impertinence.

"She's delightfully frank, Lion," Lady Frockman said with a laugh. "And right, of course."

Denbigh gave Claudia an icy look that silenced her. He turned back to the girl and said, "My age is not at issue here. And you may address me as 'Lord Denbigh' or 'my lord.' "

"My friends call me Charlie," the girl replied with a smile that was as guileless as it was enchanting.

"Charlie is a boy's name," he said in his most

disapproving voice. "I will address you as 'Lady Charlotte.' "

"I wish you wouldn't," she said, the smile replaced by a frown that made him feel like a churl. "I'm not an English lady. I'm an American."

"Your father was Lord Edgerton, was he not?"

"I suppose he was. But that was a long time ago, before he moved to New Orleans, before he married my mother, before I was born. There aren't any lords and ladies in America, only common folk. Couldn't you just call me Charlie?"

"No female ward of mine is going to be called *Charlie* in public or in private," he said in a withering voice.

"Good!" she retorted. "Because I don't want to be your ward. You can put me on the next ship back to America and make us both happy." She turned and threw herself onto the stallion's back in a movement of strength and grace that so astonished him he didn't even try to stop her.

She looked down at him and said, "I'm glad you finally came, so you could see I don't belong here. I have friends in America who would be delighted to let me live with them. Please leave enough money with your steward to pay my passage back to New Orleans. You can keep the rest of my fortune until I'm ready for it."

He realized she was turning her horse to leave without waiting to be excused by him. Nowhere in her speech had there been a single "Lord Denbigh" or "my lord." In fact, she had forgone the "sir," as well. He was irritated at having been forced to make the trip to Sussex from London in the first place, worried at finding his sister out riding the country-side unchaperoned, and appalled at the sight of his ward attired in breeches. Being dismissed by her as though she were the one in charge was the last straw.

"Stop right there, Lady Charlotte," he commanded.

To his amazement, the chit jabbed her booted heels into the stallion's sides. If Lion's reflexes hadn't been quick, she would have been gone before he could stop her. If he hadn't been as strong as he was, the stallion would have run him down, instead of being yanked to an abrupt halt by his lightning quick grasp of the bridle.

The stallion curvetted and crowhopped, neighing his fury at the contradictory signals being given by the rider and the man on the ground. Denbigh was sure the girl would be bucked off, but she kept her seat, crooning to the animal until he stood docile at last.

"That was a terrible thing to do to Mephistoph-eles!" she accused.

"You shouldn't have tried to leave without my permission," Denbigh retorted.

"I don't need your permission to ride my horse."

"From now on you need my permission to do anything and everything you do."

"That's monstrous!"

Denbigh had been called a lot of things over the past year and had fought several duels as a consequence. He didn't have to listen to this spoiled American brat call him names.

He reached up and wrapped an arm around her waist, hauled her down from the saddle, and slung her over his shoulder like a sack of mangel-wurzels. Then he called to the coachman, "Take the reins, Henry, and return Lady Charlotte's mount to the stable. Make sure he's cooled down before you put him away."

"Yes, milord," Henry answered, eyeing the big black beast askance.

Of course, Lion said all this over the shrieks of the slender girl, who was kicking and wriggling and yelling like a banshee. He gave an inward sigh. The girl had a temper, and she wasn't afraid to display it. She was a far cry from the demure young lady he had expected to find. He experienced a sinking feeling as he realized no English gentleman would willingly pay court to such a hellion. He was likely going to be stuck with her for—God help him!—the next four years.

"What are you going to do with her, now that

you've got her?" Lady Frockman asked with an amused smile.

"Take her to her room, of course. Excuse me, Lady Frockman. Make yourself comfortable in the salon. I will join you shortly."

"I won't stay in my room!" the girl cried. "You can't make me obey you. I'll run away!"

Denbigh ignored her—insofar as that was possible—as he marched up the front steps.

Samuels, the butler, had apparently heard the commotion, because he opened the front door even before Denbigh reached it to knock.

"Thank you, Samuels," Lion said as he entered the massive tiled hallway. It opened onto a double set of curving marble stairs, each leading to a separate wing of the house.

"It's good to have you home, milord."

"Which is Lady Charlotte's room?" he asked.

"The Blue Room, milord," Samuels answered.

Denbigh headed up the left set of stairs, his boots muffled by the Persian carpet that covered them. The Blue Room had belonged to his mother. He was surprised that his housekeeper, Mrs. Tinsworthy, had allowed this American troublemaker to occupy it.

He realized, with chagrin, that if he slept in his father's room, as he usually did, she would be right next door. He hoped she did not plan to keep up her caterwauling all night. He had plans later in the evening for Lady Frockman that he did not want disturbed.

The girl wriggled so much that he nearly dropped her on the stairs. "Be still!" he roared.

She fell limp so suddenly he thought she had fainted. When he loosened his grasp to shift her in his arms, she jerked herself free. Before he could catch her, she tumbled head over heels down the carpeted stairs.

He took the stairs two at a time and caught her just as she reached the bottom. "Are you all right?" he asked as he turned her over.

Her green eyes looked dazed, and a knot was already growing on her forehead. He felt guilty about her injury, but angry, as well. If she had not been resisting him, she would not have been hurt in the first place.

"Are you all right?" he repeated, gently brushing what turned out to be incredibly silky blond curls from her brow. Her bowed lips pouted in a way that made her look half her age, but her square chin was outthrust enough that it could have belonged to a grande dame of the *ton*.

She slapped at his hand. "I'm fine," she said, gulping back a sob. "Leave me alone."

"I say there, Charlie—"

Denbigh glanced up to see one of his footmen starting toward the girl. He was appalled to hear the chit addressed by that impossible nickname—and by one of his servants!

The footman, Galbraith, recognized his mistake immediately and said, "Begging your pardon, milord, but Char—Lady Charlotte is—" He cut himself off again and shifted from foot to foot.

"What Timothy is trying to say is that we're friends, and he's worried about me," the chit said.

Timothy Galbraith—Denbigh had not known the man's first name before Charlotte mentioned it—flushed to the roots of his hair at this confession and stiffened as the earl gave him a narrow-eyed look. For the first time Denbigh noticed the footman was young and handsome.

The earl's gaze shifted from the footman to his ward and back. What he was thinking must have been plain on his face, because Galbraith hurried to reassure him, "Lady Charlotte is only what she said, milord. A friend. She doesn't see class, the way we do in England. Char—Lady Charlotte says that in America everyone is equal."

Denbigh turned to stare at his ward. Had she been spouting that sort of heresy ever since she arrived? No wonder Mrs. Killington was upset. He looked into the faces of the collection of servants who stood watching them. "Go get the housekeeper," he instructed them. "Tell Mrs. Tinsworthy to bring whatever she needs to care for Lady Charlotte's bruises to the Blue Room."

The servants stood unmoving, obviously protective of the girl, until he said, "If you have nothing better to do than stand there and gawk, perhaps it is time I reduced the staff," whereupon they dispersed hurriedly.

"Are you going to come upstairs with me peaceably?" Denbigh asked his ward.

"I don't see why I should."

"I should think the threat of more bruises would be reason enough," Denbigh said.

"Are you planning to beat me?" the girl demanded.

"The idea has definite appeal," Denbigh muttered to himself. The girl was looking him right in the eye, and he would not have put it past her to spit in it. "Are you going upstairs on your own two feet, or must I carry you?"

She wrapped her arms around her knees. "I'm not going anywhere with you. I wish I'd never met you. I want my life back the way it was before my papa died. I can't imagine what Papa was thinking. He can't have meant for you to be my guardian. You're a bully and a brute. You're a worm in the grass. No, you're a snake. You're a—"

"You've made your point exceedingly plain, Lady Charlotte," he said, cutting her off.

His pulse was throbbing in his temples, and it sounded as if she were just getting warmed up. He had no intention of waiting around until the servants returned to hear her diatribe. Without any warning, he scooped her up in his arms, intending to take her where she would not go on her own.

She gave an outraged shriek when his hand accidentally brushed against her breast. If it had given her as much of a jolt as it had given him, he could understand her response. She might be dressed like a man, but she was most definitely a woman. His body had reacted swiftly and surely to the feel of soft female flesh beneath his hand.

"You . . . You're . . ." she sputtered.

Obviously she was having trouble coming up with a word disgusting enough to describe him. He was horrified at the thought of the servants racing to her rescue—and finding him in the condition he was in. The current fashions left absolutely nothing to the imagination.

"You're despicable!" she finally managed. "You're—"

He put a hand across her mouth to cut off a new spate of insults, gathered her more tightly into his arms, and began marching back up the stairs.

He was careful not to underestimate the chit again, but she nevertheless managed to bite the hand that cut off her muffled cries before he got her to her room.

He threw her onto the canopied bed and sucked on the painful, blood-red row of teethmarks on his forefinger. She picked up where she had left off.

"You're lower than a snake in the grass," she hissed. "I can't even think of anything as low as you."

"That will be quite enough! If I haven't already, I want to make it perfectly clear that before I allow you out in public again you will reform your behavior to the standards expected of an English lady."

"I'm not a damned English lady!" she cried.

"Not yet," he agreed. "But before you leave this house again, you will dress and act and talk like a lady."

"I won't!"

"You will not leave this room until I have your agreement that you will," he said implacably.

She faced him unrepentant, undeterred. Denbigh had to admire the girl. It almost seemed a shame to curb her spirit. It was hard not to be impressed by the militant fire in her green eyes or to find beauty in the disheveled golden curls that fell free across her shoulders. The rosy flush on her cheeks made her look as though she had been engaged in . . . in something he had no business even thinking of in association with the young lady who was his ward.

He backed away toward the door. Before he had gone two steps she was heading for the door, as well.

"Where do you think you're going?" he asked.

"You can't keep me a prisoner here."

"I can do anything I believe is necessary for your welfare. I'm your guardian."

"I don't need a guardian. You don't want me here. Why won't you let me go home to America?"

"Your father obviously believed you needed a guardian. And I can see why." She had turned out to be something less—and more—than he was expecting. "You're my responsibility until you marry—although lord knows where I'll find an Englishman who'll take you.

"When you have learned the necessary female arts, you will be presented at court and receive an invitation to Almack's, where you will seek out a suitable husband. A selection which, of course, I must approve. Until then—or until you come of age—you will do as I say."

"I won't!"

"Very well. We'll talk again when you're ready to listen to reason." Instead of arguing further, he stepped out of the room, closed the door, turned the key in the lock, and stood waiting to see what she would do.

Lady Charlotte did not disappoint him.

She pounded on the door with her fists and kicked it with her boots. She rattled the knob, but the door was firmly locked.

"Are you ready to do as I ask?" he demanded through the door.

"Never!" she shouted back.

He had not expected her to give up without a fight. But he was not going to give up, either. He would leave her alone to think. Eventually, his charming—disarming? disturbing? delightful?—captive would come to understand that she had no choice except surrender.

Charlotte had never been so furious or felt so frustrated. *Keep her prisoner, would he? Marry her off to some stuffy old Englishman, would he? Like hell he would!* She would never give up or give in. She would die an old maid before she would concede the battle to him! After all, it was only four years until she was one and twenty. Oh, God. Four years!

The sound of her stallion trumpeting his anger as he resisted those who held him captive sent her running to the window. She peered through the leafy branches of the majestic oak that grew there and saw two stable boys trying in vain to subdue Mephistopheles. She and her horse were alike. They were both renegades, used to doing as they pleased, used to running wild. Until *he* had come along.

Charlotte paced from corner to corner of the elegant bedroom, tears of anxiety falling unnoticed. She felt sore and bruised all over from her fall down the stairs, but her aching bones were not what concerned her. She could not bear the thought of living under that man's thumb for years to come.

How dare the earl confine her! She would never

make the promises he was demanding in exchange for her freedom. Dress like a *lady*. Act like a *lady*. Talk like a *lady*. She would dress and act and talk just as she always had and be damned to him!

Despite the fact her father had been an English lord, she was not an English lady. She was an American. The high-handed guardian who had been appointed in her father's will was wrong to try and force her into a mold she didn't fit. It was like squeezing her feet into dainty satin slippers when leather riding boots would fit so much better. She liked wearing trousers. She liked riding astride. She liked saying exactly what was on her mind.

And what was wrong with the way she was? It had been fine for dear Papa. Oh, how she missed him! If only he had not taken ill and died. If only she had been allowed to stay at her plantation home in New Orleans instead of coming to live in this damp, drafty castle in England.

Suddenly the raging horse fell silent. Charlotte ran back to the window to see what had happened to Mephistopheles.

He was there. His hand lay on Mephistopheles's nose, calming the stallion, who stood quietly for him. Charlotte quivered with indignation that Mephistopheles should stand tamely for anyone but her, and that her horse had conceded the battle so easily to their mutual foe.

A soft knock at the door drew her attention away from the window. "Charlotte, I'm sorry."

She ran to the door and spoke through it. "Oh, Livy, thank goodness. Turn the key and let me out."

"I can't, Charlotte. Lion would be furious if I did."

"Don't be such a nodcock," Charlotte chided. "How will he know you unlocked the door?"

"He would ask. And I couldn't lie to him."

Charlotte leaned her forehead against the cool wooden door. Lady Olivia, the earl's sister, was eight years her elder, already five and twenty. But she was as timid as a mouse—and looked a great deal like one, too, with her plain brown hair and large hazel eyes.

Charlotte had done all she could over the past four months since she had arrived to encourage Livy to rebel against the strictures in her life. So far Livy was a butterfly still stuck tight in her chrysalis.

"I don't know what your brother was so upset about in the first place," Charlotte complained. "All we did was race his carriage to the house."

"You cannot blame Lion for being angry at finding his ward dressed in trousers and riding astride that huge black beast," Livy said through the door. "You know I nearly fainted myself when I first saw you mount Mephistopheles wearing breeches."

"Mephistopheles would never hurt me," Charlotte protested. "And I refuse to ride sidesaddle when riding astride makes so much more sense."

"I'm afraid Lion won't be swayed by your arguments, Charlotte. I warned you, did I not?"

'Why have you stopped calling me Charlie?' Charlotte asked softly. "I thought we were friends, Livy."

A pause and then, "Lion doesn't approve."

"You have a mind and a will of your own, Livy. You don't always have to do what your brother says."

There was a long pause before Charlotte heard the key move in the lock. The door opened, and Olivia stepped inside. "Oh, Charlie, look at your face! What happened?"

Charlotte's forehead was throbbing, but too many other things had been on her mind to worry about it. She crossed now to the standing mirror in the corner and gingerly touched the black-and-blue goose egg.

At that moment Mrs. Tinsworthy arrived at the door. "Oh, my dear Charlie," the elderly lady said as she entered with a handful of medicinals. "What on earth was that poor boy thinking?"

Charlotte had never been a very good patient, and it was hard to sit still for Mrs. Tinsworthy's attentions to her bruised face. What kept her silent during her ministrations was Mrs. Tinsworthy's references to the Earl of Denbigh as "that poor boy."

The housekeeper sounded almost sympathetic. As far as Charlotte could tell, the earl could take care of himself. After all, she was the one with the bruises.

Charlotte had discounted all the stories she had heard about the earl since she had arrived at Denbigh Castle. How he had killed a man simply because he didn't like the way he tied his neck cloth. That he was so dangerous with his fists that no one would go into the ring with him at Gentleman Jackson's salon. That his fencing bouts at Angelo's had resulted in serious injury to at least three young bucks of the *ton* who had wanted to try their hand at besting him. And that he was an unbeatable whip, risked life and limb to race his cattle, and always won.

Now that she had met him, she believed every word.

Worse than all of that, in her mind, however, was the way he ignored his family. He had elderly, sickly grandparents that he rarely visited, and his younger sister, Olivia, had been left alone in the country to wither away into an old maid. It was no wonder, Charlotte thought, that his bride had killed herself rather than marry the man.

But she could see why Lady Alice had been attracted to Denbigh in the first place. His eyes were startling to behold, such a light, silvery gray they had made her breath catch in her throat the first

time he looked at her. He had an aristocratic nose
and angular cheekbones. His mouth was wide and
generous, though he kept it pressed flat most of the
time in a grim line. Even more impressive was the
man himself. His tightly fitted jacket emphasized his
broad shoulders, while his flat stomach and strong
thighs were shown to advantage in skintight buckskins. Oh, he was attractive, all right.

She wasn't going to let that sway her opinion of
him. What good were looks when the man himself
was so flawed? Imagine, ordering his sister around!
Livy obeyed him like some English spaniel. Charlotte would never come to heel.

The Earl of Denbigh had finally met his match.
It was time he learned to treat his family better. His
servants, too, for that matter. And he could use a
little instruction in the proper care and consideration of a ward. Oh, yes, Charlotte Edgerton had a
few lessons to teach the arrogant earl.

"Come on, Livy," Charlotte said, when Mrs.
Tinsworthy was finished with her ministrations.
"Let's go talk to your brother."

"I don't think that's a very good idea, Charlie.
He's in the salon with Lady Frockman. Besides, you
don't have Lion's permission to leave this room."

Charlotte gave a derisive, unladylike snort. "I
don't see anyone to stop me."

"Lion won't appreciate being interrupted,"
Olivia said.

"I don't care," Charlotte replied. "I didn't want to be locked in my room. Did your brother care? No, he locked me in, anyway." She took a few steps toward the door, but Olivia held back. "Are you coming?"

"No. I'm not."

"All right, Livy, have it your way. I'll beard the Lion by myself." She grinned at her play on words.

Livy wasn't the least amused. Her brow furrowed anxiously, and her eyes looked worried. "Good luck, Charlie."

"Are you suggesting I'll need it?" Charlotte asked.

"Oh, yes. More than luck. Courage. And fortitude. And a stiff British upper lip."

Charlotte laughed as she headed out the door. "You're forgetting I have something much better than a stiff British upper lip."

"What's that?"

"A strong American backbone."

2

 CHARLOTTE SHOVED OPEN THE DOOR TO the earl's study without knocking, intending to confront him—and gasped.

The earl sat on the edge of a claw-footed sofa, his dark head pressed against a reclining woman's naked bosom.

Charlotte stood frozen, her eyes riveted to the sight of the earl's mouth releasing a damp, rosy crest. "My lord," she whispered.

He rose like a hungry lion above its feast, his dark mane wild, his eyes feral, then viciously angry as they focused on her.

"Out!" he rasped. "Get out!"

She backed away, then turned and ran. But not to her room, where he had ordered her to stay. She headed instead out the front door—where she was forbidden to go——slamming the heavy portal defiantly behind her.

Denbigh rearranged the immaculate waterfall his valet had created with his neck cloth, shoved a hand through dark curls cut in a Brutus, and bowed gracefully to the half-naked woman draped on the sofa. "You will have to excuse me, Lady Frockman," he said through tight jaws. "Duty calls."

"Stay, Lion," Lady Frockman cajoled. "The brat is gone, and we can be alone."

Denbigh's gray eyes turned cold. "Take care, Claudia. You are speaking of a young lady."

"But, Lion, you've called her worse yourself!" Lady Frockman protested.

Of course he had. The incorrigible minx was driving him mad. But he could not allow his young ward to be disparaged by a lady who was, despite her title, no lady. "You will be gone when I return, Claudia. Samuels will arrange to have a carriage take you back to London." Without another word he pivoted on his booted heel and headed out the door of the salon.

"If you send me away, Lion, I'm not coming back," Lady Frockman threatened.

Denbigh did not even pause. He should never have brought his mistress to his home in the first place. It was an outrageous thing to do. But there had been no one to say him nay for a very long time. His grandfather, the Duke of Trent, had been ill for years, keeping him and his duchess housebound on their estate in Kent. Responsibility for the family had fallen on Denbigh's shoulders when he was still a boy himself, but along with it had come a great deal of freedom to do as he pleased.

That was no excuse for subjecting his sister and his ward to the presence of his mistress. He was suddenly glad that Lady Frockman was leaving. It was plain he would be needing all his time and attention to deal with his new ward. He made a mental note to have his steward send Lady Frockman a diamond bracelet, along with a letter ending their relationship. But his mind was already racing ahead to the inevitable confrontation with his ward.

Assuming he could find the rebellious chit.

Samuels, the butler, was standing ramrod straight, cheeks ruddy with color, holding the front door open for him. "Sorry, milord. She caught me by surprise. I had no idea she would—"

"Never mind, Samuels. I doubt the devil himself could have stopped her."

Denbigh took one step outside the portals of Denbigh Castle and looked past the long, sloping lawn to the forest of ash and oak trees beyond. They provided a leafy refuge that could easily hide Lady Charlotte. But it was too far a distance for her to have managed to travel in the few moments since she had so precipitately ended his lovemaking.

Denbigh shuddered as he thought of what the girl must have seen. A picture of her wide-eyed, ashen face rose before his, and he felt something he had not believed he could still feel after an entire year of excess. *Shame.* What if it had been Olivia who had opened that door? Of course, Olivia would have knocked, but that was no excuse. He probably owed the chit an apology. Damn and blast her.

He glanced to the east, to the cliffs above the sea, and the treacherous path that led down to the pounding surf. He tried to imagine her running that far in the time since she had slammed the front door. Impossible. She was fast, but not that fast.

He looked west to the stable. It was closer than the other two hiding places she could have sought. He began striding toward it without further consideration. She was probably saddling that stallion of hers right now to make good her escape. She was a bruising rider, especially astride. If memory served, the chit had still been wearing trousers when she interrupted him in the study.

Denbigh frowned. The girl had no sense of decency. Dressed in trousers, every delectable line of her body was visible to any rake or rogue who cared to look. Heaven help him, he was as guilty as the worst of them. And every time he looked, he was reminded that his ward was a grown woman.

Not that she acted like one.

It was time Lady Charlotte Edgerton learned that he would not tolerate her crotchets. He was the one in control. He gave the orders in this house. It was her duty to obey them.

He stepped inside the stable and waited for his eyes to adjust to the dark. It was cooler inside than out, and he stood quietly, inhaling the familiar scents of leather and horse and manure, listening, waiting for her to reveal herself. He could not see her, but he knew she was there.

One of his pair of chestnut geldings swished its tail to whisk away a buzzing fly. A tiger-striped barn cat brushed against his Wellingtons, weaving itself between his legs, purring softly. He strained to hear some human movement, anything that would give away the girl's location.

And heard her panting.

The sound came from the loft above him. He looked up but could not see her through the narrow cracks in the wooden floor. Was she frightened of him? She ought to be. He was furious enough to give her a lesson that would keep her standing for days. But he could not very well spank her. She was not a child. She was a young lady. Hard as that was to remember at times.

He looked around for the hostler but remembered he had asked Jeremy to take his favorite hunter into the village to have a loose shoe replaced.

"I know you're up there, Lady Charlotte," Denbigh said. "I can hear you breathing. There is no one here but the two of us. You might as well come down and take your punishment."

He heard the rustle of straw, and several wisps floated down from above to land on the dirt floor. But no mutinous, heart-shaped face surrounded by golden curls appeared over the edge of the loft.

"If you do not come down here at once, I will have to come up there after you," he warned.

Still nothing.

"Very well." Denbigh put his hands on the rough-hewn ladder and began to climb.

He could hear her scrambling around above him and hurried his ascent. When his eyes breached the edge of the loft he saw her racing toward the open second-story doors through which hay was loaded into the barn. For an instant he thought she was going to jump out through the doors to escape him. She would break a leg at the least, and most likely her neck.

"Don't do it!" he yelled, clambering up into the loft and racing toward her. At the precise moment he lunged for her, she whirled. Too late he saw she held a pitchfork braced defensively in front of her.

There was no way he could stop his momentum. Two of the four razor-sharp tines were driven deep into the flesh of his upper thigh. He was too shocked even to cry out. His eyes widened in pained surprise as he raised them to meet the girl's startled, green-eyed gaze.

"I didn't mean to hurt you!" she cried. "If you hadn't attacked me like that—"

"I was trying to save your life," he said through clenched teeth. The pain was growing as the shock wore off. "I thought you were going to jump."

"Jump?"

"Out the loft door," he explained, gesturing toward the double doors with his chin.

"Are you crazy?" she said incredulously. "I would have broken my neck."

"My point precisely."

He saw the moment she became aware that she was still holding the wooden-handled pitchfork that was deeply imbedded in his flesh. She started to let go, and the angling tines drew a cry of agony from his throat.

"Don't let go," he rasped.

She grasped the weight of the pitchfork again and held it steady. "Oh, God," she croaked. "It's really stuck." She looked around wildly for someone to come and take it from her. There was no one. They were alone.

"What are we going to do now?" she asked.

"You're going to pull it out."

"I couldn't possibly!"

"You stuck it in. You can bloody well pull it

out.'' Beads of perspiration had formed on his upper lip, and his hands were curled into fists, one of which he pressed against his injured thigh to counter the pain of his wound.

He bit back a groan as the girl gave a slight tug. The tines did not come free.

She shot him a desperate look. ''It's really, really stuck.''

''I know,'' he said. ''You'll have to try a little harder.''

She stared fixedly at the worms of blood crawling from the two wounds on his thigh. Her body began to tremble, and she swayed on her feet.

For the first time, he saw a trace of vulnerability beneath the facade of bravado she wore. Before him stood a young woman still grieving the death of a beloved parent, forced to come to a strange land, and faced with a situation that would have sent any delicately nurtured young English lady into a swoon long ago.

''You aren't going to faint on me, are you, Charlotte? I thought you Americans had better bottom than that,'' he chided her gently.

As quickly as the mask had dropped, she pulled it back into place. Her shoulders squared, and she answered, ''We do.''

Before he was ready, and with all her strength, she yanked on the pitchfork. When it came free, she fell backward onto the straw. "It came out!" she said with a relieved laugh.

He felt light-headed and for a moment was afraid *he* was going to faint. Before he could falter, she was beside him with her arm around his waist, lifting his arm onto her shoulder for support. She was holding him closer than his affianced bride ever had.

"Lean on me," she said.

He did not want her help, but it was either lean on her or fall down. He expected his weight would be too much for her, but though she was small, she was surprisingly sturdy.

"How are we going to get you down from here?" she asked, looking up at him.

"I'll have to climb down."

"It's going to hurt like the devil when you do," she said.

"Thanks for pointing that out," he said. "Do you see any way around it?"

She shook her head. "At least let me tie something around your wound to stop the bleeding first."

He stared down at her. A moment ago she had been about to faint. Now she was offering to doctor him. Lady Charlotte was a most unusual woman. He found himself admiring her again, and realized that was a mistake. She was the reason he had ended up impaled on a pitchfork in the first place. And he would not have been out in the barn if she had not disobeyed him and left the house.

She pulled her lawn shirt from her breeches and tore a strip from the hem of the gauzy material long enough to tie over his wounds. He was still standing stunned at that bit of nursing ingenuity when she reached toward his thigh as though to bind up his wound.

"I'll do it," he said, taking the strip of cloth from her.

It was small satisfaction to see the relief in her face.

"Let me go down first," she said. "That way, if you fall, I can catch you."

"I'm not going to fall."

"Of course not," she said in a voice he found irritating because it was intended to soothe his ruffled ego. At the same time she was urging him toward the ladder. "Can you stand by yourself?" she asked.

As she let him go, he realized he was able to balance on his uninjured leg. "Yes, I can manage."

She headed down the ladder as quick as a monkey and stood on the floor below him looking up with anxious eyes. "Come on down," she said, gesturing with her hands. "I'll catch you if you fall."

It made him smile to picture her squashed beneath his bulk. But not for long. His leg was killing him.

"I'm not going to fall," he gritted out as he turned and began making his way down the ladder. By now the left leg of his buckskins was soaked with blood, and he could feel it pooling in his boot. It hurt like the very devil every time he moved his leg. He kept his mind off the pain by imagining the injured look on his valet's face when he showed up in such disarray. Theobald prided himself on keeping his master looking top-of-the-trees.

As luck would have it, his boot slipped on the last rung of the ladder, and he very nearly did fall. If she had not been there behind him to support him, he would have landed flat on his back. His ears turned red with embarrassment.

"You can let me go," he said, removing her arms from around his waist. "I can make it to the house by myself."

She was chewing on her lower lip, something else English ladies never did in public. Now he knew why. It was unbelievably erotic to imagine himself doing the same thing to her.

"You'd better let me help you."

"I said I can manage on my own," he snapped.

"Fine! Go ahead."

She took off for the house at a run—English ladies never ran anywhere, they walked sedately—shouting at the top of her lungs for help. Ladies did not shout, either, he could have pointed out. Before he was halfway to the house, which he was forced to admit he never would have reached on his own, she was back with Samuels and Galbraith, who made a chair for him with their arms and carted him back to the house.

Meanwhile, the chit was not satisfied with ordering around his servants. He heard her giving commands to his sister, as well.

"Have Mrs. Tinsworthy pull down the covers on your brother's bed, and get his valet—what is that man's name?—to come and undress him. I'm going to ride for the doctor."

She was racing—not walking, not ambling or strolling—but running at full speed back down one side of the stairs as Samuels and Galbraith carried him up the other.

"Slow down, Lady Charlotte," he called to her. "Walk."

"The sooner I can get my horse saddled, the sooner the doctor will be here to look at your leg," she countered.

"You're not riding to the doctor dressed like that!" She was still wearing those damned skintight breeches.

"Try and stop me!" she called up to him as she flitted down the stairs.

"Charlotte!" he roared. The chit completely

ignored him. He winced as he heard the front door slam.

"That girl is unbelievable!" he muttered.

"She certainly is," Galbraith agreed. "Astounding really, wouldn't you say, milord? Can't think of an English lady who could manage the situation half so well."

Denbigh realized his footman had misunderstood him. He had been criticizing Charlotte, not commending her. He had to admit that Lady Alice, or even his sister, Olivia, would not have marshaled everyone to do her bidding nearly so effectively. Unfortunately, Charlotte Edgerton utterly lacked the ability to be the only thing required of her in England—a perfect lady.

His valet was every bit as appalled as Denbigh had expected him to be. Theobald had been dressing the earl since he was a boy, and on occasion still treated him like one.

"Your buckskins are ruined, my lord," Theobald scolded, shaking his head as though the crown jewels themselves had been damaged. "While I could clean your boots, they will never be what they were. I am afraid I could not recommend that you wear them again."

"Then get rid of them," Denbigh said.

"Very well, my lord. If that is all, I will leave you until the doctor arrives."

"Go, Theobald. Please go." The man was turning green. Theobald never had been able to stand the sight of blood.

Denbigh had stripped naked, because the tines of the fork had pierced his smallclothes, as well, and put on a dressing gown to wait for the doctor in bed. Unfortunately, he had a great deal too much time to think before the doctor arrived.

The more thinking he did, the more convinced he became that he had handled the matter of Charlotte Edgerton all wrong. He should have sent her to his grandmother in the first place. The Duchess of Trent would have known how to smooth the rough edges off the girl.

However, the longer he pondered that alternative, the less he liked it. His grandfather was in ailing health. Imagine having someone as rambunctious as Charlotte around day in and day out. It was exhausting just to think about it. His elderly grandparents should not be saddled with what, after all, was his responsibility.

He had a lot of work to do if he was going to turn his ward into someone who could be presented to the queen and become a diamond of the first water at Almack's. He would have to bring in a modiste from London to make gowns for her—and burn all her trousers. He would have to teach her not to look at a man so directly or answer him so defiantly. Could she dance? He had better see to that, as well.

Charlotte had a great deal to learn in order to become a proper English lady. And he was just the man to teach her.

A knock at the door interrupted his thoughts.

"Lion? May I come in?"

He made sure he was as decent as possible. "Come in, Olivia."

She peered around the edge of his bedroom door before she entered the room, like a mouse checking for the cat before leaving its hole, then limped awkwardly across the room. Her broken leg had not healed properly, and one leg was slightly longer than the other. It had sadly curtailed her come-out, but in the years since her accident, she had never expressed any desire to rejoin Society.

"From my bedroom window I could see the doctor coming down the drive in his carriage," she said. "I thought I'd let you know he'll be here soon. Are you in much pain?"

"Not much." His leg was on fire, but there was no sense worrying her about it.

"Can you tell me what happened?"

"It was an accident."

"Did Charlotte have anything to do with it?"

"She happened to be holding the pitchfork at the time I ran into it," he said with a wry twist of his lips.

"Oh, dear." Olivia stood at the foot of his bed wringing her hands. "I'm sure she didn't mean to do it, Lion. It's only that she's such a lively girl. And so often she doesn't think before she acts."

"What I would like to know is how she got out of her room in the first place."

She lowered her gaze and said, "I unlocked the door."

"Why?"

It annoyed him that she would not look at him. Which made no sense, when he had found equal fault with Charlotte's more direct gaze. He realized he had no way of telling what Olivia was thinking when she hid her eyes from him that way. "I can understand the girl's defiance, Olivia. What I do not understand is why you would disobey me."

Her fingers toyed with the folds of her plain merino day dress. "You were wrong to confine her, Lion. I let her out because you had no right to lock Charlotte in her room in the first place."

"I'm her guardian, Olivia. I have every right."

"Because you *have* the right does not mean it *is* right," Olivia persisted.

"Come here, Olivia."

She took two awkward, tilted steps. When she reached his side, he lifted her chin. She kept her eyes lowered despite his efforts to see into them. "I'm surprised at you defending her, Olivia. The girl has no sense of maidenly modesty. She does not obey even the most basic rules of etiquette. In short, she is a disaster."

Olivia flashed him a quick look before she lowered her eyes and said, "I like her, Lion. She's my friend."

Lion sighed. "I cannot argue with that. Very well, Olivia. So long as you do your best to influence her to the good, instead of allowing her to influence you in the other direction."

"There is no badness in her, Lion," Olivia said earnestly. "She has a huge heart, and it is open to everyone."

"It's her mixed-up head that is causing the problems," he said.

They were interrupted when Charlotte came bursting through the door with the doctor, Mr. Rowland, right behind her.

"Charlotte!" Denbigh roared. "What are you doing in my bedroom, and why didn't you knock?"

"I brought the doctor," she said with asperity.

"A young lady does not enter the bedroom of a gentleman to whom she is not married," Denbigh retorted.

"Then what is Olivia doing in here?" she asked.

"Olivia is my sister."

"So?"

"You are my ward."

"So?"

Olivia laughed. "Oh, Lion, you won't win an argument with Charlotte. Believe me, I've tried."

Denbigh glared at his sister. "Unless you would

like to see your brother naked, I suggest you leave the room, Olivia. And take this young lady with you.''

"Come along, Charlotte. There's nothing for us to do here," Olivia said, putting an arm around Charlotte's shoulder.

"I could help," Charlotte offered.

"Get her out, Olivia, before I strangle her."

"Lion never was a very good patient, Charlotte. And Mr. Rowland will take very good care of him."

Denbigh watched as Charlotte allowed herself to be led from the room. She looked over her shoulder at him one last time before she left. He felt a pang of some emotion, one he refused to identify, when he recognized the look in her eyes. The chit had glanced back at him with . . . concern.

He reminded himself of what Olivia had said. The girl had a big heart and offered it to everyone. There was nothing personal in the look she had given him. He meant nothing to her. Which was fine with him. He wanted nothing to do with her, either. Except, of course, to prepare her to become some other man's wife.

3

CHARLOTTE KNOCKED ON THE EARL'S bedroom door and said, "It's Charlotte. May I come in?"

She heard the earl and his valet speaking in quiet, indistinguishable tones, then the earl's voice saying, "Can this wait?"

"I don't think so," Charlotte said.

His sigh was so loud and plaintive she heard it even through the door. A rustling sound followed, as though sheets were being rearranged. The door opened, and she found herself facing the earl's valet, Theobald.

"You may come in now, Lady Charlotte."

Charlotte crossed directly to the bed and stood before her guardian. "I hope your leg is feeling better," she said.

His wounded thigh was hidden beneath the

sheet, and she thought perhaps that was what all the rustling had been about. He was still wearing a dressing gown, which she supposed meant it still hurt too much for him to pull on trousers over the bandages.

"It will heal," the earl said. "Eventually," he added.

"His lordship has been in a great deal of pain," Theobald announced.

Denbigh shot him a reproving glance, but his valet didn't seem the least bit cowed by it.

"I'm very sorry," Charlotte said. "That's why I've come, you see. To make amends."

"And wearing a dress," the earl said. "That is an improvement I can applaud."

Charlotte looked down at the willow-green sprigged muslin she had donned for her visit to the earl. The dress made her look even less than her seventeen years, if that was possible. But she was hoping to melt the earl's cold heart, and she had decided it could not hurt to look young and vulnerable. So far it appeared her plan was working.

"These are for you to do with as you please," she said, holding out her arms, which were stacked eight inches high with folded clothing.

"What, exactly, do you have there?" the earl asked.

"Every pair of breeches I own," she said. *Except the pair hidden under my mattress.*

58

"Ah," the earl said. "You may give them to Theobald, Lady Charlotte."

Theobald's eyebrows had risen to his hairline, but like the true man's man he was—that is, no task was too revolting, and all were handled with utmost care—he accepted the pile of grass-stained, oft-mended breeches from her hands. "What shall I do with them, my lord?" Theobald asked.

"Burn them."

Charlotte saw the earl watching for her reaction, and she barely managed to avoid wincing. All those wonderful breeches going up in smoke. Such a waste!

"It shall be as you wish, my lord," Theobald said.

"Do it now, Theobald," Denbigh said.

"Very well, my lord," he said. "Excuse me, Lady Charlotte. Do you need anything else before I leave?"

Charlotte caressed the smooth buckskin inseam on her best riding breeches one last time and said, "No thank you, Theobald. But . . ." She turned to the earl and said, "Do you think you could give the breeches away instead of burning them? There are several boys in the village—"

"See to it, Theobald," the earl said.

"Yes, my lord. Will there be anything else?"

The earl gestured to Charlotte, and Theobald turned to see if she needed any further assistance.

"There is one more thing," Charlotte began. Too late she realized this probably was not the time to bring up this subject. But the earl and his valet continued to stare at her, so she blurted, "Theobald needs a raise."

"What?" the earl exclaimed.

Theobald's face turned red as a boiled crayfish. Charlotte had eaten a lot of them in New Orleans, so she was a good judge of the color.

"My lord, I would never deign to suggest—"

"Stubble it, Theobald." The earl turned to Charlotte and said, "That is an unusual request, Lady Charlotte. I wondered if you might have some particular reason for making it."

"Well, Mrs. Tinsworthy told me Theobald's sister has gotten herself in the family way and her man has been gone to India for ever so long and she has just heard that the natives *killed* him, and she has No Hope except her brother. And though Theobald has been the most frugal of men, he simply hasn't enough to be of any real help. So she is going to have to go to the poorhouse and give her babe to an orphanage.

"So you see, you are his Only Hope," she said dramatically.

"Is this true, Theobald?" the earl asked.

"Essentially, yes, my lord."

"Consider the matter taken care of, Lady Charlotte."

Charlotte flashed the earl a grin and gave Theobald a hug. The poor man nearly expired from apoplexy on the spot. He escaped as quickly as he could and left the room without another word. Charlotte thought it was because he was overcome by the earl's generosity. She felt the same way herself.

"You can be a kind man," she pointed out to him. "If you would only try a little harder."

The earl's lips flattened. The kind look went away.

"If you have accomplished the purpose of your visit, you may leave," he said.

"Oh, but there's more," she said.

"I was afraid of that."

She dropped onto the foot of his bed and heard him gasp as his leg bounced under the covers. "Oops! I'll be more careful."

"You shouldn't be sitting on my bed at all," he said. "You shouldn't even be in this room without a chaperon."

"I'll be quick," she said, jumping to her feet.

He groaned as his leg got jostled again.

"Oh, I'm so very sorry," she said.

"I'm sure you are," he said. "I believe that's what brought you here in the first place," he reminded her.

"Oh, yes. Well. You may have noticed that I

have decided to defer to your wishes regarding the dresses and the breeches.''

"I have."

"I will even ride sidesaddle," she conceded.

"Very commendable."

"But I think, if it's all the same to you, I'd rather choose a husband who will like me just the way I am. I'm perfectly willing to buy my freedom from your authority with matrimony, but that won't do me much good if I end up married to another tyrant."

She realized, when he scowled, that perhaps *tyrant* was not a politic word to use. "I mean, another man as inflexible as you." *Inflexible* drew a tic in his cheek.

She tried once more. "I mean, I want a husband who will love me for who I am." This time he looked incredulous.

"Where are you planning to find such a paragon?" the earl asked.

"I hear there are a lot of men to choose from in London."

"How are you planning to get there?"

"You're going to take me, of course."

For another half hour, until she could see the earl's leg was paining him too much to continue, they discussed her needs and his demands. When the interview was over, Charlotte had not gotten everything her own way. The earl had agreed to take her to London, but only after she agreed to endure a series of lessons in etiquette—she had to meet his rigid standards of correct social behavior—and acquired a completely new wardrobe and learned all the newest dances, including the waltz.

She was suspicious of the way her guardian had given in so easily. She made a vow to herself that no matter what tricks the earl tried, she would be the one to choose her husband. If for some reason Denbigh did not like the man she chose, and tried to forbid the marriage, she would elope.

Being remade in someone else's image turned out to be more of a trial than Charlotte had expected. Two weeks later she still did not recognize the "new" Charlotte.

"You look lovely, Charlie," Olivia said from her perch on the edge of Charlotte's bed.

Charlotte eyed herself in the standing mirror. She felt naked wearing the short-sleeved gown that was gathered under her bosom with a thin silk ribbon. It was cut low in front, exposing a great deal of her chest.

"Your brother can't really believe this is less revealing than a shirt and breeches," Charlotte said, covering the wide expanse of naked skin on her chest with her hands. "Why, any man taller than me can see my bosom!"

Livy grinned. "I believe that's the general idea. You're setting bait to trap a husband, Charlie."

Charlotte grimaced.

"You don't know how lucky you are," Olivia said. "I'd give anything to be in your shoes."

"No you wouldn't. They pinch." Charlotte stepped out of the uncomfortable satin slippers, bent over to pick them up, and held them out to Livy. "But be my guest."

Livy smiled. "I wish it were that simple." Her smile faded. "I cannot dance, so what would be the point?"

"Why can't you dance?" Charlotte asked.

"Be sensible, Charlie. I walk like a lopsided duck. How could I possibly manage to dance?"

"I remember you telling me you would never ride again. You managed that," Charlotte reminded her. "What's so different about dancing?"

"When I'm riding, the horse does all the work," Olivia said. "On the dance floor it would just be me and my awkward hobble." Olivia stared off into the distance. "Don't worry about me, Charlie. In my dreams, I'm a very good dancer."

Charlotte climbed up onto the bed beside Olivia, pulled her skirt up practically to her waist, exposing her gartered stockings, and sat cross-legged like one of the red savages for which America was famous. "Tell me about your dreams, Livy."

"I don't want to bore you."

"I wouldn't be bored. Tell me. I'll bet you're being courted by a devastatingly handsome man."

"Oh, yes. He's blond and blue-eyed and very tall. When we waltz, he can't take his eyes off me. He's graceful, but strong. And he has a warm and friendly smile."

"Oh, Livy, he sounds wonderful. Who is he?"

Olivia laughed. "He isn't real, Charlie. I made him up."

"But he could be real. You could come to London with me and find him."

"I've already told you why that's impossible."

"Because you have a limp? That's no reason. The queen will understand if you can't curtsy as low as everyone else. I know your handsome suitor is out there looking for you. All you have to do is go to London and let him find you."

"You're the one who's dreaming now, Charlie. No man is going to want a woman who's . . . who's crippled. I don't have any illusions about my looks, either. I would never have been a belle of the ball. And at five and twenty, I'm firmly on the shelf."

Olivia paused and swallowed hard. "I've resigned myself to being a maiden aunt to my brother's children."

Charlotte grabbed Olivia's hand and squeezed it tight. "Any man would be lucky to have you, Livy. You're the kindest, most thoughtful person I know.

I'm not going to let you give up on yourself. You're going to dance at a ball with a handsome beau, just as you've always dreamed. All you have to do is come to London with me."

"I can't, Charlie. Please try to understand."

"I won't take no for an answer, Livy. You have to go to London. Otherwise, I'm not going, either."

"Oh, Charlie, no! Lion has everything planned. He'll be furious if you change your mind about going now."

"I'll be glad to make my bow to the queen and behave myself at Almack's," Charlotte assured her. "As long as you come with me."

"I don't have the proper wardrobe for a sojourn to London," Olivia protested.

"The modiste has several more fittings to do for me. We'll simply get her to make up the necessary gowns for you, as well."

"Oh, Charlie, you're impossible," Livy said.

But Charlotte noticed her eyes positively glowed with excitement. She couldn't wait to see Livy dressed for a ball. In no time at all she would find a real beau just like the man of her dreams.

Now all Charlotte had to do was convince her guardian that he needed to bring his sister along for the journey.

* * *

In the weeks since his arrival at Denbigh Castle, the earl had closeted himself with his steward in the mornings, spent the afternoons lecturing to Charlotte, and usually accepted an invitation from one neighbor or another for an evening of entertainment and supper. Olivia had told Charlotte that the earl was much in demand as a dinner guest in the neighborhood, despite his rakish reputation.

"He's rich as Croesus," Olivia confided, "the heir to a dukedom, and you must have noticed his features are very well put together."

"I hadn't noticed," Charlotte lied.

The truth was, she could not take her eyes off the man when they were in the same room together. She was purely disgusted with herself but could not seem to break herself of the habit. It was disconcerting because the earl had spent at least two hours with her every afternoon giving her what he called "lessons in deportment."

She was scheduled for another one in a very few minutes. She crawled off the bed and forced her toes back into the uncomfortable slippers. "We had better get to the salon before your brother sends someone after us," she said to Olivia.

"What is it today?" Olivia asked.

"Flirting lessons, I think."

Olivia was startled into a laugh. "You're teasing me."

"Your brother didn't call it that, but he mentioned at breakfast this morning that he wants me to learn how to behave when a gentleman exhibits an interest in courting me. It's a good thing you're going to be there, Livy. Maybe you can learn something useful."

The earl's sister acted as a chaperon during the lessons. She also happened to play the piano, which had been convenient on the afternoon the earl decided to teach her to waltz.

Charlotte shivered as she recalled the debacle.

She had learned a great many country dances in America, but she had no knowledge of the waltz. It had amazed her to discover that the woman stood within the man's embrace, that he put his arm around her waist, and that one of her hands rested on his shoulder while her other hand rested in his palm.

"Are you certain this is the right way to do it?" she had asked the earl when he had the two of them stationed in a virtual embrace.

"I'm sure," he replied. "Music, Olivia."

She had turned to Olivia in desperation, but Olivia had simply smiled from her seat in front of the piano and said wistfully, "It's a wonderful dance, Charlotte. It's almost like flying."

"You've danced the waltz?" she asked, surprised.

"Oh, no. But I've seen it danced."

"Are you ready?" the earl said, obviously impatient to begin.

"I guess so," Charlotte said. But really, she wasn't ready at all for the emotions rioting through her. She felt gauche for the first time in her memory. Flustered when she was ordinarily never discomposed. She was achingly aware of the earl's hand on the center of her back, and the warmth of his palm holding hers. She was ice; he was fire. Any second now he was going to see a puddle at his feet.

"Relax, Charlotte," the earl ordered.

"I'm trying." She unlocked her knees and nearly collapsed.

"Not that much," he said, holding her breathtakingly close as he helped her regain her balance.

"Count one-two-three, one-two-three, one-two-three," he said, as he began whirling her around the room. "Ow!"

"I'm sorry. Did I get your foot?" she asked.

"Concentrate, Charlotte. Keep counting."

"One, two, three," she repeated dutifully. She could have been saying "cat, cow, pig" for all the attention she was paying to the dance. She could not take her eyes off him. His gaze was so intense, she got lost in its depths.

She felt quivery inside and a little frightened, too, because she had never felt this way before. His arm tightened around her waist, and he pulled her close as she tripped over the edge of the carpet they had moved out of the way.

"Careful, Charlotte," he said in a rumbly voice that made the hairs stand up on her arms. "Careful."

It was far too late to be careful. Something very dangerous was happening to her, and she was helpless to prevent it. She had known she was attracted to the earl from the first moment she had seen him. She had been resisting that pull with all her might and main. But she had not counted on the waltz. Waltzing was so much more intimate than she had imagined a dance could be.

Her nipples peaked when the tips of her breasts barely brushed the earl's waistcoat. Her belly curled with desire when he pulled her tight against him as they whirled faster and faster. She felt lightheaded—which was obviously the result of all that whirling. Except she had never felt quite like this before. Breathless—and why not? It was an energetic dance. Euphoric. There was no explanation for that except the joy she felt at being held in his arms.

Abruptly, he stopped dancing and shoved her away to arm's length. "You're not paying attention, Charlotte. You won't have much success on the Marriage Mart if you persist in losing count and stumbling and stepping on your suitor's toes."

It was a lowering experience for someone as coordinated as Charlotte Edgerton knew herself to be to fail at something so simple. But how could she be expected to dance with boneless knees? How could she be expected to keep count when she could barely remember her own name? How could she be expected to keep from bumping into him, when her body wanted more than anything to be next to his?

Worst of all was the knowledge that while she was mooning over him like some calfling, he was busy planning how best to marry her off to some other man.

Surely everything she was feeling could not be all one-sided. Surely he must feel the attraction, as well. But when she looked up at him, there was no sign of anything except annoyance on his face.

"Are you ready to try again?" he asked.

No, she was not. She had suffered quite enough humiliation for one afternoon. "I'm sure I'll do fine at Almack's," she said. "I promise to practice with Timothy."

He frowned. "I didn't know Galbraith knew how to waltz."

"If he doesn't, I'll teach him," she replied.

"I don't approve of such familiarity with the servants, Charlotte. Each person has his place in this household. Galbraith is a footman, not a dance instructor."

"Timothy is my friend."

"English ladies don't make friends with the servants," he admonished her.

"I thought we had established that I'm not an English lady."

"That's precisely the point," he said. "I'm trying to teach you the right way to act."

"Is it right to treat people differently simply because they weren't born with a title? I can't subscribe to that point of view, sir."

He gave an exasperated snort at the "sir." "Every society has its own rules, Charlotte. Ours in England are different, but we have our reasons for them."

"What reason can account for making a butler less of a man than a baron? Explain that to me please," she demanded. "Or an American custom less civilized than an English one."

"That's simply the way it is," he blustered. "A man's hereditary birthright and position—"

"Don't say any more." She took a step back from him. Maybe the earl was not so admirable, after all. She wasn't sure what it was that had made her act like a silly goose for a moment. Now she saw him clearly. He was narrow-minded and shallow and not at all the kind of person a woman would want as the father of her children. Imagine the awful things he would teach them!

She had left the room without another word. And had not spoken to him for two days. Of course, he had not said a word to her, either. Until this morning at breakfast, when he had demanded her presence in the salon for flirting lessons after luncheon.

Thank goodness Olivia would be with her. Thank goodness she had realized what a reprehensible character the earl really was before she lost her heart to him. He could flirt all he wanted with her—she could flirt all she wanted with him—and it was not going to affect her one teensy weensy little bit.

Unfortunately, that foolish hope was dashed the moment she entered the salon and laid eyes on the dastardly fellow. Or rather, the moment he settled his vivid gray eyes on her.

Her heart bounded around inside her like an excited puppy. At the same time, her chest felt as if it were being squeezed by the sugar press that crushed the cane on her father's plantation. She felt dazed and disoriented, fluttery and faint.

"Charlotte? Are you all right?" Denbigh asked.

His husky voice sent a frisson of awareness skittering down her spine. "Of course—" She had to clear the frog in her throat before she could say, "Of course I'm all right."

Olivia took her place in the upholstered wingback chair near the fire and took up her knitting, while Denbigh reached for Charlotte's hand and led her over to sit beside him on the claw-footed sofa.

Unfortunately, the instant he sat down beside her, the vision rose in her mind of what he had been doing to Lady Frockman on that same sofa. And what it might feel like if he did that to her.

She made the mistake of looking at him, and found him staring back at her intently. She quickly lowered her gaze—a very unCharlottelike thing to do. Which she realized, too late, had revealed her distress.

"What's wrong, Charlotte?" Denbigh asked in a voice soft enough not to be overheard by his sister.

"Nothing."

"In any other woman, I would believe you're simply being demure," he said. "But not you, Charlotte. You brazenly look a man in the eye. So I ask you again. What's wrong?"

He lifted her chin with his forefinger. The last thing she wanted to do was look at him, but it was the only way she could prove she was not upset. She lifted her lids and stared into his eyes. And felt herself falling.

He removed his hand reluctantly. Before he did, his thumb brushed across her chin in what might almost have been a caress. "Charlotte . . ."

She waited for him to complete whatever it was he wanted to say. He didn't use words. He simply looked deep into her eyes, took her hand in his, and stroked his thumb across her knuckles. He lifted her hand to his lips, and kissed the back of it, leaving a damp spot that cooled in the air.

Suddenly, he dropped her hand. "You've let me go too far," he announced.

"What?"

"It is perfectly appropriate to gaze lovingly into a gentleman's eyes," Denbigh said, "but when he begins kissing—even your hand—he has gone too far. It is not to be allowed. Not before you have my approval to continue the courtship. Is that understood?"

"What?" She was still having trouble grasping the fact that Denbigh's intense gaze, his gentle touch, had all been part of the lesson. He had not been affected in the least by her presence. He had not been moved at all by the touch of her hand, as she had been by his. She rose abruptly.

"Oh, I understand, all right," she said. "All you're interested in is seeing that some man—with the correct heritage and birthright—is fooled by an act long enough to be tricked into marriage. Have I got it right?"

He rose to face her. "I did not mean— I suppose it must seem—Damn and blast, Charlotte. You're twisting everything."

"You mean I'm not supposed to flirt? I thought that was what this lesson was all about." She batted her eyelashes at him.

"Stop that. You look ridiculous."

"I can't be what I'm not," she cried. "I refuse to put on an act that I wouldn't be able to keep up forever. What do you suppose would happen after I married a man whom I had deceived as to my true nature? What would happen when he woke up after the honeymoon and realized who—and what—he had married?''

Denbigh had the grace to flush.

''Don't you think it might be better if I choose a man to suit me, rather than try to change myself to suit a man?''

Denbigh's jaw tightened. ''Choosing your husband is my prerogative.''

''How can you know who would make me happy?''

''Happiness is not the purpose of marriage. Marriages are alliances where property and bloodlines are considered foremost.''

''No wonder Lady Alice left you at the altar,'' Charlotte blurted out. ''I don't blame her for fleeing from a loveless marriage.''

Olivia's knitting needles clattered into her lap. ''Oh, Charlotte, please don't say such things!''

The blood drained from Denbigh's face. He stood rigid for a moment longer before he turned and left the room.

Charlotte felt wretched. She had never purposely hurt another human being in her life. Accidentally, yes. Through carelessness, yes. But she had wanted to make Denbigh feel the same pain she was feeling at his rejection. She had said what she thought would wound him the most. Her unerring aim had hit a very vulnerable mark.

She saw Olivia through a blur, and realized Olivia's eyes also welled with tears. She crossed and dropped to her knees in front of the earl's sister. "I'm sorry, Livy."

Olivia brushed her hair back from her face soothingly as she looked out the window past Charlotte's head. "You must never, ever say such things again. You will never know how much Lion suffered when Lady Alice abandoned him. It was a love match. At least on his side. Something happened . . . It was awful."

"What happened?" Charlotte asked.

Olivia shook her head. "Please don't ask. He told me once. When he was in his cups. It was awful."

"I'm sorry," Charlotte said again. "I promise I won't ever do such a thing again."

But she was more than ever convinced that the choosing of her husband should not be left to the Earl of Denbigh's discretion. He did not have the same values as she did, or embrace the same ideals. She would be better off choosing a husband of her own.

Or staying single. That idea also had considerable merit.

The only problem was, Charlotte did not think she could last four years as the earl's ward.

4

"MAY I HAVE THE PLEASURE OF THIS dance?"

There was nothing demure about Lady Charlotte's gaze as she examined the blond Adonis standing before her. He was older than the young bucks of the *ton* who had crowded round her ever since she had entered Almack's. Lines webbed his piercing blue eyes and creased his sharp-boned cheeks. He was broad-shouldered and lean-hipped, altogether an admirable male specimen. Before Charlotte could accept the gentleman's offer, Denbigh answered for her.

"The lady's dance card is filled, Your Grace," her guardian said in clipped tones.

Charlotte's eyes goggled. A *duke* had just asked her to dance, and Denbigh had turned him down! And unless magic elves had been at work, her dance card most certainly was not filled. Denbigh had been picky about the sprigs of fashion he allowed to pay court to her. But what was wrong with *this* man? The duke looked fine to her, even if he was at least ten years older than Denbigh, maybe even old enough to be her father—at least thirty-seven or eight.

She perused her dance card and looked up at the duke with a twinkle in her eye. "It seems there is one dance—"

That was as far as she got before Denbigh's hand clamped tight on her wrist. He tugged her from her seat and, when she glared mutinously at him, settled her hand on his arm with an unspoken dare to try removing it. Charlotte was rebellious; she was not stupid. She left her hand where her guardian had put it.

"Excuse us, Your Grace," Denbigh said. "This dance is promised to me, and the set is about to begin." He turned and began leading Charlotte onto the dance floor.

"But, Your Grace, Lady Olivia, the earl's sister, would love to dance with you," Charlotte called back over her shoulder.

Charlotte felt Denbigh's arm go rigid beneath her fingertips as he stopped abruptly. He gave her a narrow-eyed look that would have kept a Gunter's ice chilled for a week. Charlotte wrinkled her nose at him and heard him growl as he turned his attention back to the duke.

Well, it was his own fault for leaving his sister sitting there all alone like a wallflower, when she should be enjoying herself, Charlotte thought.

Olivia sat stiff as a buckram hat brim in the chair next to the one Charlotte had vacated, her hazel eyes lowered modestly in a way Charlotte's never were.

Charlotte watched the duke's eyes and saw them settle on her friend. Charlotte knew the duke was seeing a rather plain, rather shy woman, her oval face surrounded by mousy brown curls topped by a lace-edged spinster's cap. Under his perusal, Olivia's face turned crimson and then, as the duke's heels snapped together and he bowed over her hand, faded to a ghostly white.

"My lady?" the duke said in a flinty voice. "Will you do me the honor?"

"You've done it now, Charlie," the earl muttered.

Though his features remained as immovable as one of the Elgin Marbles she had snuck out to see, Charlotte was certain Denbigh was furious. He had never, *ever* called her by her American nickname.

Charlotte watched as the blond Adonis reached out a gloved hand to the earl's sister and held it there, waiting for her hand to be laid in it. "I am Braddock," he said.

Olivia gasped. Braddock was an infamous rake.

Charlotte would have gasped, too, if she hadn't been afraid a too-deep breath would cause her bosom to fall completely out of her gown. Her nearly naked—though charmingly exposed—bosom was another of her plans to upset Denbigh that had gone awry.

She had instructed the *modiste* to lower the bodice to a level she was sure would leave Denbigh howling with outrage and then pranced down the stairs of the town house in London where they were staying, confident that her guardian would be forced to leave her at home this evening. She had no desire to be paraded on the Marriage Mart like a filly for sale.

Denbigh had taken one shocked look at her décolletage and roared, "Charlotte! You will go right back upstairs and—"

That was when she had made the mistake of smirking in triumph. Denbigh recognized the trap she had set, snapped his jaws shut, swallowed hard, and in a remarkably calm—if cold—voice said, "Get a scarf. It will be chilly this evening."

In spite of Denbigh's black looks, she had refused to wear the scarf once they arrived at Almack's. But she feared she had suffered more than Denbigh. It was like dangling a worm before trout. The gentlemen simply couldn't resist. Now it seemed she had attracted a very big, very dangerous fish indeed. Braddock, as in Reeve Somers, the Duke of Braddock.

Denbigh had killed the Duke of Braddock's younger brother, Lord James, in a duel barely a year past. As a result, the two powerful men had become mortal enemies. It wasn't bad enough she had landed the dangerous duke, she had thrown him—sharp teeth and all—to Denbigh's innocent sister. *Good Lord,* she thought. *What have I done?*

On second thought, the two men's enmity for each other was no reason, so far as Charlotte could see, to cheat Olivia of her chance to dance with a handsome man. And the duke was handsome, a striking contrast with his blond hair and blue eyes, to Denbigh's black hair and silvery gray eyes.

Charlotte met Olivia's panic-stricken gaze and pleaded with her eyes for Livy to accept the duke's offer. *Take a chance on life. Don't let your brother's disapproval keep you on the shelf.*

Then, to everyone's amazement—not least of all her brother's—Lady Olivia Morgan stood and said, "I will be glad to dance with you, Your Grace."

"But—" Denbigh spluttered.

Charlotte's fingernails dug through three layers of cloth—her gloves and the earl's snug velvet coat-sleeve and fine lawn shirt—to silence him. Her heart sank when she saw Braddock frown as Livy's

first two steps revealed her uneven, almost un-
steady, gait.

The duke took a step closer, offering his entire
arm, rather than merely his hand, to support Livy.
"You're hurt," he said. "I would be glad to sit
out—"

Before Charlotte could tell the blasted man that
Livy yearned to dance, Livy surprised Charlotte by
saying so herself.

"It is a long-ago injury, Your Grace, and has
healed as well as ever it will. I prefer to dance, if
you please," she said in a trembling voice.

"Very well, then. Shall we?" The duke's arm
slid around Olivia's slim waist, and the earl's sister
went whirling onto the dance floor, leaving Charlotte and the earl staring after them. Charlotte
watched long enough to see that the duke was supporting Livy's weight with the arm he had around
her waist, pulling them almost indecently close.
Lucky Livy.

Charlotte grinned.

Denbigh snorted.

Before Charlotte could say another word, Denbigh circled his arm around her waist.

"I thought I had to have permission from one of
the patronesses to dance a waltz," she protested.

"While you were busy with that idiot Lord
Fairchild earlier this evening, Lady Jersey gave permission," Denbigh said through clenched teeth.

Then they were waltzing, whirling around the ballroom at a dizzying speed. It was like floating, like flying, like heaven on earth—so long as she ignored the scowl on Denbigh's face. And the fact she could have been an Indian pachyderm in his arms, for all the attention he gave her. His gaze was riveted on Braddock and his sister.

Which wasn't all bad, because it gave her a chance to look at his face up close without being observed. It wasn't a bad-looking face, she supposed, but it would be vastly improved if he would smile more often. And she liked his eyes better when he was laughing. They turned a lighter, softer gray than the stormy color they were now, when he was angry.

She purposely stepped on his toe, to get his attention.

He took his eyes off his sister and Braddock barely long enough to say, "Remember to count, Charlotte," and then swiveled his head to follow the other couple as they twirled past him.

"Dancing is quite as nice as I thought it would be," Charlotte said. "I thank you for the lessons."

"I'm glad you're enjoying yourself. Now stubble it." He pulled her close to avoid a collision with Lord Bottomly and a giggling heiress.

Charlotte was suddenly aware of her breasts crushed against Denbigh's chest and the feel of his muscular thighs pressing against her own through her gown. For the first time all evening, her bosom was definitely in no danger of escape from her bodice, yet she felt more exposed than ever. Her feelings, the yearning she felt for Denbigh's approval, but even more for his touch, were naked on her face. She glanced up at him, wondering if he had divined her dreadful secret—that she was attracted to him.

To her chagrin, Denbigh did not seem at all affected by their closeness. He merely set out to give her yet another scold. "I cannot imagine what came over you, Charlotte. A lady does not offer her chaperon as a dance partner to a gentleman she cannot partner herself."

"Why not?" Charlotte asked. "Especially when her chaperon is far too young to be put in that role and . . ." Charlotte cut herself off. She could not tell Denbigh about Livy's secret dream of someday being whirled around a dance floor by a handsome young man. That was something Livy had told her in confidence. "Livy did not seem to mind being forced into the duke's arms."

"I think I am the best judge of what is appropriate for my sister," Denbigh said.

"I beg to differ," Charlotte said.

"You would," Denbigh muttered. His eyes remained riveted on the other couple.

Perturbed at being so totally ignored, Charlotte

demanded, "What is it you think he's going to do to her in the middle of the dance floor?"

Denbigh's gray eyes left the other couple and turned back to her. "I don't know. I wouldn't put anything past him. The man has sworn to ruin me."

"Surely he wouldn't hurt Livy," Charlotte protested. "And certainly not here at Almack's. He wouldn't dare!"

"There's no telling what an angry, desperate man will dare."

"Is that why you didn't want Braddock to dance with me? Because you were afraid he might do me harm?"

"Braddock is a confirmed bachelor. No woman is going to get him to the altar. Since my goal is to get you married and out of my hair, it made no sense to let you dance with him."

Charlotte's chin jutted mulishly. "I thought we had settled that I will choose my own husband. I might like to try attaching Braddock."

"Don't."

"Don't what?"

"Don't try my patience by saying provoking things," Denbigh said. "I won't allow you to marry Braddock, and that is final."

"You can't stop me once I'm of age from marrying whomever I choose," Charlotte retorted.

The earl's lip curled in amusement. "Are you

willing to be my ward and obey my dictates for four more years, Charlotte?''

Charlotte quivered with fury. Trust Denbigh to remind her she was only seventeen. She blinked back the tears of frustration that welled in her eyes. She was captive to the earl's whims until she was twenty-one or until she was married. Charlotte had already figured out that her only hope was marriage. She had determined to marry a man who would give her the freedom to be herself, a freedom that had been bred in her bones, a freedom that was as American as she was. It would serve Denbigh right if she married his enemy.

But from what Denbigh was saying, Braddock hadn't really been interested in courting her, but in somehow hurting him. ''Are you saying the duke only asked me to dance to cause trouble for you?''

''I think he asked you to dance because you're beautiful. And because he wanted to cause trouble for me. It is common knowledge you are my ward. His intentions cannot be honorable.''

''Why not? Is the duke a dishonorable man?''

''His brother was.''

''What did Lord James do that was so terrible?'' Charlotte asked. Olivia had refused to discuss the matter.

Denbigh did not answer.

Charlotte opened her mouth to pursue the issue but closed it again when she looked up into Denbigh's eyes. They were filled with anguish. Something terrible had happened, that was for sure. Someday she was going to find out the whole story. Clearly this was not the time or the place.

She sought for some safe subject on which to converse. Of course, with Denbigh, there was little they could discuss without arguing. Then she recalled what Denbigh had said, that the duke had wanted to dance with her because she was beautiful.

"Do you think I'm beautiful?"

Denbigh looked startled at the question, and then uncomfortable. "Why do you ask?"

"You said the duke wanted to dance with me because I'm beautiful. Do you think I'm beautiful?"

Charlotte was looking right into Denbigh's eyes when she asked and saw a flare of some emotion, quickly shuttered. He continued staring at her until she felt a disconcerting heat rising in her cheeks. She refused to look away, focusing instead on his individual features, the wide-spaced gray eyes, the black brows, the aquiline nose, the square jaw, the mobile mouth that hardly ever smiled.

She watched him lick his lips and felt a strange shiver of excitement run through her. She wondered if he had felt it, too. She lifted her gaze to meet his and found his eyes were heavy-lidded, his nostrils flared, his lips somewhat full. Charlotte suddenly felt threatened, but there was no escape from his embrace.

"My lord . . ." She didn't finish the sentence because she couldn't remember what she had wanted to say.

"Your eyes are too big," the earl said in a husky voice, "and as green as a cat's. Your hair tumbles about your face like a fallen stack of goldenboys. Your lashes, on the other hand, don't match your hair at all. They're coal black. And you have freckles marring those alabaster cheeks."

"You refused to let me cover them with powder, my lord," Charlotte reminded him in a voice that quivered with hurt as he listed all her faults.

"And your mouth . . ." Denbigh made a *tsk*-ing sound and shook his head as though in dismay. "You have the mouth of a courtesan. Red and plump and rosy. It is easy to see what Braddock found to like. But Braddock is a rake."

Charlotte lifted her chin pugnaciously. "Are you finished, my lord?"

"No, I am not. Your chin defines you, Lady Charlotte. Defiant. Stubborn. Square and honest to a fault."

"Now are you done?"

"One more thing."

"What is that?"

Instead of answering, Denbigh danced her toward the edge of the floor, toward a curtained anteroom that concealed them from the assembly. Once inside, he stopped dancing. When she tried to step back, his arm firmed around her waist, holding her in place. "You make a man want to keep you safe from the evils of the world, to kiss you and touch you and hold you close."

Charlotte fought back a momentary panic. She had no idea why Denbigh was saying such things. He most certainly could not act on such a statement. After all, she could hear the dancers whirling past them on the other side of the curtain. There was nothing the earl could do to her here that would be any worse than the insults he had hurled on the dance floor.

Or so she thought, until he lowered his head and his lips touched hers.

Olivia could hardly believe she was waltzing at Almack's. She had dreamed of it for so many years—since the accident when she was seventeen—and been so very certain her dream would never come true. Now, thanks to Charlotte, it had.

The reality of it was even more wonderful than she had imagined. She could feel the muscles in Braddock's shoulder under her fingertips, feel the strength of his arm around her waist, the warmth of his body, the scents of soap and male sweat, which were not at all unpleasant.

And she could feel his gaze on her. That is, when he was not watching her brother.

"Do you think your brother will call me out for the insult?" Braddock asked abruptly.

She glanced up at him in surprise. "What insult, Your Grace?"

"For daring to dance with his sister," Braddock said. It was plain he would have welcomed a duel.

"It is an honor you do me, Your Grace."

"The honor is mine," he replied grimly.

She knew he was responding with what courtesy demanded. Even if he did not mean it. "It is kind of you to say so, Your Grace."

"Kindness has nothing to do with my feelings toward you or your family," Braddock said harshly.

Olivia faltered and missed a step at the virulence in his voice, and Braddock's arm tightened around her. "I'm sorry to be so clumsy, Your Grace."

"The fault was mine."

Olivia shook her head. "No. I should not have accepted your offer to dance, given as it was under duress. Sometimes Lady Charlotte does outrageous things." *That was an understatement.* "Inveigling you to dance with me was one of them."

For the first time, she saw his features relax in amusement. "No one forces me to do anything, my dear."

"You could not have wanted to dance with me," Olivia managed to say, glancing at him from beneath lowered lashes.

"Why not?"

"Because . . ." Because she was a twenty-five-year-old spinster, with mousy brown hair and nondescript hazel eyes and a painfully awkward limp. "What will people think?"

"Are you worried about my reputation as a rake?"

"Hardly. I mean, who would think . . . surely no one would believe . . ." She flushed, unable to conceive of herself as the female in such a relationship.

Braddock grinned, and she was amazed to see the years fall away. He looked younger, almost care-free. "I assure you, my lady, from the indecently close way I am holding you, we are already setting tongues to wagging. And I must say, I am not suffering at all from the experience. Beneath that dreadfully unstylish frock you are wearing, I believe I am holding quite a handful of woman."

Olivia would have stopped dancing entirely if the duke had not chosen that moment to whirl her around so that she was forced to grasp his shoulder or go flying into the air. Her cheeks burned with humiliation. No gentleman spoke in such terms to a lady. He must mean to insult her, and thus provoke her brother into a duel and perhaps kill him. She refused to allow that to happen.

She wished she were like Charlotte. Charlotte would have confronted the duke and slapped his face. She hadn't even the courage to raise her eyes to the man. But she could make it plain in words that the duke could not hope to use her to destroy her brother.

"You may insult me all you wish, Your Grace. I will repeat nothing you say to my brother. I will not allow you to provoke him to a quarrel because of me."

"I would hardly expect your brother to challenge me to a duel because I called your dress unfashionable," Braddock said with a cynical curl of his lip.

"You purposely misunderstand me. That was not what I meant. I meant . . . the other thing you said."

"It is no insult to say a lady has the figure of a woman," Braddock said in a soft voice.

"It is unseemly to speak of such things." Olivia felt her face heating with embarrassment.

"Then I will not speak of it again. At least not tonight. May I call on you tomorrow?"

Olivia felt a flash of joy followed immediately by suspicion. "For what purpose?"

"Why, to take you driving in the park, of course."

Olivia wished she knew what the duke was really thinking. Was he truly interested in her? It seemed too much to hope. More likely he wanted to cause trouble for her brother. However, she did not want to turn down his offer to go driving if it had been made because he was sincerely interested in her, however unlikely that seemed. Maybe, if she had a chance to talk with him, she could somehow manage to bring peace between Braddock and her brother.

To judge the duke's intentions, she needed to see his eyes. But that meant lifting her chin and looking up at him. She simply could not do it. Which meant she would have to turn Braddock down. "I don't think—"

"I have him now," Braddock muttered.

"What?"

Instead of answering her, the duke whirled her toward the edge of the dance floor. Before she realized what he was about, he came to a halt near one of the alcoves and, with a flourish, pulled the curtain aside.

Lionel Morgan had become the Earl of Denbigh, Viscount Leighton, and several other lesser titles when he was eighteen, and his father had tried to jump a fence with a nag that could not do the job. His mother had died years before, giving birth to a stillborn child.

He had done a creditable job over the past eleven years, of managing the life of his sister and a great many properties, with all their attendant servants and tenants. Or so he had thought, until Lady

Charlotte Edgerton had come along and told him everything he was doing wrong.

The chit was driving him crazy. They had clearly been engaged in a war of wills since the moment they met. He had refused to be manipulated, cajoled, or entreated to fulfill the girl's demands to be returned to America. He had made it clear that the only way she would ever be free of him was if she fulfilled the requirements of her father's will. The stubborn minx had vowed to buy her freedom with matrimony, and he had been doing his best to help her ever since. He would rejoice and be glad when she was finally out of his life.

So why was he standing here behind a curtain, a few feet from the dance floor at Almack's, kissing her? And worse, much worse, enjoying it!

Her lips were soft and supple and pliant. Not at all like the Charlotte he knew. Because her response was so unexpected, he was held in thrall a moment longer than was safe under the circumstances.

The bright candlelight from the ballroom chandelier hit his closed eyelids before he realized what had happened. The collective gasp he heard told him before he opened his eyes that their indiscretion had been discovered. It was not until he turned to see who had exposed them that he realized how neatly he had been trapped.

"Braddock!"

"Well, well, Denbigh. Enjoying the company of your ward a bit too much, I should say."

Lion's lips pressed flat. The duke would love it if he slapped a glove in his face, but he refused to be taunted into creating a scene. Lion saw the shocked look in Olivia's eyes and felt sick to his stomach. What had he done? He was supposed to be the responsible one. Damn it all.

The music stopped, and those who had merely been glancing at the unfolding spectacle as they danced by stopped to gape. Denbigh could see the patronesses conferring. Soon he would be joined by one or several of them, demanding an explanation for his behavior.

There was no help for it. The Earl of Denbigh had jeopardized—all right, ruined—a young woman's reputation. There was only one way to repair it. A glance at Charlotte's blushing, but untroubled, face revealed she had no idea how great the calamity that had befallen them.

Denbigh waited for Lady Jersey to reach his side before he took Charlotte's hand in his, forced a smile, and said, "I have proposed to Lady Charlotte, and she has accepted me. I hope you will be the first to congratulate me on my good fortune."

He held tight to Charlotte's hand when she tried to snatch it free. He saw the relief on Olivia's face. She gave him a supportive smile, and he realized his sister was not in the least upset by the prospect of having Charlotte as a sister-in-law.

Charlotte had turned a chalky white. He could feel her quivering, as though she were going to explode any minute. He had to get her out of here before she did.

Denbigh saw the approving look in Lady Jersey's eyes before she signaled through her congratulations that he was forgiven his solecism.

"You should have told us, Denbigh. We would have brought in some champagne."

"Lemonade will be fine to toast our nuptials," Denbigh reassured her, since weak lemonade was the strongest drink ever served at Almack's. "If I could be allowed a moment of privacy with my fiancée—"

"A moment only," Lady Jersey said, making it clear there were limits to her tolerance. The patroness stood guard as the curtain dropped to give them privacy.

Denbigh turned to his ward, certain Charlotte would have a potent opinion about the situation to share with him. He was caught off-balance by her silence.

Tears brimmed in her eyes, and she caught her lower lip in her teeth so hard he winced.

A lump formed in his throat. He swallowed painfully and said, "Well, Charlotte, do you have something you would like to say to me?"

"You're an idiot and a fool and I wouldn't marry you if you were the last man on earth."

"I see," Denbigh said, a chilling smile curving his lips. That was more like the Charlotte he knew. He held out his arm to her. "Shall we join the others to toast our nuptials?"

Her troubled gaze locked with his. "I . . . I can't marry you, sir," she said. "I . . . I don't love you."

"I'm truly sorry, Charlotte. There's no help for it now. We have to marry. I know this is all my fault—and Braddock's," he added bitterly. "But I'm willing to pay the necessary price to preserve your good name."

"You could let me go back to America."

"No, Charlotte. I can't. Your father made me responsible for your well-being. I'm doing the only thing I know to do under the circumstances."

"You don't love me, Lion," she whispered. "You don't even like me. Please don't do this to us."

She had never called him by his name before. It sounded like a caress coming from her lips. His chest hurt. He opened his mouth to say he would find some honorable way to release her, but at that moment the curtain was shoved abruptly aside.

"Join us, children," Lady Jersey said. "We want to wish you joy."

Denbigh waited to see what Charlotte would

do. Her chin came up, and her eyes blazed with sudden light. She laid her hand on his arm and, as they left the alcove, said to Lady Jersey, "Did Denbigh tell you we've decided on a very long engagement?"

"No, Lady Charlotte, he did not."

"Oh, yes. Four years, to be exact."

Denbigh gave her a stunned look. The conniving chit! She had no intention of marrying him. She intended to wait until she was twenty-one and had the use of her inheritance to escape him. He would be stuck dancing attendance on her, while she would be entitled to the freedom—God help him!—of an affianced lady.

Charlotte shot him a triumphant grin and whispered, "Who's the captive now, my lord?"

5

 WHEN LION AWOKE, HAVING DRUNK ONE too many toasts to his impending nuptials at his club, he had no idea where he was. One by one, he eliminated the places he was not. Definitely not in his bedroom at Denbigh Castle, nor his bachelor apartments near Whitehall, nor Lady Frockman's boudoir, nor even his grandfather's London town house on Grosvenor Square, where he had established his sister and his ward.

The room was lavishly appointed, but he saw no frills that indicated it belonged to a woman. Nevertheless, he tensed when he heard a knock at the door, wondering if he was about to come face to face with some irate husband.

When he looked down at himself, he realized that was unlikely. He was still completely dressed except for his cravat and the fancy silver-buckled shoes he had worn with the required stockings and knee breeches to Almack's.

He hesitated, then said, "Come in."

The door opened to reveal . . . Percival Porter. Lion winced at the brilliant puce waistcoat his friend wore buttoned around his substantial girth. Percy had an execrable sense of fashion, and he deplored exercise beyond lifting his fork at the supper table. He had not been anywhere near the top of his class at either Eton or Oxford. But he had no vices. And a man could not hope to have a more staunch or steadfast friend.

"Good morning, old man," Percy said as he stepped into the room. "Or perhaps I should say good afternoon, since it is almost noon."

Once upon a time, the sight of his friend would have been a source of relief. But ever since Alice's death, Denbigh had forced Percy out of his life, even refusing to receive his friend because it was too difficult—too painful—to discuss what Alice had done. Her death had thus become a double tragedy. He had lost both the woman he loved and his best friend at the same time.

The year of mourning for Alice had ended. He noticed Percy no longer wore a black armband on his Devonshire brown sleeve. Time had dulled the edge of his own grief, as well. But not his anger. He would never forgive what Alice had done.

He saw the wariness in Percy's eyes. His friend seemed no more certain how to proceed than Lion was himself.

"Good afternoon," Lion said at last. It came out as more of a croak, his throat was so parched.

"I had my valet leave some claret by the bed," Percy said, pointing to a crystal decanter. "If you would like a hair of the dog."

"I would, thank you," Denbigh said, pouring a small amount of claret for himself. It took some of the fuzziness from his mouth, if not his head. "How did I get here?" he asked.

"We met at White's early this morning," Percy said. "You were a bit foxed from celebrating your engagement to Lady Charlotte Edgerton."

Lion had not wanted to celebrate at all, but he'd had no choice when an acquaintance who had been at Almack's arrived at White's and congratulated him on his engagement. One drink had led to another.

Lion met Percy's gaze, and they stared at each other somberly. He should have been celebrating the birth of his first child by now, not marriage to another woman. He had no recollection of meeting Percy, but he was glad his friend had brought him here. He shuddered to think where he might have ended up otherwise.

"I saw the note Alice left at the inn, Lion," Percy said in a quiet voice. "Her maid pulled it from the fire. I am so very sorry things turned out the way they did. I wish . . .''

He did not finish the thought. It was not necessary. They had been friends for a long time before Lion realized he was in love with Alice. A bond existed between them from the days when they were boys growing up on neighboring estates in Sussex. Even before Lion knew Percy would become his brother-in-law, they had been as close as any two brothers.

Lion realized suddenly that nothing had changed between them. All the things Lion had not allowed Percy to say a year ago, did not need saying. Percy was still—had always been and always would be—his friend. His throat tightened with emotion. He tried to smile, but failed. ''It has been a difficult year,'' he admitted.

Percy cleared his throat. ''I have missed your company, Lion. May I be among the first to congratulate you on your forthcoming marriage to Lady Charlotte?''

Lion put a trembling hand to his forehead. He was immensely glad to have a friend with whom to share the truth. ''Bloody hell, Percy. I've made an awful mess of things.''

Percy crossed and settled himself in a wooden armchair beside the bed. ''I'm all ears, Lion.''

Denbigh told him everything that had happened since he had gone to Denbigh Castle to chastise Lady

Charlotte—and ended up engaged to the brat. "Braddock must have been watching and waiting for his chance," he said.

"The man has been the bane of my existence for the past year. Everywhere I go, he is there. He stole that opera singer I fancied from beneath my nose before I could claim her as my mistress. He bought up all the space on the merchant ships headed for America at harvest time, leaving me with no way to ship the wheat from my farms. I had to take a disastrous price for it here in England.

"I cannot prove he is responsible, but someone meddled with my best team of chestnuts before a race on which I had bet a great deal of money. I very nearly lost.

"Braddock seems determined to make my life as miserable as he can. I wish he would confront me and demand satisfaction. That would be better than never knowing where he will strike next."

"Have you tried to talk to him?" Percy asked.

"I've left my card more than once. He refuses to see me," Lion replied. "Trapping me in a compromising situation with Lady Charlotte is the latest effort in what I can only guess is a plan of convoluted revenge for the death of his brother. I feel a fool getting caught kissing behind a curtain, Percy. I can tell you that."

"You are honor bound to go through with the

wedding,'' Percy advised, ''no matter how you were manipulated into it.''

''Oh, no, Percy, I am most certainly *not* going to marry the chit!''

''What of the girl's reputation?''

''All I have to do is find some other clunch to take her off my hands,'' Lion said. ''Have you any suggestions?''

''I know my share of clunches,'' Percy said with an amused grin. ''I doubt whether any of them is in search of a wife.''

''She's an heiress, Percy. And not bad to look at. She has a few small faults that will need attending to by whoever marries her. But the right man will be able to manage her. I will have to look around at the next few balls and routs and fêtes and see who is available. Surely there is someone who will want her.''

''Have you no feelings at all for the girl?'' Percy asked.

Denbigh opened his mouth to say ''absolutely not'' and snapped it shut again. The problem was he felt a dozen things when he thought of Charlotte Edgerton—all of them contradictory.

''I'm not in love with her,'' he said at last. He would never trust another woman enough to put his heart in her hands. ''But I cannot deny there are things about her I admire.'' He smiled wryly. ''But the list of her admirable qualities is outweighed by one at least twice as long of traits that make me want to wring her lovely neck."

"Ah, then she is beautiful?"

"Not in the conventional sense," Lion replied, bringing Charlotte's face to mind. "Her complexion is not as fair as it might be, because she refuses to wear a bonnet to protect herself from the sun. I know freckles are considered a flaw, Percy, but I rather like them on her.

"She smiles more than the usual miss, but her teeth are straight and white. Her eyes are a striking green color, and believe me you will notice them, because they are never downcast. Her chin is continually outthrust, as though she is out to fight the world.

"And our world disappoints her a great deal, Percy. The chit has picked up quite a few revolutionary ideas in America. My servants jump to do her bidding because they like her, not because she expects them to wait on her. You see, Charlotte believes every man should be treated equally, no matter what his station."

"I say!" Percy exclaimed. "What a radical point of view! The girl sounds a veritable bluestocking."

"I've caught her many times with her nose in a book," Lion said. "But that's not all. We now have schools for the servants' children on my lands, Percy. And she has repaired the crofters' roofs. After all, as Charlotte pointed out to me, they suffer as much from the rain and cold as we do.''

"Good heavens," Percy breathed.

Lion's smile broadened. "She has even got Olivia riding again.''

"I thought her injury prevented it.''

Lion shook his head. "Apparently it was only fear that kept her from trying to ride again. I tell you, in many ways Charlotte is a wonder. Then there are the times when she does something so outrageous I cannot believe my eyes and ears.''

"Like what?" Percy asked curiously.

"Like suggesting that Braddock dance with Olivia when I refused to allow him to dance with Charlotte.''

"What? Olivia dancing, too?''

"The waltz, no less, with the Duke of Braddock.''

"I can hardly believe it. How wonderful for her!''

"Were you not listening? I said it was Braddock who took my sister in his arms. The duke has some rig in mind, you can bet on it. I'm worried that he will find a way to hurt Olivia.''

"Do you have any reason to believe he will see your sister again?" Percy asked.

"I warned him not to try.''

"Perhaps he has honorable intentions toward Olivia," Percy suggested.

Denbigh shook his head. "You've seen Olivia, Percy. Do you really think one of the richest men in the kingdom—who, by the way, hates me for killing his brother—would seek out my sister for any but a nefarious purpose?"

"Olivia is a very fine girl," Percy said.

"You've made my point for me," Lion said. "Olivia is my sister, and I love her, but no one would ever call her beautiful, or even pretty. She is shy and retiring and will not speak at all if you do not prompt her. Despite the progress she has made, there are too many men who could never accept a crippled wife. And if we are being perfectly honest, she is fast reaching an age when she will be too old to bear children."

"I say, Lion. Surely she has a few good years left."

But they both knew Olivia was well past the age when she could be expected to make a favorable match.

"Mark my words, Percy. If the Duke of Braddock seeks her out, he can only have mischief in mind. I intend to nip any such attempts in the bud."

"What does Olivia think about all this?"

"Unlike that rebellious hellcat I call my ward, my sister will do as she is told."

At that very moment, Olivia was contemplating the very decision her brother believed he had already made for her. Should she, or should she not go driving in Hyde Park that afternoon with the Duke of Braddock?

Olivia examined the profusion of roses and orchids and daffodils that had been delivered to Charlotte that morning by the young bucks she had devastated with her charms at Almack's. Olivia was happy for her friend. Unquestionably, Charlotte had taken.

Olivia had received a single bouquet of violets . . . from the Duke of Braddock. He had enclosed a note that said, "Because they remind me of you."

She had puzzled over that for most of the morning, because she could not imagine what he had meant. He had also invited her to drive with him and named a time when he would pick her up. She had only to send him a note that she was willing.

Olivia had sat poised, quill in hand, at the desk in her grandfather's library for almost an hour, trying to make up her mind whether to accept the duke's invitation.

She knew all the reasons why she should refuse. None of them held as much sway as the one reason why she wished to accept.

Braddock was the man of her dreams.

To refuse him would be to give up her dreams forever, because a man of his prominence was not likely to pursue her without encouragement. She could not give up the hope that he had some other motive for inviting her than revenge against her brother. She dipped her quill and began to write.

"You're up early."

Olivia turned and saw Charlotte standing at the door. "So are you. Did something awaken you?"

"I couldn't sleep," she admitted.

Charlotte wandered around the library, picking leatherbound tomes from the shelves and leafing through them before replacing them again. Olivia was afraid to continue writing for fear Charlotte would want to see her missive. She had hoped to have at least this first meeting with the duke without fanfare. That way, she could ask him his intentions and determine his motives before she let herself fall any more deeply in love with him than she already was.

Eventually, Charlotte settled into one of the two leather wing chairs in front of the fireplace. Except, since it was Charlotte, instead of sitting with her feet on the floor, she had draped herself sideways in the chair with her legs hanging over one arm.

Olivia had just dipped her quill again when Charlotte asked, "Can you spare a moment to talk?"

Olivia laid down her quill and rose from the desk, turning her letter, with its revealing salutation, facedown on the blotter, in case Charlotte should start to roam the room again and come upon it. Then she crossed and sat properly in the other brass-studded leather chair. "What is it, Charlie?"

She gave a long-suffering sigh. "Lion."

Olivia smiled. She couldn't help it. Personally, she believed Charlotte and her brother were well suited for each other. Lion was too rigidly set in his ways and often authoritarian. He had become an embittered man after Lady Alice had abandoned him at the altar. Many times over the past year when she had heard about her brother's exploits, she had feared he would end up dissipated or dead.

Everything had changed since Charlotte came into their lives. As far as she was concerned, Charlotte was Lion's salvation. Charlotte would help her brother learn to enjoy life again.

"What about Lion?" Olivia asked.

"I can't marry him, Livy." She scooted forward over the arm of the chair and said earnestly, "I'm going to look around and see if I can find someone else."

"Oh?" It wasn't necessary to say more than that with Charlotte. She could easily carry a conversation all by herself.

"Your brother doesn't want to marry me any more than I want to marry him. We fight like dogs and cats, like weasels and wolverines, like——"

"Husbands and wives," Olivia inserted. "Every couple has disagreements. The secret is to learn how to compromise."

Charlotte shook her head. "We're too different. And he's too stubborn to change his mind."

"And you're not stubborn?" Olivia queried.

"I can be reasonable."

"Prove it. Give Lion a chance. Try to understand him. Try to like him. Try to see his point of view."

Charlotte wrinkled her nose. "What purpose would that serve?"

"You might find out Lion is nicer than you think."

Charlotte bounded out of the chair as though the stuffing had exploded under her. "I think you're wrong, Livy. But since it's your brother I'm going to be rejecting, I suppose I owe it to you to give him a fair chance. How long do I have to be reasonable?" she asked.

Olivia laughed. "Is a month too long?"

"Oh, Lord. That's *forever!*"

"Three weeks then."

"All right," Charlotte conceded. "For the next three weeks I'll try to understand his point of view. But I'm going to keep my eyes open for someone else to marry."

"That sounds fair," Olivia said.

"Thanks, Olivia," Charlotte said. "Oh, by the way. Be sure to give the duke my regards."

Olivia's cheeks grew hot. "I don't know what you mean."

"I saw the violets, Livy."

Olivia looked at her questioningly. "How did you know they were mine?"

"Who would send me violets?" she said. "Violets are for someone mysterious and delicate and lovely. That isn't me at all. That's you, Livy."

"Mysterious?" Olivia repeated. "Delicate and lovely?"

Charlotte nodded. "Tell him yes, you'll go driving with him, Livy. And have a wonderful time."

She was gone before Olivia could argue with her. Olivia could find nothing mysterious about herself. She was plain and ordinary and forthright. And how could someone who walked like a lopsided duck be delicate? Lovely was the worst lie of all. She knew how plain she was. She had lived with her looks long enough to be honest with herself.

She put her hands to her warm cheeks. Was that really how the duke saw her? Could he really find her intriguing? Could he really find her lovely?

She rose slowly and returned to the desk in a daze. She lifted the quill and wrote, "I will be glad to go driving with you this afternoon." She signed her name and folded the letter and sealed it with wax. She stared at it for a few moments more before she called Galbraith to come and deliver it.

The instant the note was gone, Olivia wished it back again. She was a foolish old maid, long past her Last Prayer, who was only going to be hurt by a vengeful man. Charlotte's fanciful explanation for the violets was no more than that. It would probably turn out that Braddock had asked his steward to send the flowers, and he actually had no idea what variety the man had chosen.

But the dream was too strong to die.

She wanted to be mysterious. She wanted to be delicate and lovely. She retired to her room alone to transform herself into the vision Charlotte had painted for her.

It wasn't easy.

It amazed her to discover that despite the fact she had purchased as many gowns from the *modiste* as Charlotte had for her trip to London, everything in her closet was a shade of brown or green—including the gown she had worn last night to Almack's. Had she really chosen those faded, unfashionable colors for herself? Something bright at the end of the row of dresses caught her eye. She pushed everything else aside and drew it forward.

She remembered the dress very well. Charlotte had picked the soft peach-colored muslin over her protest and the design from a stack of fashion plates she had already rejected, saying, "The day will come, Livy, when you will want something special to wear. When you look through your gowns, there it will be."

She took the high-waisted dress out of the wardrobe and laid it on the bed. It had a deeply cut square neck and a ruffled hem. She was tempted to call for her maid to help her, but she knew the woman would be likely to remark on something so foreign to what she usually wore. Olivia already felt self-conscious about dressing in something so obviously intended to attract a man's attention. She decided she would have to manage alone.

Once she had the gown on it became apparent the bodice was cut even lower than she remembered—Charlotte again, she was sure. Weren't such short, puffy sleeves too youthful for a woman of her age? The ribbon tied beneath her breasts emphasized the difference between her slender body and her bountiful assets.

She walked slowly to the mirror over her dresser, almost afraid to look at herself.

A stranger peered back at her. Her ordinary brown hair, which she kept pinned up and out of her way, had taken on red highlights. Her hazel eyes looked as warm and rich as sherry. And against the peach fabric, her skin looked vibrantly alive.

Olivia smiled and received another pleasant surprise. The lady reflected in the mirror was no schoolroom miss, but a mature woman, serene, poised, and . . . No, she was not beautiful. That would have been saying too much. Not even pretty, if she were brutally honest. But soft and lovely, like a violet.

"Livy, why is the door locked?" Charlotte called from the hall.

"Because otherwise you would burst in without knocking," Olivia answered with a laugh.

"What are you doing in there? I've been looking everywhere for you."

Olivia crossed to the door, opened it wide, and stood waiting for Charlotte's verdict. Charlotte, being Charlotte, didn't disappoint her.

A smile as big as the ocean split her face. She grabbed Olivia's hands and whirled her exuberantly in a circle. "Oh, Livy, look at you! You're a beauty! You'll have the duke on his knees declaring himself before you know it. He won't be able to take his eyes off of you. When is he coming? Can I be there when he does I want to see his face. He won't believe it's the same Livy he met last night."

That was what worried her. Braddock would know she had gone to a great deal of effort to improve herself for him. Would he mention the difference? Would he appreciate it?

"I'd rather meet the duke alone, if you don't mind," she said. "I'll be nervous enough without someone there to watch every move I make."

"I won't say anything. I promise I'll be as quiet as a mouse."

Olivia arched a disbelieving brow.

"All right, so I wouldn't be able to keep my

mouth shut for long. But I wouldn't say anything to embarrass you."

The brow arched higher.

"At least, not on purpose. Oh, please, Livy, let me be there," Charlotte begged.

"I suppose I owe you something for insisting I have this lovely dress made," Olivia said. "All right, Charlie. You may be present in the drawing room when he arrives. But you must promise to act like a lady."

"I'll do my best," Charlotte said. "Now, before the duke arrives, we need to do something with your hair."

Olivia reached up to touch her neatly arranged hair, looking for something out of place. "Is anything amiss?"

Charlotte wrinkled her nose. "You might as well put on one of those old-maid lace caps of yours. That hairdo cries out for one."

Olivia hurried to the mirror and stared at herself. The look of serenity was gone from her eyes. Panic had replaced it. "What can I do, Charlie? I've always worn it like this."

"Always?"

"Since my accident, anyway."

"Then it's time for a change, Livy. Sit down, and let me see what I can do." Charlotte urged her onto the cushioned bench in front of the mirror and began pulling pins willy-nilly from her hair. It fell in soft waves around her face.

"My goodness," Charlotte said. "I had no idea your hair was so long. Or so full of curls."

"I can't get it to hang straight," Olivia complained. "So I keep it pinned up."

"Look how bouncy these curls are on your shoulders," Charlotte said as she brushed Olivia's hair. "We'll just pin a little of it away from your face and let the rest hang free. There. That's perfect!" Charlotte announced.

Olivia looked at herself in the mirror. Another transformation had taken place. Now she was almost pretty.

It was terrifying.

"Put it back like it was, Charlie." She quickly gathered her hair back against her head, stabbing pins in so hard they hurt her scalp.

"What are you doing, Livy? You're messing up my creation."

"It isn't me, Charlie. I'm not that woman in the mirror. I'm plain and ordinary. Any man who wants me will have to want me for who I am inside. I'll never trap him with my looks."

Charlotte stood aside without interfering while Olivia pinned her hair back smooth again, brushing every single stray wisp into place.

"Why are you so afraid of being pretty, Livy?" Charlotte asked quietly.

Livy turned startled eyes on the girl, who saw too much for one so young. "I'm not afraid of being pretty. It's just that I know I'm not. Lion has told me so."

"Lion doesn't know everything, Livy. I thought you had learned that lesson by now."

Olivia wasn't sure where the anger came from, but it bubbled up inside her like some witch's brew. "You don't know everything, either, Charlotte. I—"

Her brother appeared in her bedroom door like some apparition. His shirt points were wilted, as though he had slept in his clothes. His neck cloth hung shapeless at his throat. Theobald would probably have an attack of the vapors when he saw the ruin of his handiwork.

Olivia would not have minded having one herself. It would have allowed her to avoid seeing the look on Lion's face as he perused her from head to foot.

He leaned against the door frame, layered his arms across his chest, put one booted foot over the other, and asked in a lazy voice, "What is the occasion, Olivia?"

"For your information, she's going driving with the Duke of Braddock this afternoon," Charlotte answered for her.

"You may speak when you're spoken to, Lady

Charlotte," Lion corrected her in a chilly voice. "I was addressing my sister."

Charlotte's lower lip formed a six-year-old's pout, and her eyebrows lowered mutinously over angry green eyes. "Don't think you can stop her," Charlotte warned. "She's going whether you like it or not."

"This is none of your business," Lion retorted, legs and arms coming uncrossed at the same time as he settled his weight on both feet, ready to take up the cudgel and fight. "I'll thank you to keep your nose out of places where it doesn't belong."

"Both of you stop!" Olivia cried. Her brother and his ward both looked at her as though she were the scapegrace for interrupting their argument. "I am going driving with the Duke of Braddock this afternoon," she told her brother.

"I forbid it," he replied in a stony voice.

"I am not seventeen, I am five and twenty. I am not your ward, I am your sister. You have no authority over me, Lion. I may do as I please. And I am going driving this afternoon with Braddock."

"Hurrah for you, Livy!" Charlotte cheered.

"As for you, Charlotte," Olivia said, "You made a promise to me earlier today. Have you forgotten it already?"

Charlotte grimaced. "Do I have to?"

"A promise is a promise."

Charlotte rolled her eyes and turned to the earl.

"I guess Livy can take care of herself." She sniffed the earl's breath and said, "Have you been drinking this morning?"

"That is none of your business, either."

"If you say so." She turned back to Olivia. "I'm trying, Livy. But it isn't going to be easy." A moment later she had left Olivia alone with her brother.

"I knew that girl would be a bad influence on you," Lion said. "What is that you're wearing?"

"A dress."

"Why do you look so different?"

"Do I?" Livy asked.

"You don't look like yourself."

Livy felt the tension ease from her shoulders. It would take time for Lion to adjust to a sister who wore bright colors and believed she could attract a beau. It was taking time for her to accept that fact herself.

"Everything will be all right, Lion. I'm only going driving in the park. What could possibly happen to me with hundreds of other people around?"

"The last time I thought something like that, I ended up engaged," Lion said.

Olivia smiled. "In my case, that wouldn't be such a bad result."

"Be careful, Olivia."

"I will, Lion. Oh, believe me. I will."

6

"WHY DID YOU CHOOSE VIOLETS?"

Reeve Somers, sixth Duke of Braddock, Earl of Comarty, Viscount Greenwich, Baron Hardy, and several other lesser titles, nodded to the couple in a passing carriage to avoid looking into Lady Olivia's eyes when he answered her. "I should have thought that would be obvious."

She fidgeted with the peach-colored ribbon that hung down beneath her bodice, drawing his attention back to it. He had suspected she hid a ripe figure beneath the awful bronze gown she had worn at Almack's. The more fashionable carriage dress she wore for their ride in Hyde Park confirmed what he had only suspected. She had everything a mistress needed to make him happy.

Which made her the perfect foil in his plans of

revenge. His year of mourning was up. At long last, the Earl of Denbigh would be made to pay for the death of Reeve's brother.

Reeve had been in India when he got the news of what had happened. It seemed the Earl of Denbigh had challenged the duke's younger brother, James, to a duel for the most frivolous of reasons. The earl had not liked the way James tied his cravat.

The duel was held at dawn on the first day of July, with bets laid at White's as to the outcome, considering the relative reputations of the twenty-one-year-old Lord James, and the twenty-eight-year-old Earl of Denbigh, with firearms.

James had fired his pistol and missed. The earl had not.

Reeve's brother, his only living relative, the only person in the world who cared whether he lived or died, had been murdered. During the several months before the news reached him, while Reeve had been imagining his unlicked cub of a brother in London getting a bit of town bronze, James had been buried six feet underground.

Reeve's first inclination had been to return at once to England and challenge Denbigh to a duel and end his life. But Denbigh's death was not nearly enough recompense for what he had done. James would still be dead. Reeve would have to live a lifetime knowing his brother had died a senseless death, while Denbigh was relieved of all mortal suffering. No, Reeve had needed more satisfaction.

He had hounded the earl and harried him, decimated his properties and ruined his investments. Then he had conceived the most fitting revenge of all . . . to destroy someone he loved.

Reeve had known from the beginning that the earl had a sister, but when he heard she was crippled, he had looked for someone else the earl cared about. To his surprise, he had discovered there was no one.

Then, quite by accident, he had discovered the sister was not as crippled as he had been led to believe. He decided on the spot that he would make the earl's sister his mistress and ruin her reputation. When Denbigh confronted him to redeem his sister's honor, he would take delight in killing him.

He had not delayed in putting his plan into action. He had sent a bouquet of violets and invited the earl's sister to go driving with him.

Olivia sat rigidly at his side as they drove through Hyde Park, seeing the fashionable world and being seen by them. He had seen her surprise when he appeared at her door driving a curricle, since it meant her maid would have to be left behind. But she had not refused to come with him. She had clutched his arm once with her gloved hand when he took a corner too fast but let go as soon as she regained her balance. She was clearly agitated, clearly uncomfortable. He needed to put her at ease, needed to gain her trust, in order for his plan to succeed.

"I sent violets because they have dark, mysterious depths. Like you," he said at last.

She shot him a startled look, then broke into a radiant smile that completely transformed her face. For an instant she seemed almost pretty. Almost. Her features were too ordinary for real beauty. Except, perhaps, for her hazel eyes, which were wide-spaced and warm as the sun and unbelievably innocent for one of her advanced age. Aside from an occasional brief peek at him, she kept them lowered demurely. He felt the oddest urge to lift her chin and demand that she look at him.

"Charl—Lady Charlotte guessed that was why you sent violets," she said. "I . . . I didn't believe her."

"You don't believe you're mysterious?" he teased.

An enchanting blush raced upward from her throat to land in two rosy spots on her cheeks. "No one has ever said so," she confessed.

She was a green one, a mere babe in the woods, and not much of a challenge for an experienced rake of thirty-five. It was almost going to be too easy, Reeve thought. He wanted to draw out his seduction of the girl, goading Denbigh with his utter helplessness to prevent his sister's ruination, so the earl would suffer all the more when it became a *fait accompli*.

"Is this your first visit to London?" the duke asked, knowing that it was.

"Yes, Your Grace."

"Are you enjoying the sights?"

"Yes, Your Grace."

"Have you been to Astley's to see the performing horses?"

She chuckled. "Lady Charlotte insisted we go there the day we arrived. If you can imagine, she was determined to see the Elgin Marbles, as well. My brother absolutely forbid it."

The famous collection at the British Museum included several sculptures of nearly naked male bodies.

"Would you like to see the statues?" he asked.

She angled her head to observe him past the edge of a stylish straw bonnet that ostensibly protected her complexion from the sun, but also managed to keep her face neatly hidden from him when she looked straight ahead. "Are you inviting me to go with you, Your Grace?"

"If you would be interested in seeing them, I will take you," he said.

He saw the flicker of yearning on her face before she slowly shook her head. "My brother would not approve, Your Grace."

"Do you always let your brother dictate your behavior?"

She kept her eyes hidden, but her hands gave away her agitation. Her gloved fingers twined in her lap, the peach ribbon laced between them. At last she turned to face him, her eyes lowered so her lashes sat like coal crescents on her cheeks.

"I have not been out much in the world," she said at last. "I trust my brother to have my best interests at heart."

"What if I promised to protect you from the dangers that lay in waiting for a young miss in London?"

Her fingers went still. "I am hardly a young miss." She took a hitching breath and announced, "I am five and twenty," as though she were sounding the death knell for any possible relationship between them.

"That old?" he said with a chuckle. "But still in need of a protector, I hope."

Her brow wrinkled in confusion. Protector was a term ordinarily used by a man in relation to his mistress.

The duke did not want to give away the game too early, so he clarified, "I stand ready to offer my services as your escort for any future outings in London."

He could see she was still trying to sort it all

out. She turned completely away from him and stared at the passing carriages.

"Good afternoon, Lady Hornby," he said, nodding to the notorious gossip.

"Good afternoon, Your Grace," Lady Hornby replied. "Is that Denbigh's sister with you?"

"It is." He gave his prime cattle a taste of the whip to keep them moving, even though it was plain the old lady wanted to continue the conversation. It had served his purpose to be noticed with the girl. Driving alone with an unmarried woman in Hyde Park was tantamount to a declaration in some circles. That was to the good, if it helped him to mislead Lady Olivia regarding his designs on her virtue.

"You have not answered me, Lady Olivia," he said when she had sat silently for five entire minutes. "Will you allow me to be your escort?"

"Are you . . . ?" She stopped to clear her throat. "Why would you . . . ?"

He turned his horses down a less used lane in the park where they would not be observed and pulled his team to a halt. He turned and reached for her balled fists, straightening her fingers and holding both of her hands in his. "Perhaps I have not made my intentions plain enough," he began. "I find you . . ."

At the last moment he realized he could not say "beautiful," because she would recognize it immediately for the lie it was. ". . . an admirable woman," he said. "And I would like your permission to court you."

Her hands began to tremble. But she did not pull away.

"If only I could believe you."

She had spoken so softly, he was not sure he had heard her correctly. "You don't believe my intentions are honorable?" he said, acting affronted.

"No," she whispered.

For the length of a heartbeat, he thought Lady Olivia was actually going to raise her eyes and look at him. He quickly wiped the calculating look from his face. Her lids rose slightly, then lowered again, along with her chin, and he was saved from her scrutiny.

"You see, Your Grace, I have no illusions about myself," she said. "I cannot understand what a man such as you would find to admire about . . . about someone like me. And it is a well-known fact you bear a great enmity for my brother."

He was surprised at her resistance to his proposition. The mamas of each new season's crop of schoolroom misses had been trying for years to bring him up to scratch. Of course she was right to be suspicious. His intentions toward her were not, in fact, honorable. But he was a duke, and she was an ape-leader with no realistic hope of finding a husband. She could not really be refusing him!

"It is true there is no love lost between myself

and your brother," he began. Better to admit a little of the truth to hide the wealth of lies. "But my interest right now is not in him."

"Then you don't mean to use me to provoke him to a duel?" she asked in a tentative voice.

That was plain speaking. Perhaps she was not as simple as he had first thought. "I am with you for the pleasure of your company, Lady Olivia." It was not precisely a lie, merely an omission of the entire truth.

"And for no other reason?" she persisted.

"There is one other reason," he admitted.

Her hands clutched his tightly. "What is it?" she asked.

He gave her the only answer he knew would stop her questions. "Because I find you desirable."

She gasped and tried to withdraw her hands from his.

Reeve indulged the need he had felt the entire hour since he had taken her up in his curricle to turn her face toward him and lift her chin. "Look at me," he said softly.

"I cannot."

"Look at me, Lady Olivia."

She raised her eyes, and he saw why she had kept them lowered. Everything she felt was bared for him to see. All her hopes and longings . . . and fears. For a moment he considered giving her a reprieve. Then he remembered the loneliness of coming home to an empty house and the feel of the cold marble that marked his brother's grave, and his resolution returned.

"Believe we can be together, Lady Olivia," he urged, "and we will be."

She swallowed hard. "Very well, Your Grace. You have my permission to court me."

He made himself smile. It was more difficult than he had expected to present himself so falsely to her. He kept reminding himself she was a means to an end. She would suffer, it was true, but more importantly, so would her brother.

"May I take you to the theater next week?" he asked.

"Oh," she breathed. "I would love to go. Could I invite Lady Charlotte to join us? She has been begging to go and Lion—my brother," she corrected herself, "—has not had the time to take us yet."

His smile became brittle, but he managed to keep it on his face. "Of course. The more, the merrier."

Olivia was still floating on air when the duke set her down in front of her grandfather's town house fifteen minutes later. The last person she wanted to see was the person who confronted her the instant she entered the door. Her brother followed her to the drawing room, where she drew off her gloves and untied the ribbons on her hat.

She turned to face him and said, "All right, Lion. What is it you want to say?"

"I am asking you, as a brother who cares deeply for you, not to see Braddock again."

"He wants to court me, Lion. His intentions are honorable," she said breathlessly.

"He wants to get back at me for killing his brother. He only means to lead you on. He will do something dishonorable before he is through, believe me."

"I asked him, Lion, and he said he only wanted to keep me company."

"You don't want to believe I'm right," Lion said gently. "I don't want to hurt you, Olivia, but it's time for honesty between us. Look at yourself. Look at him. Tell me you believe the Duke of Braddock could choose you over all the other women in London."

Her chin began to quiver. "I know . . . I know it seems a bit odd—"

"Odd? It's downright peculiar."

Olivia was trying desperately to believe in the duke's promises. But what Lion said made too much sense. Of course the duke would lie to her about his true intentions if he meant to harm Lion. But she didn't want to believe it!

She tried to brush past her brother and escape up the stairs before she burst into tears, but he stepped in front of her. "I'm sorry, Olivia."

He put his hands on her shoulders. They felt more oppressive than comforting. She knew he loved her. She knew he only wanted the best for her. But he had not lived the isolated life she had. He had not had his dreams dashed by a riding accident at an age when other girls were enjoying their first season in London. He had not wished and hoped and yearned for the impossible.

How could she turn away from Braddock? How could she give up even a frail hope of becoming a wife and mother?

"I'm willing to take the risk, Lion. I'm willing to give Braddock a chance."

"I'm not," he said implacably. "I want you to stay away from him."

Olivia had seldom defied her brother. It felt strange to do so now. She could not have said whether seeing Charlotte's face appear beyond her brother's shoulder gave her the courage to speak her mind, or whether she would have spoken anyway. She was as amazed at her temerity as Lion was when she replied, "The duke has invited Charlotte and me to the theater next week. I have accepted for both of us."

"Bravo, Livy," Charlotte said, clapping her hands. "Just imagine, you and me attending the theater. It will be such an adventure!"

"It will be no such thing, because you aren't going," Denbigh said, his glance shifting from one to the other like a baited bear caught between two nipping terriers.

"You may, of course, keep Charlotte home. But then I will be alone with the duke," Olivia pointed out.

"Damn and blast, Olivia—"

"Excuse me, Lion. I'm tired after my outing. I would like to go to my room."

She gathered up her hat and gloves and fled up the stairs. When Charlotte pursued her, she turned and said, "I would rather be alone, Charlotte, if you don't mind."

Charlotte stopped where she was. "All right, Livy. Are you sure the duke said nothing to upset you?"

Olivia smiled. "Oh, no, Charlotte. Quite the contrary." But she needed privacy to relive the whole exciting afternoon, from the moment she had first seen the handsome duke, to her last shy glance at him before he left her at her door. "I'll talk with you later, I promise."

Charlotte watched Olivia's awkward ascent up the stairs with a furrowed brow. "Something happened," she murmured.

"What did you say?" Denbigh asked.

She turned and skipped back down the stairs to stand before him. "I said something happened between her and Braddock."

Denbigh scowled and headed back to the drawing room. Charlotte followed in his wake.

"It's a good something, I'm sure," she said. "Did you see the way she practically floated up the stairs?"

"Olivia had the same difficult time she always has with stairs," he retorted. "I noticed no difference."

"That's because you weren't looking close enough." She was barely inside when he closed the doors behind her, closeting them together. Charlotte settled herself in a chair sideways, ignored the disapproving frown he gave her, and said, "You are going to let me go with her to the theater, aren't you? Please?"

He cocked a brow. "Please? I don't believe I've ever heard you use that word before. At least not to me."

She gave him an impish grin. "Is it working?"

He turned to face her, one hand tucked behind his back. "You may go. But I will accompany you."

She bounded out of the chair and stood toe to toe with him. "Oh, no! You can't come. Everything will be spoiled if you do."

"If you mean Braddock will not have a free hand with my sister, then you are correct. Neither will you be free to indulge in whatever mischief you had in mind."

"I was only going to leave them alone for a little while," she confessed.

He shook his head. "At least we will be able to use the occasion to some advantage. Any number of gentlemen attending might be considered as a suitable husband, Charlotte."

"But I've already got you," Charlotte replied with a teasing grin. "I saw the notice of our engagement printed in the *Times* just this morning."

"It was?" Denbigh exclaimed. "Who sent it to them?"

"You must have done it," Charlotte said. "Didn't you?"

Denbigh closed his eyes to try and remember whether he might have done such a thing. Then it came back to him. He had dictated the notice to someone at White's while foxed and bet he could induce the *Times* to do a special printing and have it included in the next day's issue. "Good God."

"What's wrong?" she asked. "Didn't you want to announce our engagement?"

"Why would I want to do that when I live in expectation of finding some other man to be your husband before the season is done?"

"I will find my own husband, thank you," she retorted.

"I will do the choosing," Denbigh said. "You will do as you're told."

"I want to marry for love, or not at all," Charlotte announced dramatically.

"What does a chit like you know about love?" Denbigh scoffed. "And what does love have to do with marriage? I believe we've had this conversation before."

"I know your opinion on the matter. It simply doesn't happen to coincide with mine. I've done some thinking, and it seems to me that it might not be such a bad thing for me to stay engaged to you."

"What?" His mouth gaped like a fish yanked out of water.

"As long as I'm going to be stuck with you as my guardian for who knows how long, I might as well be enjoying the social freedoms granted to an affianced lady. I'll be able to go all sorts of places and do all sorts of things without you tagging along."

"You will leave this house unaccompanied over my dead body."

"But, my lord," she said with a sparkle of laughter in her eyes, "affianced couples rarely spend much time together. It simply isn't done."

"In the first place, we aren't really engaged."

"But the *Times*—"

"Charlotte!" he roared. "I am running out of patience with you. After an appropriate time, a notice will appear in the *Times* announcing that you have had a change of heart and cried off."

"You can't force me to break our engagement," she said stubbornly.

His silvery gray eyes narrowed. "Very well. If we are an engaged couple, there are certain liberties that I am allowed with your person."

As he stalked toward her, she backed away from him. She bumped into a chair, went around it, and then kept it between them.

"Liberties? What kind of liberties?" she said, her breath coming in shallow pants.

"I may be seen holding your hand in public."

"Oh," she said, palpable relief appearing on her face. Charlotte supposed this sort of compromise was what Livy had been talking about when she had urged her to meet Denbigh halfway. She extended her hand over the top of the chair. "Be my guest."

He took her hand, and a frisson of excitement skittered up her arm.

"Uh oh," she murmured.

"What did you say?"

"Nothing."

He led her around the obstruction, so they were standing toe to toe. She felt a little jittery with him holding her hand, but she was adjusting. In no time at all she figured she would hardly notice his touch.

"And I may kiss your hand when I bid you adieu," he said.

A little kiss on the hand. What could it hurt?

She smiled brightly and said, "That's fine with me."

She had not expected him to turn her hand over, exposing her wrist and palm. She wriggled against the unfamiliar sensations when he traced the lines in her palm with his fingertips. She nearly jumped out of her skin when he lowered his head and tasted her wrist with his tongue.

The touch of his damp lips against her flesh sent a curl of desire streaking straight up her arm and all the way back down to her belly. She ripped her hand free of his, accidentally smacking him hard on the nose.

"Ow!" He rubbed his nose gingerly, while she stared up at him in confusion, quite unable to catch her breath.

He dropped his hand, and a self-satisfied look appeared on his face. "Are you ready to back out now?"

"Was that supposed to scare me off? It didn't work," she taunted.

A muscle in his jaw jerked, and his lips settled in a determined line. "An affianced gentleman is also expected to steal a kiss behind the palms at balls and routs and musicales."

Charlotte's heart began to ricochet around inside her like a bird that finds itself in a cage for the first time and cannot believe there is no escape. "Kisses?" she squeaked. "Are you sure?"

He nodded. "Oh, yes, my darling affianced bride," he said in a dark, silky voice. "Most definitely kisses, and perhaps a bit of fondling, as well, if the woman is willing. Are you sure you don't want to change your mind and break this engagement?"

Charlotte wished she knew more about such things. If a kiss on her wrist could excite such feelings, what might happen if he touched her . . . wherever. She was treading in dangerous waters. But she could not run until she knew there was no chance she could win by staying to fight.

"Go ahead and kiss me," she said. "I can stand it if you can."

She had not meant to make it sound like a challenge. She had not meant to suggest that she was not going to enjoy it. Maybe then, he would not have kissed her the way he did. Maybe then he would not have put his heart and soul into the thing. Maybe then she would not have found herself drowning in feelings that were overwhelming.

His lips, that she so often saw pressed flat in an uncompromising line, were amazingly soft and supple against her own. They brushed against her lips in a feather-light touch while he murmured, "Kiss me back, Charlie."

Maybe if he had said Charlotte, instead of Charlie, she would have been able to resist him. But there was something so intimate about the sound of his voice saying her name that she willingly surrendered to his demand.

She wasn't conscious of her arms going around his neck or his arms closing around her waist and pulling her body tight against his. She only knew she needed to be closer, she needed to be a part of him, she wanted him to be a part of her.

His hands tightened suddenly on the flesh at her waist, and the single devastating, entangling kiss became a series of kisses pressed against her closed eyelids and nose and cheeks.

"We have to stop, Charlotte," he murmured, his breath hot against her skin.

"No."

He chuckled, then gasped when her lips found his again.

She wanted to be Charlie again. She wanted the intimacy he had stolen from her when he backed away from the kiss.

His mouth closed once more on hers. And she dove again into waters deep and dangerous.

"Where is that grandson of mine?" a gruff voice bellowed from the hallway. "And where is my new granddaughter?"

Before they could separate, the drawing room door slammed open. Denbigh turned to stare with dazed eyes into the astounded, then delighted, eyes of his grandfather, who was joined an instant later by his grandmother. He pushed Charlotte away from him and tried in vain to pretend that nothing had happened.

Something had happened.

Denbigh took a step back from the gamine baggage who had tricked him into compromising her yet again—this time in full view of his grandparents. He was still reeling from the effects of her kiss, and he felt disoriented by the sudden appearance of the only two people in the world who could, without effort, remind him he had not always been a confident Corinthian, a man of the world, a pink of the *ton*. That instead, once upon a time, he had been a clumsy, heartbroken boy in short pants.

"Caught them kissing, Lizzie," his grandfather said to his grandmother with a naughty grin.

"Shame on you, Arthur, bursting in without knocking," the duchess replied.

"God help us now," Denbigh muttered.

"Who are they?" Charlotte asked.

"My grandparents, the Duke and Duchess of Trent." He shoved a hand through his hair, leaving his valet's careful efforts at a perfect Brutus standing askew.

"I should have realized he would see the announcement," he said in an aside to Charlotte. "He has the *Times* delivered before noon every day. Although how he got here so quickly, I can't imagine. He must not even have stopped to pack."

"I'm glad they're here," Charlotte whispered.

"In my opinion you don't spend nearly enough time with your grandparents."

"There are reasons why I keep my distance," Denbigh said in her ear.

"What reasons?"

"You're about to find out," he said.

His grandfather thumped his way farther into the room, leaning heavily on a gnarled hickory cane. His right foot was swathed in an immense bandage, and he yelled for a servant to bring him a footstool as he settled himself in one of the chairs that faced the fire. "Damned gout is making a grumpy old man out of me," the duke admitted.

The duchess was so tall she had been called a Long Meg in her youth. She wore her pure white hair in a braid across the top of her head that looked like a silver crown, and she crossed the room to stand behind the duke with a grace so regal she might have been a queen. She brushed her hand lovingly through the few gray hairs that remained on the duke's head and said, "The journey is over now, my dear. Put your foot up and relax."

She turned and offered her cheek for Lion's kiss, then opened her arms wide to Charlotte. "Come to me, child," she said. "I want to welcome the young miss my grandson has chosen to present him with his heir."

Denbigh shot Charlotte a warning look. She snapped her mouth shut on whatever correction she

had been about to make to the duchess's pronounce-
ment and allowed herself to be fondly hugged. The
duchess held her out at arm's length and looked her
over with a discerning eye that Denbigh was sure did
not miss a thing. He would have given anything for
five minutes to repair the chit's dishabille.

Blond curls had slipped free from the ribbon
that supposedly tied her hair in place at her nape.
Her hands were dappled with paint from the fence
around the garden in back of the town house that he
had caught her whitewashing. And her skirt was
dusty across the front from lying on the floor of the
library, her legs up in the air, reading a book.

In addition, her lips were swollen from his kisses
and her cheeks were rosy and she looked thoroughly
delectable, as though she had just stepped out of his
bed. He hoped his grandmother would not notice
any of that.

Charlotte had forgotten to curtsy to the duchess, and she was staring up at his grandmother without the least deference to her exalted station. He
groaned, but kept the sound to himself.

He was astounded to hear his grandmother say,
"She will do, Lion. She will do very well, indeed."

Were they both looking at the same person, he
wondered? Maybe his grandmother's eyesight was
failing.

"You should have told us, Denbigh," his grandfather said, holding his chilblained hands out to the

fire that was always kept burning in case he should come visiting his London residence unannounced. "It is an important day when a man chooses his bride."

"I was afraid that Lady Alice had put you off women permanently," his grandmother said in her no-nonsense fashion, as she led Charlotte over to greet his grandfather. "I'm glad to see I was wrong."

"But Grandmama, I—" He realized he could not tell his grandparents the truth, that he had no intention of marrying Charlotte Edgerton. Under the circumstances—having caught the two of them *in flagrante delicto*—they would insist he go through with the marriage. Honor demanded it. He would have to pretend that his engagement was real. At least until he could come up with another husband for Charlotte.

He realized the vixen was enjoying his discomfort immensely. His grandfather put an end to that when he said, "Go stand beside Denbigh, and let me see the two of you together."

Charlotte crossed and stood at his side, the smile gone from her face, replaced by wariness.

"She's a little bit of a thing, isn't she?" the Duke of Trent observed.

"I'm not tall, sir, if that's what you mean," Charlotte said.

"Did you hear that, Lizzie?" his grandfather

said to his grandmother. "The chit called me 'sir'! I like that. Familiar address is good for family, I always say. None of this 'Your Grace this' and 'Your Grace that.' Come here, girl, and give your new Grandpapa a kiss on the cheek."

Charlotte's face relaxed into a relieved smile as she gave the old man a hug and a kiss. "I'm glad to meet you at last, sir. It will be nice to have another Papa. I lost mine, you know."

"I heard Edgerton had died," the duke said. "Always liked your father."

"Did you know him, sir?"

"Certainly. Why do you think he sent you back to us?"

Charlotte shot Denbigh a questioning look. "I thought it was a mistake, sir."

"No mistake, my dear Charlotte," the duchess said. "Your father was a close friend of the family."

"What Lizzie doesn't like to admit is that she almost married the man!" his grandfather said with a chortle.

"Really?" Charlotte said, her eyes wide with wonder. "I might have been your daughter, madam."

"You might have been," the duchess agreed. "But this is so much better," she said with a smile. "I've had all these lovely years with Arthur, and I can still have you for my granddaughter."

The duke harrumped.

The duchess laughed.

Charlotte grinned.

Denbigh sulked. If anyone had ever wondered why he kept his distance from his grandparents, they would only have to witness this scene to understand. The Duke and Duchess of Trent did not act like any other duke or duchess he knew. They had embarrassed him as a boy when he brought his friends to visit. People expected dukes and duchesses to be remote and haughty. His grandparents were as open and friendly as the local innkeeper and his wife.

His friends always came away from holiday visits saying what "good'uns" his grandparents were. But he could not help wishing they were not quite so eccentric. He had avoided his grandparents as he grew older and shouldered more responsibilities, because he never knew quite how to act with them. He liked to follow the rules; they were forever breaking them.

Maybe that was why Charlotte got along so well with them. And why he had found it so difficult to deal with her.

"Lady Charlotte, someone is waiting to see you in the kitchen," a footman announced.

Charlotte had already started for the door of the drawing room, when Denbigh called after her, "Where are you going?"

"I'm supposed to meet my new maid before supper."

"Your new maid? What's wrong with the one you have?"

"Nothing." She crossed back and laid her fingertips soothingly on his crossed arms. She looked up at him and said, "Yesterday a woman came begging for scraps at the kitchen door. When she told me she had once been a lady's maid, I thought I would hire her to help."

"You can't hire every beggar off the streets, Charlotte," Denbigh began. "She—"

"She's in a family way, Lion. I can't turn her away. You don't really mind, do you?"

When she looked up at him with those green eyes, earnest and innocent and anxious for his approval, Denbigh found he could not tell her no. Even though servants were usually *fired,* not *hired,* when they began to show signs of increasing. Of course, leave it to Charlotte to get things backward. "This is the last time, Charlotte. From now on, let my steward do the hiring."

"I will." She turned and ran toward the door.

"Walk, Charlotte," he admonished.

She slowed down, but not much. At the portal she turned and said, "Thank you, my lord. I know Sally will be grateful for your generosity."

Denbigh shook his head. Charlotte Edgerton would never be a proper lady. Unless he wanted to end up buckled to her for the rest of his life, he had better find her another husband.

7

CHARLOTTE HAD TRIED FOR NEARLY A week to see Denbigh's point of view, as she had promised Olivia, and met with frustration at every turn. He was to be her escort to the theater that evening and had already dictated how she was to dress—in white; when she was to appear downstairs—precisely at eight; how she was to act upon their arrival at Covent Garden—demure, modest, reserved, and retiring; and what she was to say to Braddock— nothing at all, if she could manage it.

"He's given me a half-dozen orders, at least," she said as she paced Olivia's room. "And he expects all of them to be obeyed to the letter. He's high-handed, arrogant, arbitrary, overbearing, domineering, and . . . and . . . arrogant."

"You already said that."

"It bears repeating," Charlotte retorted.

"Why do you persist in seeing the worst in Lion?" Olivia asked.

"Wear the jonquil gown, Livy," Charlotte said, ignoring her question. "It picks up the gold in your eyes. The green is too . . . green."

"Do you not think the gown you have on this evening is too . . . thin?" Olivia asked.

Charlotte ran her fingers over the fragile gauze skirt of the gown she had commissioned from a *modiste* who catered mostly to the demimonde. It was virginal white, as Denbigh had ordered. There, she was sure, all resemblance to what he had in mind ended. The nearly transparent dress clung to the shape of her body, and the bodice was cut so low it had given even her second thoughts. It was fit only for a Cyprian, a woman of easy virtue.

But she was proving another point to Denbigh.

"Of course it is too revealing," Charlotte conceded. "How else am I to make it plain to your brother that I will make my own decisions about what to wear?" Charlotte tugged at the bodice, but it covered no more skin than before.

"I thought you were going to try to get along with Lion," Olivia said.

Charlotte snorted. "We've given the appearance of getting along so well that, if I'm not careful, your grandparents will have me married off to your brother before the season is over."

"They like you, Charlie. It's only natural they want you to become a part of the family as soon as possible."

"I'd love having you for a sister, Livy. It's your brother I can do without." When Olivia shot her an exasperated look, Charlotte changed the subject. "Are you nervous about tonight? You look so calm. You haven't seen the duke all week. Aren't you the least bit anxious about seeing him again?"

Olivia gave a tremulous laugh. "I'm terrified. Why do you think I'm not dressed yet? When I am, I'll have to go downstairs and face him. What if he has changed his mind? What if he no longer wishes to court me?"

"How could he not want to court you? I've told you over and over what a rare catch you are, Livy." Charlotte reached for the jonquil silk and held it ready for her. "Here. Let me be your maid. It's half past eight. The sooner you're dressed, the sooner we can go. I'm dying to see a play with real actors. Aren't you? I'm sure I won't be able to take my eyes off the stage."

"No one else in the theater will be able to take their eyes off of you in that scandalous gown," Olivia said.

"Do you think some of the gentlemen might show an interest in me?"

Olivia laughed. "Count on it. During the interval, they will come to the duke's box to present themselves. All you have to do is sit and wait."

"Even though I'm engaged?"

"There are many satisfied to be a *cicisbeo,* a man who keeps company with an engaged lady. And there are others, rakes, who will want to see if they can steal a kiss, now that you are engaged.

"And there are the curious, and Lion's friends, who will want to meet you. From them all, you may find one you like."

"That sounds easy enough," Charlotte said. "I think we should already be downstairs when the duke arrives, don't you, Livy? That way we can keep our escorts from getting into an argument over nothing and throwing gloves in one another's faces."

"You're right, of course. My brother and the duke won't need an excuse to fight. They have reason enough already."

Once Olivia had the right incentive, it didn't take any time at all for her to finish her toilette.

"Wait, Livy," Charlotte said before Olivia rose from in front of her mirror. "My new maid, Sally, gave me some things she said would aid your appearance." Charlotte used a hare's foot to dust sandalwood rouge over Olivia's cheeks. Then she dampened a colored paper and dabbed the resulting red stain across Olivia's lips with her finger.

"All done," she said.

Olivia looked in the mirror and frowned. "You don't think it is too much?"

"I don't know," Charlotte answered honestly. "At least now your whole face isn't as white as a ghost."

Olivia groaned and urged Charlotte out of her bedroom and down the stairs.

Charlotte got the anticipated response from Denbigh when she appeared in the drawing room arm in arm with Olivia.

"You're late," he said from his chair by the fire when he heard the door open. He angled his head to look at her and roared, "Charlotte!"

She had figured out long ago why his nickname was Lion.

He leapt to his feet, ogling her with disbelief. "What in heaven's name are you wearing?"

"A white gown, as you requested."

"You know I had nothing like . . . like that . . . that wisp of muslin in mind," he stuttered out.

Charlotte left Olivia's side and crossed to where he stood, his legs widespread, his hands militantly perched on his hips. She noticed he didn't take his eyes off her indecent décolletage until she was standing directly in front of him. The tips of his ears were red when his eyes finally met hers.

"That dress is—"

"Beautiful on her," Olivia interrupted. "Don't you think so, Lion?"

Charlotte dutifully twirled in a circle. The dress did little to conceal her assets. Denbigh's color was high when she faced him again. "Do you want me to change into something else?" she asked.

He tugged at the snow-white cravat that Theobald had tied in a precise Mathematical. "Knowing you, whatever you replaced it with would not be an improvement." He reached out to gather up a bit of thin muslin from her sleeve and rubbed it between his fingertips.

His silvery eyes locked with her green ones, and Charlotte shivered as though it was her flesh he was caressing.

"Do you want to marry me, Lion?" she asked in a voice too quiet to be overheard by Olivia.

"You know I do not," he said stiffly.

"Then I must find another husband," she said. "I think this dress might help."

"With net this flimsy," he said, letting the gauze fall against her skin, "you're liable to attract exactly the sort of loose fish you *don't* want."

His eyes were on hers again, but the disapproval she saw was not nearly so strong as the desire.

"A dress like this one . . ." he began.

He licked his lips, and her mouth went dry.

"Does it make me look beautiful, Lion?"

"It makes you look bed-able," he corrected.

"Both will do to catch a husband, I think."

"I don't think—"

The Duke of Trent's butler, an elderly gentleman named Stiles, for whom Charlotte had procured a better-fitting set of false teeth, announced, "His Grace, the Duke of Braddock," without his wooden top teeth even once falling out and having to be pushed back into place. Charlotte gave him a broad smile, and he beamed back.

She held her breath as Braddock entered the drawing room, not sure what sort of fireworks might erupt when the duke finally entered the home of the man who had killed his brother.

The two men, both pinks of the *ton,* were a formidable sight when viewed together. Braddock was turned out in dark Spanish blue. Denbigh wore black. It was hard to admire them when they immediately faced off against each other like two stiff-legged barnyard dogs fighting over the same bitch.

"Denbigh," the duke said.

"Braddock," the earl answered.

They sounded perfectly civil.

Then Charlotte saw the tic in Braddock's jaw, and the pulse pounding in Denbigh's temple. Tension simmered under the surface and threatened to boil over.

"Shall we go?" Charlotte said, slipping her arm through Denbigh's. "Stiles has my wrap by the door."

Olivia quickly followed her lead, slipping her arm through Braddock's. "Yes. Shall we?"

"My carriage is waiting," Braddock said.

"So is mine," Denbigh countered.

The two men stopped in their tracks, pulling both women to a stop beside them.

"My sister rides with me," Denbigh said.

"I'll be glad to take your ward with me in my carriage," Braddock said, his lip curling cynically.

Even Charlotte recognized the folly in that.

"Why don't we all go together in one carriage?" Olivia suggested.

"Mine will hold four comfortably," Denbigh said.

"So will mine," Braddock countered.

"Would you like to draw straws to see who wins?" Charlotte asked with a shake of her head at their ridiculous competition.

Neither man ceded the point. They glared at each other, shirt points high, shoulders back, neck hairs hackled.

"I think I feel a headache coming on," Olivia said. "Perhaps I had better stay at home tonight."

Braddock stood mute, but he was clearly disappointed. It was not the gentleman's place to tell a lady she was lying to spare them all an uncomfortable situation.

Charlotte knew no such bounds. "Well, I don't have a headache, and I've been looking forward to the theater all week. If you don't go, Livy, I shall have to stay home, too. Is there any possibility a little hartshorn might help?"

"Perhaps you would be more comfortable in your brother's carriage," Braddock said. He turned to Denbigh and continued in a dry voice, "If it is agreeable, Lady Olivia and I will be happy to join you and your ward for the ride to Covent Garden."

Denbigh nodded. "It is."

"Thank goodness that's settled," Charlotte said with a bright smile. "Shall we go?"

"Some hartshorn for Lady Olivia?" Braddock reminded Charlotte.

"Oh, yes," Charlotte said, realizing the play must be acted to the finish before they could leave for the theater.

A footman was sent to find Lady Olivia's maid, who located the hartshorn in her bedroom and gave it to the footman, who brought it down to Lady Olivia in the drawing room.

No one said a word while they waited.

All four heaved a silent sigh of relief once they were all seated in Denbigh's carriage.

Sometime during the first act of *She Stoops to Conquer,* Olivia realized she really did have a headache. There was no way she could ask to leave; they had all come in one carriage. Even if she could have persuaded her brother to take her home without creating another scene, she didn't want to spoil Charlotte's obvious enjoyment of the performance. So she suffered in silence.

She and Braddock were sitting in the two seats behind Denbigh and Charlotte in Braddock's box, only because Charlotte had raced to the balcony rail the instant they arrived, enthralled by the glittering sights, and remained until the curtain came up.

It was clear Lion would rather Olivia and Braddock had been sitting in front, so he could keep an eye on them. Several anxious glances over his shoulder had so far sufficed to convince him that Braddock had no designs on her person.

"Is your headache worse?" the duke whispered in her ear.

"I only made it up," she said.

"I have seen you twice wince when the crowd roared with laughter. If you did not have a headache before, I suspect you have one now. Am I right?"

What was the use of lying? She nodded.

"Come," he said.

"But—"

He didn't give her a choice. He took her firmly by the hand and led her from the box. To her surprise, Lion didn't even look back. He was too busy trying to keep an exuberant Charlotte from leaning over the balcony rail to ogle those in the pit.

The duke laid her hand on his forearm and walked slowly down the hall, where it was surprisingly quiet, and where the dim light was more soothing to her eyes.

"Feel better?" he asked.

"Yes, thank you," she said. "Perhaps it was all the noise and the smell of oranges from the pit." Oranges were a popular refreshment at the theater, and the immense numbers of peeled fruit, combined with the smell of the unwashed masses, gave off a pungent aroma.

Braddock ignored that excuse and supplied the truth. "Perhaps it was the tension between myself and your brother."

Olivia halted and looked up into the duke's eyes. No one could really have eyes that blue. Braddock did. They crinkled at the corners in a marvelous spray of joy as he smiled.

"Have I grown two heads?" he asked.

Appalled that she had been caught staring, she lowered her gaze and said, "Your frankness surprised me."

"It would be foolish to deny what any gudgeon could see. There's no love lost between Denbigh and me. He killed my brother. If it were not for you . . ."

"You would kill mine?"

He pressed his lips flat, refusing to answer.

"I am glad, Your Grace," she said, "if I am a reason to curtail your revenge. But . . ."

Olivia had not allowed herself to admit, until

this evening when she saw the two men together, how very dangerous it was to let herself love Braddock. There was no changing history. Denbigh had killed Lord James. That death would always lie between her family and Braddock.

It was possible, if she continued to see him, that the two men might make peace. Possible. But not probable. More likely, the enforced proximity would produce exactly the result Charlotte had predicted. Some day, when Olivia was not around, Braddock would throw a glove in Lion's face. And one, or both men, would end up dead.

She opened her mouth to tell the duke she would no longer be at home to him if he came to see her at the house on Grosvenor Square in the future. She simply could not get the words to come out.

"Is something wrong, Lady Olivia?" the duke asked.

"It is only the headache."

"Let me arrange for a hackney, and I will see you home."

"I don't think my brother—"

He put a fingertip to her lips. The touch was electrifying. She gasped, and he went still. She looked up into his eyes and saw surprise and . . . something else. The brief moment of doubt she had seen in his eyes was gone almost before she recognized it for what it was. Doubt about what? she wondered. Too many things came to mind for comfort.

"It is improper for me to be with you unchaperoned," she pointed out. "The gossips would tear us to bits if they discovered it."

"Nothing will come amiss," he said in a low, vibrant voice. "Trust me."

Her heart ached with wanting to do exactly that. "Very well," she said. "I must tell my brother I am leaving."

"I will take care of that, as well," he assured her.

He escorted her outside and settled her in a hackney he summoned with a wave of his hand. The ancient cab had cracked leather seats, rather than the plush upholstery she was used to, and it stank of unmentionable smells.

She wanted to change her mind, but the duke had gone back inside for a moment, and she was afraid to get out of the hackney and wait for him on the curb all by herself.

"I've left a note to be delivered to your brother at the interval," the duke said as he joined her in the hackney. "With Lady Charlotte to keep him entertained, he's not likely to notice you're gone until then."

Olivia worried that Denbigh would look sooner, discover her gone, and turn the theater upside down searching for her. Braddock's unconcern helped her to ignore her own misgivings. And with him beside her, the hackney did not seem as awful.

When she was finally alone with the duke in the darkened carriage, and they were driving along the streets of London toward their destination, she acknowledged the impropriety of the situation. It was easy to tell herself no one would ever know. But it was dangerous for both of them. The parson's mousetrap would snap closed tight on Braddock if they were discovered alone together.

She was so focused on the impropriety of riding home with Braddock unaccompanied, that she had entirely forgotten why custom decreed a lady must never be alone with a single gentleman. Braddock reminded her when he reached for her hand and held it warmly in his.

"This is . . . you should . . . I cannot . . ."

While she was busy concentrating on what he was doing with her hand, Braddock lowered his head and kissed her on the mouth. It was a bare meeting of lips, so fleeting that if she hadn't seen the glitter of his blue eyes in the passing street lamps as he raised his head again, she would have thought she had imagined it.

Flustered, she turned her face to stare out the window. "You should not have done that," she said, breathless and excited and horrified all at once.

"Why not?" he asked. "I wanted to taste your

lips to see if they could possibly be as sweet as the berries you must have pressed against them earlier this evening to make them so red.''

''Oh. It is only paint, Your Grace. Lady Charlotte—''

''You tasted of berries, I am sure.''

She turned to him with a protest on her lips and was caught by the force of his gaze trained on her face.

''Perhaps I was mistaken,'' he said. ''Let me see.''

She sat frozen like a rabbit, uncertain which way to bounce, as his head lowered and his lips claimed hers again.

She should have been ready. This time there had been no surprise about what he was going to do. But his second taste of her sent a frisson of feeling streaking through her even stronger than the first.

She knew she ought to pull away. She knew she ought to demand he take her home immediately. She knew she ought to keep her lips pressed tight against his exploring tongue.

But all the pent-up emotions she had stuffed down inside her for so many years cascaded over her like the rush of water over a broken dam. She moaned as she opened her mouth to him, a grating, carnal sound so foreign to her ears that she would have been mortified if she had been capable of rational thought at all.

His tongue was doing something to her, causing her body to draw up like a purse string inside. Her ears roared, and the blood pounded in the pulse at her throat as he nibbled gently at her lips, begging her to open to him.

She clasped her hands tightly in her lap to keep from reaching out to him. He had made no declaration. She was a fool to be doing even this much with him. But she could not stop herself.

She shivered at the sound he made, a raw, anguished groan, as he abandoned her mouth and drew away to stare down into her eyes. She felt herself quivering with expectation. She wanted him to kiss her again. Needed it. Craved it.

She saw he was tempted, that it would have taken only a slight move in his direction for him to take her in his arms and ravish her.

But the inhibitions of a lifetime were stronger than her newly awakened desire. She was a lady. Ladies did not throw themselves at gentlemen. She leaned back a bare fraction of an inch.

It was enough to break the spell.

She did not want the interlude to end. It was too close to what she had always imagined it might be like in her dreams—although her dreams did not hold a candle to the reality of being kissed by the duke.

"I had no idea I would feel so much," she said in a halting voice.

"Nor did I," he murmured.

The carriage came to a halt, and Olivia lifted the curtain and glanced out, expecting to see her grandfather's house. The neighborhood was dark, the houses close set and narrow. Nothing was familiar. The door to the nearest house opened, and a butler stood framed in a square of light, waiting in expectation. Olivia wondered who he thought they were. Obviously some mistake had been made.

"Where are we?" she asked the duke. "Why have we stopped here?"

Lion snatched at the sleeve of Charlotte's gauze dress to keep her from falling and felt the flimsy material tear free in his hand. He grabbed again, caught her elbow, and yanked her back from a certain fall to her death in the pit below. She was so caught up in the action on stage, she did not even notice the damage to her gown.

"Sit down," he said in a deadly voice.

"But Lion, it's all so exciting. I want to see everything. I want to feel everything."

It was hard to deny her when she cajoled him so prettily. But he had to draw the line somewhere, or she really would end up on her head in the pit.

"If you would like, we will visit the pit during the interval," he said. "But only if you promise to sit still for the rest of this act."

"Oh, I will," Charlotte promised. But she sat

on the edge of her seat, as close to the rail as she could get. A moment later she settled back fully in her chair and laid her hand on his sleeve to get his attention. "Lion," she said.

It was so unusual for her to use his name that he froze, wondering what she was going to ask for this time.

"I cannot go to the pit during the interval."

"Why not?"

"I have to wait here to be introduced to all the gentlemen who have noticed this scandalous dress and come here for an introduction."

Lion ground his teeth. Otherwise he was going to make a cake of himself by shouting at her. He turned to see if his sister could talk some sense into the girl—only to discover Olivia was missing . . . along with Braddock.

"Damn and blast!" he muttered. He could not make a scene. That would create the very scandal he was still hoping to avoid.

"It is time for us to leave, Charlotte," he said, settling her wrap around her shoulders.

"I'm not ready to go," she protested.

"Olivia has left with Braddock," he hissed in her ear.

She turned so precipitously, she almost fell off her chair. "They're gone? Where did they go?"

"I have no idea." His imagination was providing several scenes that made his blood run cold. He had known Braddock intended to take revenge on him through his sister. Why had he not watched them more closely?

The answer was sitting right beside him. Watching Charlotte took more energy than supervising a whole schoolroom full of children.

"Where shall we go to look for them?" Charlotte asked.

"*We* aren't going anywhere. You're going home. Then *I* will discover the duke's direction."

"I don't trust you to go alone," Charlotte said. "You'll end up getting killed in a duel with Braddock."

"If I do, it won't happen before dawn at the least. There are still several hours during which you will have to obey me."

"What happens to me if you're killed?" Charlotte asked. "Will I be free to do as I wish then?"

"Remove that bloodthirsty look from your eye, baggage. If anything happens to me, you will be passed along with the furniture and the paintings to the next Earl of Denbigh, whoever he may be."

Charlotte pursed her lips. "I think I would prefer to deal with you. At least we have reached a sort of understanding. So, if you please, I would rather you did not let the duke kill you."

"I'll do my best to avoid it," he assured her.

Before they could exit the box, the act ended. At least a score of fops and dandies and coxcombs collected outside the door, waiting for their chance to be presented to his ward.

In his determination not to have Charlotte importuned by a single one of them, Denbigh almost dismissed the messenger.

"A note, my lord," a fashionably dressed, but none-too-clean gentleman said, thrusting a folded parchment at him.

He grabbed for it primarily to keep it from stabbing him in the eye. Then he saw his name in bold script on the outside. "Thank you," he said.

The messenger held out his hand. "The mort said you'd have a li'l' sumthin' for me."

Denbigh searched for a coin small enough to serve as a tip and dropped it into the grimy palm. The beau-nasty quickly disappeared into the crowd.

Denbigh opened the letter and felt the blood drain from his face as he read the three words written there:

I have her.

His eyes skipped through the crowd searching for the messenger, but the man had already disappeared.

I have her. What did Braddock mean? That he had Olivia under his power and control and meant to rape and kill her? Or did he merely intend to give

Denbigh notice that his missing sister was safe some-where with her escort for the evening?

Denbigh was not comforted. An honorable man would not have disappeared. Braddock meant for him to worry. He wanted to provoke a duel.

Where had the duke taken Olivia? That was the burning question. Every moment counted. He had to find Olivia before the duke could compromise her. The sad truth was, Braddock would not even have to touch her. All he would have to do was keep her away overnight. She would be ruined.

Not that Olivia had lived in expectation of mar-riage, but she would not be able to hold her head up in company. She would be denied admittance to the best houses. And when he married, his choice of wife would be limited to those who would overlook the scandal.

Unfortunately, while Denbigh had been dis-tracted, at least three fashionable fribbles had been uncouth enough to introduce themselves to Char-lotte, who was merrily talking to them.

There was only one way to deal with fribbles. Or fops or coxcombs, for that matter. He gave them the cut direct.

Ignoring them as though they did not exist, he slipped an arm under Charlotte's elbow and ushered her through the horde and out the door.

"That wasn't very nice," Charlotte protested as

he led her down the hall. "Jerrold seemed very nice."

"Jerrold?" *She was calling a perfect stranger by his first name!* "Jerrold is most likely a gazetted fortune hunter," he said in severe tones.

His carriage was waiting in a long line, and Denbigh signaled for it to be brought to the door.

"He had nice eyes," Charlotte said.

"Who had nice eyes?"

"Jerrold, of course."

"Devil a bit," Denbigh snapped. "Since when does the color of a man's eyes matter?"

"It wasn't the color," Charlotte said. "No man could have eyes as beautiful as yours. But he looked at me as a person, and not as a bird-witted female."

Denbigh discounted the compliment to his eyes. He wouldn't put it past Charlotte to have made such an outrageous observation just to distract him from the main point of the argument.

He turned to face her and said, "Are you suggesting *I* treat you like a bird-witted female?"

She nodded.

"That's ridiculous. I—"

"You dictate every move I make. You don't allow me to think for myself, or make any decisions on my own."

"That's because, in my experience, you don't make very smart ones."

"I rest my case."

"What case?"

"That you think I'm a shallow-pated ninny."

"I said no such thing!"

Too late, Denbigh realized the cork-brained girl had provoked him into shouting. A quick look revealed the amused faces of a dozen coachmen, each of whom was sure to carry every word of his curbside argument to the *ton*'s most noble houses. He would have groaned aloud, if he hadn't known that would get repeated, as well.

The instant they were ensconced in the carriage on facing seats, Charlotte said, "I hope you realize that if you insist on scaring away potential suitors, we may be stuck in each other's pockets for years and years to come."

"I will find a husband for you, Charlotte, I promise. And—I don't believe I am saying this—he will be a man you can like. But not tonight. Tonight I have other, more important, things on my mind."

He had thought Charlotte did not realize the seriousness of Olivia's disappearance until she said, "Do you really think he will hurt Livy?"

Denbigh felt a stab of fear and fought it back. Surely even Braddock was not scoundrel enough to physically abuse an innocent woman. He did not answer the question, because he did not trust his voice.

"She's probably safe at home, and we're both

worrying for nothing,'' Charlotte said to fill the silence.

Since Denbigh had to drop Charlotte in Grosvenor Square anyway, it was worth checking to see if Olivia had been delivered there by the duke.

But he very much feared she had become a victim of the duke's revenge.

8

 "I'M NOT QUITE SURE HOW WE ENDED up here," Braddock said in answer to Olivia's question.

Olivia attributed the strangeness of the duke's voice to the fact it came out of the murky shadows. But it was unnerving to be sitting in the dark with someone who did not sound like anyone she knew.

"Perhaps the coachman did not understand my directions," Braddock said. He rapped on the roof of the hackney and gave the coachman her Grosvenor Square address.

"Make up yer mind, guv'ner," the driver called back, his voice hoarse and slurred from the effects of more than one bottle of blue ruin. "First ye tell me one thing, and then ye tell me another."

"What does he mean?" Olivia asked.

"I asked him to drive us around a bit before he took you home," Braddock explained smoothly. "I hope you don't mind."

"No," Olivia said. "I don't mind at all." She was glad he had thought of a way to give them extra time together. In fact, she did not want the evening to end. But, of course, it must.

He took her hand again and held it in his as the hackney rumbled over the cobblestones through the night.

He said nothing, and she hadn't the courage to begin a conversation with him. But she wondered when he would declare himself. Surely that was his intention.

She understood his problem. How could he speak to her brother to ask for her hand in marriage, when the two of them were barely speaking? She racked her mind to think of some solution to the problem, but could come up with no answer.

She was amazed at how the feel of his hand could be merely soothing now, when before it had seemed electrifying. She thought that boded well for their future together. Obviously the duke was willing to offer comfort as well as seek titillation in her touch.

She felt a little anxious when the hackney stopped once more, wondering if the drunken coachman had got it right this time, then was disappointed when she lifted the curtain and discovered they had, indeed, reached her grandfather's town house on Grosvenor Square.

She wondered if Braddock would try to kiss her again. She wanted him to, but she was afraid at the same time that he would consider her a light-skirt for offering him so much before he declared himself.

In the end, he did not even touch her hand after he helped her down from the carriage, but walked a step behind her as she made her way, one awkward, hitching step at a time, up the front steps and onto the porch.

"Good night, Lady Olivia," he said solemnly.

Where was his smile? she wondered. Where were the love words she wanted to hear? Why was he standing so very far away?

When will I see you again?

She managed not to say the words aloud, but she knew they were written in her eyes and on her face. Whether fortunately or unfortunately, with her eyes lowered to the toes of her evening slippers, there was little chance he would be able to read them there.

"Good night, Your Grace," she murmured.

"I will wait to make certain you are safely inside," he said.

She turned to raise the knocker above the brass lion head on the door, not wanting her time with the duke to end. But there was nothing she could do to make it last any longer.

Stiles opened the door immediately. "Welcome home, Lady Olivia." Only the lift of an eyebrow gave away his surprise at seeing her without her brother.

Olivia turned to the duke. She wanted to raise her eyes to his, but in the stark light from the open door, she feared too much of what she was feeling would be exposed if she did.

"Thank you, Your Grace. The theater was . . . the evening was . . . I enjoyed myself," she said lamely.

Nothing was coming out right. She fell silent, discomfited, unable to move in or out of the doorway.

He lifted her chin with the barest touch of his forefinger.

She glanced up briefly, long enough to see the stark look in his eyes before he said, "Good-bye, Lady Olivia."

Then he turned and walked away.

Good-bye? Not good night?

She wanted to run after him and ask for an explanation. Except, for her, running was impossible. Which was just as well, because if the duke wanted nothing more to do with her after tonight, she would only have humiliated herself chasing after him.

Olivia kept her chin tucked low as she entered the house. All she could think of was escaping to her room. Before she could, her grandfather called from the drawing room, "Is that you, Denbigh?"

"It's me, Grandpapa," she answered. "Lion is still at the theater with Lady Charlotte."

"Come in here, girl," he called in his booming voice, "and tell Lizzie and me what you're doing home so early."

Olivia wished she were Charlotte. Charlotte would have said, "No! I'm going upstairs to relive every precious moment of the evening and think about the duke's kisses and wonder why he didn't declare himself and worry over why he said good-bye instead of good night."

But Olivia was Olivia. She handed her mantle to Stiles and said, "I'm coming, Grandpapa."

"Why did you kill Lord James?" Charlotte asked.

Denbigh's whole body went taut at the question, which brought back all the memories of another time when he had raced to find someone he loved . . . and found her too late.

"You must have had a better reason than the one I've heard," she continued.

"What have you heard?" he asked.

"That you didn't like the way he tied his neck

cloth. No one kills someone else for such a frivolous reason," she said emphatically.

"Have you not heard I was mad at the time?" Denbigh replied.

"You had time between slapping a glove in James's face and the following dawn to come to your senses if you were foxed. And a true madman does not later become sane. You had a reason. I would like to hear it. Please."

"Please will not work here, Charlotte. It does not please me to speak on this subject. I bid you cease."

The chit had never obeyed him. He should have known she would not leave him be simply because he had asked it of her.

"Livy says she knows why. She wouldn't tell me the first time I asked, but eventually she will. I can be very persuasive . . . for a bird-witted female."

Denbigh snorted.

"I'd rather hear the story from you," she said in a winsome voice.

Denbigh tried to remember everything he had said to Olivia that night at Denbigh Castle. He had stayed at the dining room table long after supper and drunk bottle after bottle of claret until he was so disguised he could not stand by himself. She had heard a crash, thought a window had blown open somewhere in the house, and come downstairs to find him literally crying in his cups.

He had taken one look at the shock on her face and tried to hide his own. It was too late. She had seen his tears.

She had come to him and put her palms on either side of his face, looked down into his eyes, and told him everything would be all right. Wrapped in the comfort of her arms, he had laid his head against her bosom and cried like a lost child.

He must have told her everything.

He simply could not remember. He had woken up in his bed late the next day and felt ashamed. He had not been able to face his sister. He had returned to London without speaking to her, only writing a note to thank her for being there for him when he needed her. The next time he had come to Denbigh Castle was at the insistence of his neighbor, Mrs. Killington, to deal with his fractious ward.

"I suppose you don't owe me any explanation," Charlotte said. "But maybe if you told Braddock the real reason why you killed his brother, he would be able to forgive you."

"No man wants to believe his brother is a black-guard."

"Aha!" Charlotte crowed. "So Lord James did do something worth getting shot for!"

"In my opinion, he did."

"Aren't you going to tell me what it was?" Charlotte begged.

"No."

"I'll ask Livy," she threatened again.

"I hope you get the chance," Denbigh said in solemn tones.

As soon as he entered the house, Denbigh's fears seemed foolish. Evidently *I have her* had not had some nefarious meaning, after all. Olivia's mantle was draped across a table inside the door. However, the fact it had not yet been put away meant she had not been home very long. And Braddock had been alone with Olivia for the entire ride back to Grosvenor Square. Anything might have happened.

"Where is Lady Olivia?" he asked Stiles.

"I believe she is with the duke and duchess in the drawing room, milord."

Denbigh headed for the drawing room with Charlotte on his heels. They were both breathless when they entered the room and found Olivia sitting on a stool at her grandfather's feet, laughing at something he had just said.

"You're a sly boots," the duke said when he spied his grandson, "sending your sister home ahead of you, so you could have time alone with your future bride." The duke gave him a broad wink.

Denbigh flushed with mortification, but there was nothing he could do to deny the story without exposing Olivia, and he didn't want to do that before he had a chance to find out exactly what had happened between her and Braddock.

Denbigh tried to catch Olivia's eye to see why

she had told such a clanker, but as usual, she kept her gaze lowered.

"I take it Braddock delivered Olivia here," Denbigh said.

"That he did," the duke said. "Just moments ago. Livy has been telling us how much you enjoyed the play, Charlie."

Denbigh nearly choked when he heard the duke using that deplorable male nickname for his ward. A correction was on the tip of his tongue when he glanced at his grandmother and saw the loving concern in her eyes for his grandfather.

For his grandfather's sake, his grandmother pretended the gout was what kept him bedbound so much of the time. The truth was much more harrowing.

The doctor had said his heart was failing. The Duke of Trent did not have much longer to live.

Denbigh realized he would miss the old man's bluster when he was gone. He looked at the picture of his grandfather sitting before the fire, with Olivia perched on a stool at his feet and Charlotte—the impossible baggage—on the floor beside her, and knew it was a memory he would one day treasure.

Right now, however, he would have given his eyeteeth for five minutes alone with his sister.

Charlotte must have had the same idea. To his chagrin, she did something to arrange it.

"I'm tired, Grandpapa," she said. "I hope you'll excuse me and Livy."

"I haven't heard Livy say she's tired," the old man said.

Charlotte shot him a charming grin. "To tell the truth, I'm not tired, either. But I'm anxious to hear about Livy's evening with Braddock and to tell her about my own. You don't mind, do you?"

Denbigh watched with disbelief as Charlotte wound the Duke of Trent around her little finger. Not only was she abandoning his company for that of Olivia, she expected him to be happy about it!

"Ah, to be young again," the duke chortled. He waved a hand at Olivia and Charlotte. "Go. Go and talk. Myself, I'm looking forward to some time alone in front of the fire with your grandmother." He wiggled his eyebrows suggestively.

Denbigh was appalled at this public allusion to private romance between two people old enough to be his grandparents. Two people who *were* his grandparents!

Charlotte was obviously no more offended by his grandfather's comment than the duke had been by hers. No wonder. They were birds of a feather. Neither believed that rules were made for them.

The duke's arrogance was easily explained. He was at the top of the social order in England, second only to the king and queen. And Charlotte . . .

Charlotte was second to no one. The bird-witted female believed she was every man's equal.

Annoying as it was to admit, so far he had seen nothing to disprove it.

The end result, however, was that Charlotte and Olivia left the drawing room and headed upstairs, leaving him alone with his grandparents. At which point his grandfather, glaring at him from beneath white, beetled brows, made it plain that he was *de trop*.

Good lord, he thought. The old man really did have designs on his grandmother!

Denbigh made as graceful an exit as he could.

He could have gone to his club, but he did not want to take the chance of running into Braddock before he could speak with his sister. And now it looked like that discussion would have to be postponed until morning.

On the way to his room, he was surprised to be accosted by Olivia in the hall.

"I thought you were with Charlotte," he said.

"I must speak with you," she said. "Can we talk in your room?"

It was a bit unusual, but then, since Charlotte had come into his life, nothing surprised him anymore. "Certainly," he said, opening the door for her.

Once she was inside, and the door was closed

behind her, he gestured her to a chair near the window. "Would you like to sit down?"

He had never seen her pace, and it was disturbing that she did so now. Her lopsided gait made it difficult to focus on her face, but she was clearly troubled.

His heart sank as he became more and more certain that the duke had importuned her. He leaned back against the door, his arms crossed. "What happened, Olivia?"

She stopped abruptly and turned to face him. "What did the duke's note say? The one Charlotte said he left for you."

"It said 'I have her.' "

"And you thought he meant he had kidnapped me?" Olivia asked.

He nodded.

"What, exactly, did you think he was going to do with me?" she demanded.

She seemed incensed that he could think badly of Braddock. So he told her the truth. "I thought he would take you to a house somewhere, whatever place he has for his doxies, and keep you there overnight."

She gasped and put a hand to her mouth to keep from crying out. "Oh. Oh, no." She seemed to be struggling with some revelation, and it was obvious she was not happy with the conclusions she was being forced to draw.

Denbigh came away from the door and took a step toward her, but she shook her head furiously to indicate she did not want him to come any closer.

"What did he do to you, Olivia?"

"Nothing," she said in a paper thin voice. "We rode around for a while in the hackney, and then we . . . and then he brought me home," she corrected herself.

And then we . . . what? Denbigh tried to fill in the blank. It came to him like a bolt of lightning and was equally devastating. Then we *stopped at a house.*

The duke had done exactly what Denbigh had expected him to do, but for some reason he had not gone through with his dastardly plan. Why? Had this merely been a trial run, to see how difficult the deed would be to manage? Had Olivia said something that had changed the duke's mind? Had Braddock merely wanted to show how impossible it was to keep Olivia safe, so Denbigh would not sleep another night in peace?

The simple solution was to challenge the man to a duel and kill him. But before tonight, he'd had no reason to kill Braddock, even though his brother had deserved to die.

Maybe Charlotte was right. Maybe he should tell Braddock the truth. Maybe that would make a difference.

Maybe it would not.

"Why did you leave the theater with Braddock," he asked his sister.

"I . . . I had the headache. He offered . . . I didn't think . . ."

She looked up at him, her eyes glittering with tears. "Nothing happened," she said again.

Once too often to be believed, he thought. Something had happened. But she was not going to tell him what it was.

The knock at the door shouldn't have surprised him. Or the fact that Charlotte hit him in the back of the head with the door when she opened it without waiting for her knock to be answered.

"Oh, I didn't know you were standing there," she said as she edged her way inside. "Livy!" she exclaimed. "What are you doing here?"

"Talking to Lion," Livy said with a watery laugh.

"He's made you cry!" Charlotte said, giving the earl a reproving look.

"What are you doing here?" Denbigh demanded.

"I was worried about Livy, because she said she wasn't feeling well and went directly to her room," Charlotte replied. "Why did you drag her in here? What did you say to her?"

"Wait a minute. I'm not the villain here," Denbigh protested. "Braddock is. And I haven't said anything, but I was just about to."

Charlotte put a supporting arm around Olivia's waist and said, "All right. We're listening."

"This doesn't involve you," Denbigh pointed out.

"Livy's practically my sister!"

Denbigh glared, because the chit knew perfectly well he had no intention of marrying her, and that there was no way he could say so in front of Olivia.

"Very well, then. This is what I have to say: For your own good, Olivia, I cannot allow you to see Braddock again."

Olivia's chin sank to her chest. When she blinked, a tear slid down her cheek. "I understand, Lion. You may tell Stiles . . ." She swallowed hard and continued, "You may tell Stiles that when . . . if . . . the duke calls again, I am not at home to him."

"Oh, Livy, you can't turn Braddock away," Charlotte cried. "It's all a foolish misunderstanding. You'll see. At least give Braddock a chance to explain to your brother what happened."

"I . . . I don't believe there can be any explanation," she said in a quavery voice. "Not for what . . . not for . . ."

She pulled free of Charlotte and ran, her limp almost painful to watch, as she dashed tilt-legged for the door.

"Livy, wait!"

Denbigh caught Charlotte before she could stop

Olivia. "Let her go, Charlotte. She needs time to be alone."

"She needs Braddock!" Charlotte said. "She needs her hopes and dreams! You've taken them all away from her."

"Braddock is a scoundrel."

"Braddock is an angry man. You killed his brother for what he believes was no good reason. And you refuse to tell him the truth. Why shouldn't he be furious with you? Why shouldn't he want to hurt you and your family? But Livy loves him, Lion. She—"

"*Loves* him? That's absurd."

"It's not in the least absurd for your sister to fall in love. Especially with a man as handsome as the duke."

"Love is for fools."

"Only a fool would deny himself love," Charlotte countered.

"Braddock wants only one thing from my sister. And love doesn't enter into it."

"So you say. I'll bet if anyone bothered to ask, they'd discover he likes Livy a great deal."

"The man is a notorious rake. He's had some of the most beautiful demi-reps in London as his mistress. No woman has managed to bring him up to scratch in more than a dozen seasons."

"That doesn't mean he can't fall in love when the right woman comes along. Who says Livy isn't the most beautiful woman he's ever known—inside, where it counts? Why can't you see that? Why can't you let Livy fly free?"

"Olivia can barely walk, let alone fly! I'm just trying to spare her the pain and heartache of loving someone who will only betray her in the end," he said heatedly. "I know that pain, because I've endured it myself!"

Denbigh was appalled he had revealed so much. He saw the wheels begin to turn in Charlotte's head, putting together all the pieces of the puzzle he had given her so far with the latest revelation. Had he ever thought her bird-witted? Far from it. The chit was entirely too clever.

"There is only one way a woman betrays a man," she said. She looked right into his eyes and said, "With another man."

Denbigh hissed in a breath. Clever? She was sharp as a whip. He said nothing to confirm or deny her assumption, but that did not deter her from deducing the rest.

"Lady Alice betrayed you with Lord James," she breathed, her wide eyes searching his features to see whether she had guessed right. "Oh, I'm so sorry—"

"I don't want your pity," he said defensively.

Her hands landed in balled fists on her hips. "Just because you had one bad experience doesn't mean the same thing will happen to Livy."

"One bad experience was enough," Denbigh said through clenched jaws.

"Lady Alice never loved you in the first place if she betrayed you the way you say she did. No woman could betray a man she truly loved."

"I believed she loved me," Denbigh countered. "At least, it felt like love. Which only shows how deceitful a lover can be."

Charlotte's brow furrowed as deeply as an old woman's, and she began to pace. "Wait. Wait. If you're right . . . if Alice did love you . . . there has to be another explanation for what happened."

"You're reaching for straws."

"No, I don't believe you could feel that much in love with her if there was not something coming back to you in return. Which means there is a mystery here to be solved."

"There is no mystery!" Denbigh snarled. "She gave herself to him." And then, as though the words were torn from him with hot pincers, "She was carrying his child!"

Charlotte gasped. "Oh, Lion. Oh, no."

"So you see, I am not entirely an idiot for believing that Braddock may give the appearance of being interested in my sister, and have entirely different—malevolent—feelings for her instead."

"I'm not convinced Braddock is the rogue you are painting him to be. But if Lord James was so dishonorable as to compromise Lady Alice, don't you think Braddock would understand why you had to challenge James to a duel? Wouldn't it be worthwhile explaining the truth to him? That would make a match between Braddock and Livy—"

"Enough!" Denbigh said. "There's no reasoning with you."

Charlotte glared at him. "I know I'm right."

"It doesn't matter if you are or not. The matter is settled. Braddock will not see my sister again."

"We'll see about that," Charlotte muttered.

"What did you say?"

Charlotte sailed toward the door. "Nothing. We bird-witted females seldom have a useful thought in our heads."

Denbigh made a silent vow to keep a close eye on Charlotte for the next couple of days. He wouldn't put it past the chit to seek out Braddock herself!

9

 IF CHARLOTTE COULD HAVE FOUND BRAD-
dock, she would have confronted him
with the truth of what had happened
between Lord James and Denbigh. But
a note Charlotte penned to his London
address early the next morning was returned un-
opened with a second note saying the duke had left
London. All Charlotte's efforts to locate Braddock
over the next few days were futile. It was as though
he had disappeared off the face of the earth.

Livy was disconsolate.

Lion felt vindicated.

Charlotte bided her time, waiting for Braddock
to show his face in company. Unless he had gone
back to India, and gossip did not suggest it, the man
would have to turn up sooner or later. When he
did, Charlotte would be waiting for him.

Meanwhile, the idea that there was more to Lady Alice's story than she, or even Denbigh knew, niggled at her. She could not imagine how a woman who loved one man could end up in bed with another. Unless . . . unless Lord James had blackmailed Alice somehow. Or had got her drunk at a house party and taken advantage of her. Or made a bet with one of his cronies that he could have her and forced himself on her.

There were infinite possibilities, if one only had the imagination to think of them. Charlotte had a wonderfully vivid imagination . . . but absolutely no way of proving anything, since both of the parties involved were dead.

She was desperate to know the truth. Her whole life depended on it. And all because she was falling in love with a man who barely tolerated her. A man who was determined to change her into someone he could admire, as though Charlotte Edgerton, lately from America, was not an admirable person. She did not understand how it could have happened. It scared her to think she had no choice in the matter. The love was there. She could not seem to extinguish it.

The problem was, her heart had settled on someone incapable of loving her in return. The blasted man was convinced he could not trust himself to know real love when he saw it. After all, Denbigh believed he had been badly mistaken with

Lady Alice. That betrayal made him chary of trusting another woman. Clearly, something had to be done to change his mind, or her love was doomed.

The simplest solution was to prove Lady Alice had loved Denbigh all along, and that some other provocation had resulted in her coupling with Lord James. Then, and only then, Denbigh might be willing to take the chance of loving someone else . . . of loving her. Then, and only then, could they have a chance of living happily ever after.

Of course, Denbigh had a few shortcomings that needed to be corrected in order to make him the perfect husband. Not that Charlotte needed a perfect husband, but Denbigh was so far from perfect, he had long way to go. He tended to be dictatorial at times. And stubborn as a mule. And set in his ways. While she searched for an answer to Lady Alice's inexplicable behavior, she began working diligently to enlighten Denbigh to his faults, so he could correct them.

She attacked his resistance to change by constantly changing herself, and his tendency to order her around by not kowtowing to his ultimatums. The stubborn part would give way, she believed, as the other two faults were mended.

She began with small changes, like a bow in her hair.

At first she thought he might not even notice,

but at supper he said, "You look thirteen, Charlotte. Bows are for lapdogs and children."

"Bows are for anyone who wants to wear them," she countered.

"Social custom decrees—"

"That is your first mistake," she said. "Who makes up social custom? Why, it is all of us! So all we have to do is suit ourselves, you see, and the customs will change to suit us."

He took a sip of port, set down his glass, folded his hands in front of him—to keep from reaching for her throat?—and said, "If you wish to defy custom and wear a bow in your hair, you are the one who will suffer the consequences."

"Exactly!" she said, rewarding him with a smile for having been so clever as to figure that out. "And since I am perfectly happy with my bow, where is the harm?"

Once he began accepting small changes without protest, she tried something a bit more dramatic. She got the idea from her new maid, Sally, who said, as she was brushing Charlotte's waist-length hair one night before bed, "You should think about cutting off all this long, heavy hair. It is all the rage now for a lady to have her hair trimmed into a small cap of curls around her face."

When the deed was done, Charlotte was a little shocked at how different she looked. "Oh, Sally. Maybe this was not such a good idea." She felt a spasm of remorse as she looked down at all the golden locks that lay fallen around her.

"You look a pretty sight, I promise you," Sally said.

Charlotte reached up to touch her shorn head, amazed at how the curls framed her face and made her eyes look bigger. "Maybe you are right. The question is, will the earl feel the same?"

She decided not to wear a bow in her hair when she presented herself to the earl for the first time with her new haircut. That would be adding insult to injury. She put on a charmingly innocent sprigged muslin day dress, with capped sleeves and a high, square neck, and a feminine flounce at the hem, of which she knew he would approve.

"Are you busy?" she asked, as she stuck her head inside the study, where he was working.

"You forgot to knock, Charlotte," he reminded her without looking up from the papers he was perusing at the desk.

Charlotte stepped inside, closed the door behind her, and knocked on it. "May I come in?"

"I'm busy, Charlotte."

"I won't take much of your time." She kept waiting for him to look up, wanting to see his reaction to this change in her appearance. But he was determinedly focusing on the work before him.

She crossed to the desk. Eyed the spindly legs to gauge if they would hold her. And sat on the edge.

"That's what chairs are for, Charlotte," he said, an annoyed edge in his voice, still purposefully ignoring her.

She settled farther onto the desk.

He threw down his quill and looked up.

It was hard to tell, from the expression on his face, whether he liked what he was seeing. She tried a smile, to see if that would help him make up his mind.

"Charlotte!" he roared. "What have you done to your hair?"

He was on his feet and had snatched her off the desk by her shoulders before she knew what had happened. At first she thought he was going to shake her, like a terrier shakes a rat, but once he had hold of her, his grip merely tightened.

"It's all the crack," she said brightly.

"Social custom dictates—" He cut himself off.

At least he had learned that lesson, Charlotte mused.

"What possessed you to do such a thing?" he demanded.

She could not very well admit that she had done it merely to help him learn to accept change, rather than always fighting it. Changing herself to make a point was fine. But she wanted to be attractive to Denbigh, as well. Cutting off all her hair had obviously been a serious error. The expressions most apparent on his face were dismay and disapproval.

Charlotte felt like crying.

"You don't like it," she said, her chin quivering. "To be honest, I could have cried when I saw all those curls on the floor. In fact, I think I might cry now."

His gaze softened, or maybe it was only that she was seeing him through a blur of tears.

"You are never predictable, Charlotte. I will grant you that."

"It will grow back, Lion. I won't always look like this," she said woefully.

His lips curved in a tender smile. "You look charming just as you are." His hands left her shoulders and sifted into the curls at her nape, causing a shiver to roll down her spine. He angled her head upward and lowered his mouth.

The kiss was unexpected.

That is, she had not come into the study looking for it. But he gave her plenty of warning before his lips touched hers. She could have backed away. She could have told him that kisses were only going to complicate the situation. Or reminded him that kisses between unmarried couples in broad daylight were strictly forbidden by social custom.

But if he was willing to ignore social custom, who was she to argue?

This kiss was different from the first, or even the second. She was not sure exactly why, unless it had something to do with the change in her feelings for Denbigh.

Or a change in his feelings for her.

This kiss was hungry. His mouth claimed hers like a lover's would, and his tongue probed the seam of her lips, demanding admittance.

She let him in.

He gathered her up in his arms and held her tight enough that she could feel the strength of his shoulders and his pounding heart.

Nothing had prepared her for the feelings inside her. Not only the physical reactions—the melting knees, the thready pulse, the difficulty breathing—but the emotional tumult of knowing she was being held by the man she loved, and that he wanted her as much as she wanted him.

His tongue was wet and warm and welcome.

The feel of his large hand cupping the underside of her breast briefly distracted her from what he was doing to her with his mouth and teeth and tongue. When he brushed her nipple with his thumb, she was frightened by the intensity of the sensation. She would have pulled away, except he soothed her fears with murmured words that made no sense, but offered reassurance.

As his warm hand closed completely around her breast, she groaned and arched toward him. His other hand slid down to her buttocks and pulled her close. She did not know why it felt so good, only that it did. His body was hot and hard, and rubbing herself against him, even through layers of cloth, produced pleasure she had never imagined. She did what came naturally, and produced the results that nature had intended.

The male hand that had been cupping her buttocks, encouraging her to move against him, suddenly held her still. "Wait," Lion rasped. "Stop."

She pushed against him, nudging the hard part of him with her body, trying to find the exact way to press herself against him that would produce the wonderful sensations.

Abruptly he separated them. "We have to stop," he said in a harsh voice.

She looked at him and saw his eyes were heavy-lidded, his lips full, his body taut. He was aroused, and for some reason she did not understand, angry.

"What's wrong?" she asked.

"This. This is wrong," he said, letting go of her entirely, taking a step back, and shoving a frustrated hand through his hair. Apparently even that was not enough distance, because he turned and paced away from her.

"Damn and blast, Charlotte! Whenever I get near you, I seem to lose all sense of common decency. I have no business kissing you, because I have no intention of marrying you!"

Charlotte did not know what to say. She did not want to marry him, either, if he could not love her.

And as she was quickly coming to realize, love and desire were not at all the same thing.

"I only wanted to show you my hair," she managed to say past an aching throat.

"It's fine," he snapped. "Now, if you don't mind, I want to be alone to finish my work."

She retreated. But only so she could muster her forces to begin the fight again.

After Denbigh's lapse of control in the study, she noticed he was careful never to be closeted alone with her. If she came into a room where he was by himself, he left. He invited his grandparents to join them. And his sister.

Which was a good thing, because Olivia needed the company.

As the days turned into a full two weeks with no word from Braddock, Charlotte watched the light die in Livy's eyes. The butterfly who had emerged from her chrysalis under Braddock's admiring eye, folded her wings and transformed herself into . . . a mouse. Not an easy feat, when one considered the biology involved.

But the resemblance to a mouse was definitely there. Livy wore browns and grays. She peeked around corners before entering rooms. She never spoke without being spoken to. Even in company, she was quiet . . . as a mouse.

Charlotte damned Braddock aloud every chance

she got for disappearing without a word, but Olivia also felt the lash of her tongue.

Things came to a head one morning when Olivia joined Charlotte in her bedroom to share hot chocolate and toast, while Sally tried out another original creation with Charlotte's hair.

"Braddock is not the only handsome man in the world," Charlotte railed.

"He's the only one for me," Olivia replied calmly.

Charlotte whipped around to challenge Olivia and nearly pulled the curling iron out of her maid's hands.

"Sit still, Charlie," Sally said. "Otherwise I'm going to end up either searing your scalp or yanking your hair out by the roots."

In the mirror, Charlotte saw Olivia shake her head in dismay, but whether it was because she encouraged her maid to speak to her as an equal, or because Charlotte was lecturing Livy again about Braddock, she didn't know.

Charlotte examined herself in the mirror. Her head was covered in tiny golden ringlets. "This new arrangement looks awfully . . . curly," she remarked to Sally.

"That is what generally occurs when one uses a curling iron," Sally replied.

"What do you think, Livy?" Charlotte asked. "Do you think your brother will like it?"

"I doubt Lion will notice the difference," Olivia replied.

Charlotte scowled. "How could he miss noticing this?" she said, pointing to her head. "I look like Medusa with a headful of golden snakes."

"Give me a chance to finish before you complain," Sally said.

Charlotte stuck her elbows on the dressing table and dropped her chin in her hands. "It's useless. He's hopeless."

"Who is hopeless?"

"Lion. Who else have I been speaking about?"

"Braddock," Livy said.

"Speaking of Braddock," Charlotte said, perfectly willing to change the subject, "I wish you would stop moping over the man."

"I don't notice any difference in my behavior," Livy said.

Charlotte snorted. "What happened to having hopes and dreams?"

"I have accepted my lot in life, that's all."

"Accepted your lot? What does that mean?"

"I know I will never marry."

"What about Braddock?" Charlotte asked.

"Braddock is gone. He and Lion . . . with the enmity between them . . . it would never have worked."

"What I don't understand," Charlotte raged, furious that Olivia seemed determined to go back into her hidey-hole and remain there the rest of her life, "is why you didn't tell Braddock that Lord James had compromised Lady Alice the first time you had the chance!"

Livy had just taken a swallow of chocolate. She choked when she tried to speak before she had swallowed it. "How . . . ?" She set down her cup, coughed and choked and coughed again.

Charlotte jumped up from her seat in front of the mirror, leaving Sally standing alone with a hot curling iron, and pounded Olivia on the back.

"Are you all right?" Charlotte asked.

"How—did you—find out?" Olivia gasped between coughs.

"Oh. I figured it out from clues Lion gave me. First he said he had a good reason for killing Lord James. Then he confessed that Alice had betrayed him. I simply put one and one together and got . . . two men dueling."

"Do you know all of it?" Olivia asked.

Charlotte *tsk*ed. "Now, Livy, what sort of question is that? If I didn't already know it all, I would certainly know there was more I should ask about."

Olivia flushed. "I cannot believe Lion told you . . . everything. What happened was so terrible . . . and so sad."

Charlotte took Olivia's hands in hers. "He told me Alice was carrying Lord James's child when she died."

"I could hardly believe it myself when I heard," Olivia whispered.

"Why didn't you tell Braddock what you knew?" Charlotte asked. "It might have helped him to understand why your brother challenged Lord James to a duel in the strange way he did. Why Lion did not want the world to know the real reason he killed James. That if the truth were exposed, it would only hurt more innocent people, including Braddock himself."

"I stayed silent," Olivia said, "because I was fool enough to believe an explanation was not necessary. I believed Braddock wanted me badly enough to take me no matter what Lion had done. I realize my folly, now that it's too late."

"When Braddock returns, you'll have a chance to make amends," Charlotte promised. "What puzzles me is why Lady Alice betrayed your brother with Lord James. You must have seen Lion and Alice together, Livy. Did it seem to you that she loved him?"

Olivia's lips pursed. "I am not the one to be asking. I thought Braddock cared for me, and look how wrong I was about that."

"You were not wrong about Braddock," Charlotte insisted. "He has simply gone away on business somewhere. I expect him to show up at the door any day.

"But let us put that aside for a moment and go

back to Lady Alice. Do you believe she loved Lion?"
Charlotte asked.

"She did."

The voice that answered was not Olivia's. Both
women turned to look at Sally, who was standing by
the mirror, still holding the curling iron, her eyes
brimming with tears.

Charlotte rose to her feet. "Sally, did you know
Lady Alice?"

"I was her maid. I was with her that day . . .
the day she . . . I was there when the earl found
her."

Olivia's face blanched. "How could you have
ended up here, working in his house, where he
might see you and be reminded of . . . of her?"

Sally let the curling iron fall on the dressing
table and dropped her bulk to her knees in front of
Charlotte. "Please, Lady Charlotte, don't throw me
out into the street. I didn't know the earl lived here
at first, and when I found out, I had no place else to
go.

"I have tried not to let him see me, but even so,
we crossed paths once. Only, he did not seem to
know me. Please don't send me away, I beg of
you."

"Up off your knees, Sally," Charlotte said.
"It's no place for a woman unless she's sitting beside her husband at the fireplace or scrubbing
floors."

"I'll scrub floors," Sally babbled. "I'll do any-thing—"

"Stubble it," Charlotte said.

Sally closed her mouth.

"She has to go, Charlie," Olivia said. "She simply cannot stay."

"Why not?" Charlotte said. "You've already heard her say that Lion did not recognize her."

"That does not mean he won't in the future," Olivia said. "And be distressed by her presence."

"Sally was not to blame for what happened," Charlotte said. "I don't see why she should be made to suffer any more than she already has. Imagine losing your position because your mistress—"

"That will suffice, Charlie," Olivia inter-rupted.

Charlotte turned a speculative eye on the maid. "And Sally may know Lady Alice's reasons for what she did."

Olivia looked thoughtful. "Perhaps you have a point." She directed her gaze at Sally. "You said Lady Alice loved my brother. How do you know?"

"Oh, she said so many times, milady."

Charlotte frowned at Sally for using the more formal address, but it appeared the maid was taking no chances of offending Olivia.

"Then why did she take up with Lord James?" Charlotte asked.

"I cannot tell you."

"But you know?" Charlotte asked excitedly.

Sally nodded. "It was told to me in confidence by my lady. She made me swear on the cross she wore about her neck that I would tell no one. And I have not." She straightened her shoulders and said, "I have kept her secret as I promised, milady, even from the earl."

"Damn and blast!" Charlotte said. "What a coil!"

"Yes," Olivia agreed. "Quite."

"What are we going to do now?" Charlotte said to Olivia as she paced the room, her curls bouncing. She flung a hand toward Sally. "Here is the one person with the answers to all our questions, and she cannot tell them to another living soul for fear of eternal damnation. What are we to do?"

"A promise made on a cross is inviolable," Olivia said glumly.

"I know," Charlotte said. "But maybe I can come up with some way around it, if I think about it long enough." She turned to Sally and said, "I don't suppose you would consider breaking your vow."

"I cannot," Sally said. "Even if you threaten to kick me out in the streets," she added, to show how hopeless any possibility of learning the truth was.

Charlotte sighed. "At least we know a little more now than we did before."

"We do?" Olivia said.

"We know for certain that Lady Alice loved your brother. Which means we know for certain that Lord James used some sort of coercion to have his way with her."

"We have no proof of any of that," Olivia said.

"We have Sally."

"She's not talking," Olivia pointed out.

"But Lord James may have," Charlotte said. "All we have to do is find out who his friends were and ask them a few questions."

"We can't do that!" Olivia protested.

"Why not?"

"Because when we begin asking questions, people will begin to ask why we are asking questions. What happened to Lady Alice was a tragedy. If more were known, it would create a scandal."

"We'll be discreet," Charlotte promised.

"I could help," Sally offered.

"How?" Charlotte asked.

"I'm not sure," Sally said. "But if you need to know anything that I did *not* promise to keep secret, I will be glad to tell it to you."

"Thank you, Sally," Charlotte said. She turned to Olivia and said, "Just think, Livy, if Lion could be made to see that Lady Alice did not willingly betray him, his memories of her might be less painful. He might become a less bitter man."

"That is a goal worth trying to achieve," Olivia conceded. She took a sip of her chocolate and made a face when she discovered it was cold. She set her cup aside and said, "All right, Charlotte. I'll help you."

"You won't be sorry, Livy," Charlotte promised. "And don't worry. We'll be subtle. And sly. No one will even suspect us of interrogating them."

10

LION HAD DECIDED HE COULD NO LONGER delay finding a gentleman who would make a good husband for Charlotte. The incident in the study had brought home to him the dangers of leaving her unattached any longer. Maybe once she belonged to some other man, he would cease having the sort of thoughts about her that had plagued him more and more lately.

Charlotte in his bed. Charlotte naked beneath him. Charlotte's breast in his mouth. Charlotte arching up to him as he thrust inside her.

Good lord. What was he thinking? The girl was his ward. He was responsible for making sure her honor was protected.

A definite case of the fox guarding the hen coop.

That was how he had ended up standing next to

a sharp-edged palm, avoiding the stifling crush of perfumed and cologne-doused bodies at Lady Hornby's ball. Olivia was sitting along the opposite wall, lace spinster's cap firmly in place, with a cluster of young misses who had not taken and their doting mamas.

Charlotte was standing not far from Olivia, surrounded by a collection of fashionable fribbles, coxcombs, and court cards. She was smiling rather too broadly, he thought, but so long as she did not laugh out loud, he was content to let her peruse the gentlemen around her at her leisure. He had informed her earlier in the evening that she was to examine them and make her choice.

"Are you saying I may choose whatever man I wish to marry, and you will respect my choice?" she asked, brows raised high in disbelief.

"So long as he is not a gazetted fortune hunter," he said. Immediately, several other possibilities for disaster occurred to him, and he added, "Or addicted to gambling, or continually cupshot."

"Is that all?" she asked, looking amused.

"The choice is yours, as I said, but you might want to eliminate second sons."

He knew she had misunderstood his reasons for saying it when her brows arrowed down between her eyes, her lips flattened mutinously, and her cheeks puffed out like a ship at full sail.

"Because they end up as soldiers or clergymen," he explained. "One will leave you behind to go off to war. The other will bore you to death."

Her expression lightened. "Oh. I see. Any other suggestions, before I go out to make my selection?"

Choose me.

He did not know where the thought had come from. He did not want to marry anyone, least of all Charlotte Edgerton. No man in his right mind would willingly marry someone who was certain to give him heart palpitations and headaches for the rest of his life.

She was unpredictable and unmanageable. And more desirable to him than a dozen courtesans.

Maybe that was the problem. He had been without a mistress for too long. He made up his mind to find a willing demi-rep and bed her before the week was out.

"If I think of any other qualities you should avoid, I will be sure to mention them," he had said.

Now she stood on the other side of the ballroom from him sorting through the eligible suitors—and there were a great many of them—while he stood by and watched like a hawk on a promontory, waiting for her to bring him her choice, so he could tear the man to shreds. The only reason he did not shoo them all away like flies from a piece of cake, was because among them were a few substantial prospects.

Sir Fenton, for example. Although, on second thought, perhaps a rake of forty was too old for a chit of seventeen.

Lord Harrellson might do. Except he tended to corpulence. A man in his condition might not survive into old age, and with Denbigh's luck, and as her nearest relative, Charlotte might end up becoming his responsibility all over again.

Ah. The Earl of Devon. Except, Devon already had four children by his mistress of ten years and could not be expected to give her up. He did not think Charlotte would tolerate the situation, should she discover it. Or, heaven forbid—and knowing Charlotte—she would invite the mistress and the four children to come and live with them!

Viscount Canby was a definite possibility. He was said to be in trade, but that did not exclude him in Denbigh's mind. The viscount had made and lost a dozen fortunes, but had most recently lost one. Following a week-long game of whist at White's, he hadn't a feather to fly with. Canby would surely come round again, but Lion didn't like the idea of Charlotte being subjected to such financial ups and downs.

His gaze came to rest on Lord Webster. There was a suitor who could not be faulted. Webster was a large man, even taller and broader shouldered than Lion himself, but without an ounce of fat on him. Not given to excesses. Lived most of the year on his country estate, where Charlotte would be able to ride to her heart's content.

Except Webster had buried two wives already. Both lost to childbirth. What if Webster, huge man that he was, set seeds that grew too large for the women who nurtured them? What if the size of his babies ripped their mothers apart as they tried to expel them?

He could not bear the thought of that happening to his Charlotte.

She is not yours. You don't want her, remember?

His eyes scanned the room, looking for other likely marital candidates. He found few to his liking. Each one had some defect he could not accept. Charlotte deserved the very best.

"I say, Lion. Shocking crush. Lady Hornby must be delighted. Everyone who is anyone is here."

Lion turned and greeted his best friend, managing not to cringe when he laid eyes on Percy's pigpink waistcoat.

"Good evening, Percy. Everyone may be here, but I'm having a devil of a time finding a single gentleman in the throng who would make a good husband for my ward."

"Too bad, old man," Percy said, shaking his head in commiseration. He followed Denbigh's gaze to Lady Charlotte and the crowd surrounding her. "What about Fenton?" he asked.

"Too old."

"Lord Harrellson—"

"Too fat."

"You cannot fault the Earl of Devon," Percy protested.

"Except for his mistress and their four children."

"Canby is—"

"Cleaned out," he interrupted.

"Lord Webster?" Percy asked, the doubt in his voice conveying that he knew there must be some problem with the man, though he could not see it.

"He has buried two wives in childbirth. I keep seeing Charlotte ripped in two." He shook his head. "I cannot countenance it, Percy."

"Oh, dear," Percy said. "I had no idea finding a husband for a gel as taking as Lady Charlotte could be so difficult. Next you'll be looking at me," he said with a laugh.

Denbigh did exactly that. "Why not you, Percy?"

Percy's face turned as pink as his waistcoat. "You know I have no taste, Lion. The gel would turn her nose up at me."

"I promise you Charlotte would be more interested in the man inside the clothes," Denbigh said.

"I'm not ready for a leg-shackle."

"We're of an age, Percy. It is time you set up your nursery."

"I tell you I'm not ready, Lion. If you can't find another man you like for the chit, why not marry her yourself! The best part of that solution, my friend, is that you're already engaged to her."

"I don't love her, Percy."

"Love is no basis for marriage," Percy scoffed.

It was what Lion himself had told Charlotte. He could hardly blame Percy for spouting the same blasphemy. Every gentleman of their class had been brought up with the same understanding. Where marriage was concerned, property and bloodlines were more important than feelings between people.

"Besides," Percy continued, "do you think any of those gentlemen you are asking her to choose as her husband will love her? It is not the thing. At least you like her."

"I do?"

"Of course you do," Percy said. "What's more, you admire her. She's beautiful, and she has her own fortune. What more can a man ask of his bride?"

Lion could not argue with Percy's reasoning. Neither could he discuss with his friend, Alice's brother, the unhealed wounds that made him unwilling to make any woman his wife. He could not ignore the past or make it go away.

His feelings for Charlotte frightened him, because they were so similar to what he had felt for Alice. Except, what he felt for Charlotte was a hundred times more powerful. Alice's betrayal had left him wounded. Charlotte's betrayal would kill him.

Not literally, of course. He did not believe in the romantic fancy that said you could die of a broken heart. But he knew enough about heartbreak to be certain that if Charlotte betrayed him with another man, he would not want to live. He could not imagine her doing such a thing. But he had not imagined it of Alice, either.

"Be at ease, Percy," Lion said. "I will find a husband for Charlotte if I have to search the rest of my life."

But having weighed and rejected the suitors that surrounded her now and found them wanting, he could see no reason to leave her any longer at their mercy. Besides, he had arranged to have the conductor play a waltz first, so he could dance it with his ward. The orchestra had warmed up, and he could hear the music was about to begin.

"Excuse me, Percy. This dance is mine."

Denbigh started across the floor toward Charlotte, thinking how nice it was going to be to hold her in his arms.

Charlotte lying in his bed, their naked bodies entwined.

Denbigh scowled. He had better find a husband for the chit soon.

* * *

Charlotte saw the scowl on Denbigh's face and wondered who had given her away. She had tried to be subtle about asking questions, she really had. She was trying to discover where Lord James might have taken Lady Alice the day he had compromised her. So far, all she had gotten were quizzing looks from the gentlemen. Apparently English ladies never asked, "Where would a gentleman take a lady if he wanted to sneak off and be alone with her?"

Those she had asked merely cleared their throats uncomfortably. Or coughed. Or snickered.

However, Sir Fenton, a nice old man who bore a slight resemblance to her papa, had leaned in close and whispered, "Meet me at the masquerade in Vauxhall Gardens tomorrow night, and I'll tell you what you want to know. I'll be wearing a black-and-white checkered domino. Come to Lover's Walk at midnight. I'll be waiting for you there."

"How will I find you in the dark?" she whispered back.

"I will find you," he promised.

Charlotte was delighted with the prospect of intrigue, not to mention the excitement of attending a masquerade. It would be one sure way to get Olivia out of her grays and browns. She would insist that her friend dress up as someone exotic, like Cleopatra, or something charming, like a shepherdess. Yes, a shepherdess was perfect, because Olivia could carry a staff that would help her to walk.

Before Charlotte could congratulate herself on coming up with such a famous idea, Denbigh was standing before her. She was surprised to see the crowd of gentlemen had dissipated like insubstantial clouds assailed by a fierce wind.

"Shall we dance, Charlotte?" the earl said, leading her toward the small space in the center of the room that had been cleared for the purpose.

"If you don't mind me stepping on your toes," Charlotte said.

"I'll take my chances. Just remember to count."

"Cat-cow-pig, cat-cow-pig," Charlotte recited as he began whirling her in his arms.

"What?" Denbigh said, either not having heard what she said, or not believing his ears.

"I was counting." And one-two-three was too difficult to manage with her heart in her throat. It was the first time Denbigh had held her since he had kissed her in the study. It was amazing how all the hairs could stand straight up on her arms like that. She felt the prickle as goose bumps formed at the root of each one of them. Simply amazing.

She was achingly, steal-your-breath-away conscious of his hand at the small of her back, his thumb just touching her above the vertebrae exactly at her waist. One of her hands rested on his broad shoulder, while the other was cushioned gently in his gloved hand.

She blessed the wizened old general in a red uniform dotted with shiny medals who was taking up so much room with his partner that Denbigh had to pull her close to dance around him. She closed her eyes briefly to enjoy the feel of her breasts pressed against the wall of his chest.

But she quickly became dizzy and opened her eyes to regain her balance, only to find it didn't help. She still felt light-headed. Lighthearted. As if she could happily float off among the moon and stars with the earl and never come back down.

Only, they were not going anywhere together unless she could figure out what had really happened between Lord James and Lady Alice. Astounding how quickly one could get one's feet back on the ground—figuratively—when one needed them there.

"One of the gentlemen told me there is a masquerade at Vauxhall Gardens tomorrow night," Charlotte said. "May Livy and I go?"

"No."

"Why not?"

"A masquerade is no place for two gently bred ladies."

"I'm not a—"

"No."

"Why not?"

"It is not unknown for young bloods to lay in

wait for an unprotected female on the darker walkways.''

"But you'll be there to protect us."

"I cannot keep you from being ogled by every scapegrace in high shirt points," he said.

"But we'll be wearing masks, so who will know it is us?" Charlotte pointed out.

Denbigh groaned.

"Please," she said. "Livy needs some excitement to cheer her up. Pretty please." From the look on his face, this was one of those times when please was going to work. Or perhaps he changed his mind when he caught sight of Olivia, sitting along the wall in solitary, mouselike drabness, and decided she was right.

"Very well," he said. "We will go."

It was a good thing he had hold of her around the waist, or she would have jumped up and down with joy. The waltz was ending, and she had already begun to step back from the earl when he tightened his grasp on her waist.

"Our waltz is over," she said.

"I'm not through talking. We'll dance another."

"No couple dances twice in a row. Livy told me it isn't done, except by those who are promised to each other."

"We're engaged," he reminded her.

"I'm jilting you," she reminded him.

"Not before I can claim another dance," he said, whirling her into motion as the music began again.

She kept her eyes focused on his face, wondering what had provoked him to such odd behavior. Not that she minded being held in his arms. She could feel his warm breath against her cheek, and it caused her stomach to do a strange flip-flop. Once it landed, she asked, "What was it you wanted to say that required another dance?"

"I wanted to ask if you've found any gentleman who appeals to you among those you were interviewing."

"Oh. No. No one special."

If she had not known better, she would have said he heaved a sigh of relief. Apparently that was all he had wanted to know, because he did not utter another word.

But he continued looking down at her, and she could not help looking back at him. His eyes searched her face, and she wondered what he expected to find. She searched his in return, and saw too much worry and sorrow and not enough laughter in his eyes.

She could make him happy. She could make him laugh. If only he would give her the chance.

She glanced over at Olivia as they danced by and saw that she appeared agitated. Charlotte swiveled her head back to see if she could determine the problem and saw Olivia making odd gestures with her hands in her lap. Locking her hands and pulling them apart. Locking them and . . . *pulling them apart!*

She looked at the distance between her body and Denbigh's and saw that not an inch separated them. She hadn't even noticed, except that it had felt perfectly right to her.

Now that she looked, she saw others had noticed what Olivia had, including Lady Hornby herself. Charlotte gave a backward jerk, putting some distance between herself and Denbigh, and said brightly, "What are you going to be?"

"Be?"

"What costume are you going to wear to the masquerade?" It was necessary to keep continual pressure on her arms to keep Denbigh at a distance. Although why she had to be the one to observe the proprieties, she had no idea. But Olivia looked relieved the next time they danced past her, so Charlotte kept it up.

"I never wear costumes," Denbigh said.

"But you must! It's a masquerade. Why not be a pirate? Or a prince of Arabia? Or a red savage?" she said, laughing with wicked glee as she imagined him in each role.

"I refuse to parade myself before the *ton* wearing anything so outrageous," the earl said. "If you insist I come in costume, I will wear a checkered domino.''

"But—''

"But what, Charlotte? A cape and mask will completely disguise me. What more do you require?''

She wanted him to wear a costume she would not confuse with the nice gentleman she was supposed to meet at Lover's Walk. She saw the potential for trouble, but she could not very well explain her problem to Denbigh.

"A domino is fine, I suppose. But Livy and I are going in costume.''

"What did you have in mind?'' The earl pulled her close to escape the general again, pressing her breasts against his chest.

Charlotte had to wait until she could catch her breath before she could speak. It was simply too much effort to push him away again. And besides, she didn't want to. If Olivia didn't approve, she could harangue her later.

"I thought Livy could be a shepherdess, because then she could carry a staff that would help her walk more easily.''

"I approve,'' Denbigh said. "What do you have in mind for yourself?''

"I haven't thought of anything yet.''

"No breeches,'' Denbigh said firmly.

"The idea never crossed my mind.'' And it

hadn't. The pair of breeches Charlotte had saved remained hidden beneath her mattress at Denbigh Castle. She could not see the point of bringing them to London when she had left her horse in Sussex.

Denbigh had told her she could not gallop Mephistopheles in Hyde Park, and she had known the stallion would be unhappy being continually restrained. She had left instructions with the hostler at Denbigh Castle to put Mephistopheles out to pasture so he could run free while she was gone.

Now she was reminded of how long it had been since she had enjoyed a good gallop. "I miss riding," she said.

"I can take you driving in the park," Denbigh offered.

She shook her head. "It wouldn't be the same." She noticed then that Denbigh seemed disappointed that she had turned him down. "But I suppose it would be better than nothing," she said.

"Tomorrow?"

The second waltz ended before she could answer him. She felt his arm tighten around her waist again. "I'll go driving with you tomorrow, if you'll do something for me tonight," Charlotte said.

He eyed her suspiciously. "What did you have in mind?"

"Dance with Livy."

"But—"

"You know she can dance the waltz," Charlotte

said. "And I know the next dance will be another waltz, because I saw you nod to the conductor. How much did you pay him?"

"Enough to keep him playing waltzes for the rest of the evening," Denbigh said with an unrepentant grin. "Very well, baggage, I will dance with my sister."

"Thank you, Lion."

Charlotte walked with Denbigh to where Olivia sat, and was glad she had, when she heard Olivia try to refuse him.

"I won't allow you to refuse, Livy," Charlotte said. "If you won't waltz with him, I will."

"Three dances in a row?" Olivia said. "It is not done."

"I know that. So what's it to be?"

Olivia stood and stepped into her brother's arms.

Olivia was worried that she would embarrass herself, or Lion. She had never danced with him before, because when she had been learning her first dance steps he had been of an age just enough older than her that he would rather have been caught cheating at cards than dancing with his sister.

But her brother put his arm firmly around her waist and supported her as they went whirling around the dance floor. It was almost as much fun as dancing with Braddock.

"I should have done this sooner," Lion said. "I'm sorry I didn't, Olivia."

"I wouldn't have accepted, even if you had offered," she admitted. "If it weren't for Charlotte . . . we both owe her a great deal, Lion. I hope you won't hurt her."

His eyes widened. "It is not my intention to do any such thing."

Olivia wondered if he knew that Charlotte was in love with him. She knew he was fighting his feelings for her. Was equally sure he had no idea how deep-felt they were. She had watched him twirling Charlotte around the dance floor, unable to take his eyes off her. She had seen him arranging the second waltz with his ward, and the unbelievable third.

Thank goodness Charlotte had not allowed him to dance it with her. The jibes of his friends and enemies alike would have brought him awake to his actions, and forced him to admit to feelings he obviously was not yet willing to accept.

"I understand you and Charlotte are going to the masquerade at Vauxhall tomorrow," Lion said.

"We are?" Olivia barely managed not to grimace. "But why?"

"Charlotte believes you need something to cheer you up. I cannot disagree with her. I know you've been unhappy, Olivia. The only comfort I can offer is that you are better off without him."

Olivia did not agree with him, but she did not wish to argue the point. "I would like to go home to Denbigh Castle, Lion."

"What? Why?"

"For precisely the reason you mentioned. I have been unhappy here. I'm ready to go home and settle into the life I've made for myself in the country. I have my friends and the rose garden and my knitting and books. It is enough."

She saw the struggle on his face. He wanted her to go. But he knew as well as she did that she was never going to find a husband if she imprisoned herself within the walls of Denbigh Castle. Charlotte had made them both believe—for a little while—that she was not entirely on the shelf.

"It will be less painful for me to accept the life of a spinster if I do not go on hoping for more," she said quietly. "Let me go, Lion." Her throat thickened. "Let me go."

"Very well, Olivia. At least stay for the masquerade tomorrow night. I will need you to help me keep an eye on Charlotte," he said with a hard-won smile.

"All right, Lion. I will start packing tomorrow morning. I should be ready to leave in two days. I'm sure Grandmama and Grandpapa will stay to chaperon until . . . until Charlotte is safely married."

She saw the lines of worry on his face. Knew he

was as distraught by the choices he had to make as she had been by hers. She hoped he chose Charlotte. She hoped he chose love. At least then, one of them would be happy.

11

 OLIVIA WAS HOME ALONE WHEN THE Duke of Braddock came calling, because Denbigh had taken Charlotte driving in the park, and Charlotte had cajoled the Duke and Duchess of Trent into going along with them.

"His Grace would not take no for an answer, Lady Olivia," Stiles said. "He insisted I bring you his card."

She had never expected to see him again. She knew she ought to refuse him. She had promised Lion she would.

Her hand trembled as she accepted the stiff white card with one corner folded down to show the caller had come in person. Something had been written in ink beside the name inscribed in gold.

We must speak.

The duke was a man of few words, it seemed.

"Tell the duke . . ." Olivia was torn nearly in two by the divergent needs inside her. To do the safe thing. Or to take a chance.

The mouse peeked out . . . The cat was there. But so was the cheese.

"Tell the duke I will see him."

The instant Stiles closed the drawing room door, Olivia put a hand to her head to still the thrumming pulse at her temple. What had come over her? What was the use of allowing this interview? She knew what he had done. Or almost done.

Ever since Lion had said he expected Braddock to take her to a house he kept for his doxies and keep her there overnight, she knew why they had stopped at that dark, narrow house and for whom the butler had been waiting at the open door. He had been waiting for her. And Braddock.

The duke must have changed his mind at some point, but that did not excuse him. He had contemplated her ruin. In her eyes, that alone was enough to damn him.

Olivia was not certain whether she was more angry with him for the fact he had planned to seduce her, or the fact he had not gone through with his seduction.

Had he balked at bedding a cripple? Had it been

pity that made him take mercy on her? She would rather a thousand times he had taken her virtue.

It is only a crooked leg! she wanted to cry. *It does not stop me from loving or wanting to be loved . . . in every way.*

Most shameful of all was the thought that she would not have denied him. If he had wanted her, she would have given herself to him. It would not have taken much coaxing. She had wanted to touch his body. She had wanted him to touch hers.

Those thoughts brought heat to her face, turning her cheeks rosy just as Stiles knocked on the door, ushered the duke inside, and announced, "His Grace, the Duke of Braddock."

Custom and courtesy demanded that she rise from her seat on the sofa and curtsy to the duke. She performed the first part of that duty by rising, then said, "Close the door when you leave, Stiles."

The butler gave her one questioning look, but when she said nothing more, did as she bid him. When Stiles was gone, she sank onto the sofa without the curtsy because, quite simply, her knees had buckled under her.

Braddock's face looked gaunt, as though he had not eaten. There were dark shadows under his eyes, as though he had not slept. And yet his eyes glittered with some strong emotion.

"You look tired, Your Grace," she said.

"I have not slept much in the past two weeks."

"I'm sorry if you have had some misfortune."

"No misfortune. Except that I might have lost you."

Her eyes flashed up at him. It was clearly a declaration of some sort. But she did not trust him now. She dared not trust him. She lowered her eyes and said, "Where have you been?"

"May I sit down?"

He had already taken a step toward her when she held out her hand and said, "Stay where you are. Please." She did not want to take a chance that he would touch her. If he touched her, she would give herself to him. She was that weak. She was that needy. She hated herself for feeling that way. But she could not help it.

He put his hands behind his back, like a barrister waiting to present his case. "Will you let me explain?"

"I'm listening."

"I went home, to the home where I grew up with my brother, James," he said. "You would like it. My mother planted a rose garden beside the house. It is beautiful this time of year." He paused, searched for what he wanted to say, and continued, "I needed some time to think."

She watched him pace. It was all that gave away his nervousness. His Weston jacket and buckskins were impeccable. Not a blond hair was out of place. His polished boots were quiet on the Aubusson carpet. It was difficult to imagine him ever being agitated. He had always seemed so cool and aloof.

She took a calming breath and let it out. She refused to see the duke as vulnerable. She was the one whose feelings had been trampled. Let him make amends. If he could.

"Ever since I heard about James's death, about the way he was killed, I have had one goal." He stopped and turned to face her. "To see your brother dead."

She hissed in a breath at the stabbing pain of knowing for certain that Lion had been right. Braddock had never been interested in her. Only in using her to get to her brother. Her nose stung, and her eyes filled with tears. She blinked to force them back, but one squeezed out and slid down her cheek.

Braddock took a step toward her, and an anguished sound spilled forth as she rose to try and escape him.

She never had a chance. He caught her by the shoulders before she had taken two awkward, tilting steps.

"Don't leave," he said. "Please let me finish."

"I have heard all I need to hear." She could feel the heat of him, remembered the taste of him, yearned to be loved by him. But he did not want her close to him. He was the one holding them apart.

He seemed to be struggling with some great emotion, but she could not tell what it was.

"I meant to hurt you, I cannot deny that. But in the end, I could not."

"What do you want from me? Forgiveness? What you did was unforgivable. Absolution? I cannot offer it!"

She was not even aware she was looking at him until she saw the smile come into his eyes.

"You're a veritable spitfire when you're angry," he said softly. And then, "All I want from you is you."

With strength she did not know she had, she tore herself free. "How can I trust what you say? How do I know this is not some very clever ploy to arrange what you failed at the first time?"

She was almost hysterical, because he was offering her everything she had ever wanted, and she was too afraid to reach out and take it. He was saying things she had always dreamed her handsome beau would say. And she found that from a real live man, they were impossible to believe.

"Believe me," he said, reaching out his hands to her.

She took a tilting step backward and said, "Believe the handsomest, richest man in England has honorable intentions toward a shy mouse with an awkward limp? I'd sooner believe pigs can fly!"

"It's the truth," he said.

"What about your brother? And my brother?"

"If I could forgive your brother for what he did, I would. But I cannot."

"What are you saying? That you want me . . . but you still intend to challenge my brother to a duel and kill him if you can?"

"I have no choice."

"You must be insane to think I would come to you under those terms!"

"They are the only terms I am free to offer," he said.

Olivia could not believe what she was hearing. All she had to do to realize her heart's desire was tie herself in marriage to a man who intended to kill her brother! The audacity, the sheer arrogance of such an offer was staggering.

She knew now why Braddock's cheeks were sunken, and his eyes glittered with a fierce light. He wanted her. But he could not give up his need for revenge against her brother. Braddock was asking her to choose between them. She could have one, but not both.

She kept her eyes downcast. If she looked at him, she might be tempted to say yes. She loved him that much.

But she could never live with the guilt of having made such a choice. She would never be able to forgive him, or herself, if he killed Lion. They would never be able to find happiness with the death of her brother between them.

"I am sorry, Your Grace," she said in a tremulous voice. "I must refuse your kind offer."

He took a step back. He had said what he had to say. She had refused him. It was over.

She saw the light die in his eyes. And felt her heart break.

As she watched him go, she tried to think of a way to stop him. And realized there was information he did not have that might influence his decision. She need only tell him the truth about why her brother had challenged James to a duel. She need only tell him what James had done to Lady Alice, and he would be able to forgive her brother.

Maybe all was not yet lost.

Braddock was almost to the door when she said, "Your brother . . . Did it never occur to you that Lord James must have done something to provoke Denbigh?"

The duke turned to face her. "It seems your brother needed no provocation."

"You know he was engaged to—"

That was as far as she got before the drawing room door burst open. Lion stood there, his silvery gray eyes staring daggers at Braddock.

"You are not welcome here," Lion said.

"Lion, the duke has offered—"

"*Carte blanche?*" Lion said sarcastically.

The blood left Olivia's face. *Carte blanche* was the open check a man offered to his mistress. It was among the worst insults Braddock could have offered her.

"I ought to kill you for that," Braddock said. "Lady Olivia—"

"Is my sister. If I ever see you near her again, I'll slap a glove in your face and kill you, as I did your blackguard of a brother!"

Braddock went white around the mouth. "You won't have to wait. I'll be happy to accommodate you. Name the time and place. Choose your weapon. Declare your seconds."

"Stop it, both of you!" Olivia cried, her hands clapped to her ears.

"Stay out of this, Olivia," Lion said in a steely voice. "It no longer concerns you."

"What is going on here?"

Olivia ran to her grandfather, who had arrived at the drawing room door with his cane in one hand, and his other arm around Charlotte's supporting shoulder. "Grandpapa, you have to stop them. Braddock has challenged Lion to a duel. And all because of a misunderstanding!"

"What!" Charlotte shrieked. "Lion, how could you!" She helped the duke as quickly as possible toward his chair in front of the fire. Olivia kept pace with her.

"Maybe you can talk some sense into him, Charlotte," Olivia said. "He won't listen to me."

As soon as the duke was settled, Charlotte turned to confront Denbigh. "What happened?" she asked.

The earl remained stone-faced.

Charlotte turned to Braddock and demanded, "What happened?"

"Denbigh insulted Lady Olivia," he said stiffly. "I have demanded satisfaction."

Charlotte's eyes goggled. She turned back to Lion and said, "Do I have this right? You are dueling with Braddock over an insult *you* gave Livy?"

Denbigh had the grace to flush. His ears turned pink. "It was not exactly like that."

"How was it, exactly?" Charlotte asked.

"I'd like to hear that explanation myself," the Duke of Trent said, leaning both hands on his cane in front of him.

"Don't make him repeat it," Olivia said wearily. "Just please, Lion, will you take back what you said?" She crossed to stand as close to Braddock as she thought she could safely go without inciting her brother. "Will that satisfy you, Your Grace?"

She gave Braddock a beseeching look, as though to say, *If you love me, you will do this for me.*

"It is only postponing the inevitable," Braddock said in a voice meant only for her.

"Every day you are both alive is a day I

rejoice," she said equally quietly. It was as close as she could come to a declaration of how she felt about him. She would not, could not, give him more encouragement than that.

"If Denbigh apologizes," Braddock announced to those gathered in the room, "I will take back my challenge."

"Please, Lion," Olivia said.

"Olivia, you don't understand—"

"I understand honor better than you know, Lion," she said in a fierce voice. "You insulted me. And Braddock. I wish you to take back what you said. And apologize."

"Give over, Denbigh," the Duke of Trent said. "The ladies don't like to see blood spilled. And I can't say I want to take the chance of outliving my heir. Too much trouble to manage all those properties," he blustered.

Olivia waited to see what her brother would do. He was a proud man. He had been sorely hurt by Braddock's brother. But if Braddock had ever offered any insult to her, it had never been spoken aloud to him. There was no substance on which to base his insult to her and to Braddock. He was in the wrong.

At last, he acknowledged it.

"I withdraw my comments regarding your intentions toward my sister. And I apologize for any insult I may have given you''—he turned to Olivia and finished—''or my sister.''

''I accept your apology and withdraw my challenge,'' Braddock replied.

''Nicely done,'' the Duke of Trent said. ''I could use some tea,'' he said. ''How about the rest of you?''

Braddock turned and made his bow to the elderly duke. ''I must excuse myself.''

''It has been a pleasure meeting you,'' the old man said.

Olivia heard Lion grind his teeth.

Her grandfather must have heard the same thing because he said, ''Sorry you have to go, Braddock.''

Braddock turned and made his bow to Olivia. ''Until we meet again.''

Which sent a nervous tic jumping in Lion's cheek.

''Good-bye, Your Grace,'' she said firmly.

He looked at her lingeringly, and she knew that even now, he would take her. But she saw him dead upon a field of honor, and Lion at the other end of the same field, with his lifeblood dripping from him. It was a nightmare from which there was no escape.

Maybe when Braddock knew the truth, he would be able to make peace with her brother. But even then, James would always be between them.

Her eyes followed him out the door. And out of her life.

Captive

* * *

It took every bit of persuasive power Charlotte possessed to convince Olivia that they should still attend the masquerade at Vauxhall that evening.

"I have a headache," Olivia said.

"That excuse won't work," Charlotte said.

"I will have one if you make me go," Olivia retorted. "How can you even consider attending a masquerade this evening, after the events of this morning?"

"I thought everything turned out fine this morning," Charlotte said. "Lion apologized, didn't he?"

Olivia made a frustrated sound in her throat. "I don't want to go. Will that excuse do?"

"You have to come with me, Livy," Charlotte pleaded. "I'm meeting a man who may be able to give me information about where Lord James and Lady Alice met in private. We need that information to aid us in finding out what hold James had over Lady Alice to make her betray Lion.

"Don't you see? Once we know everything, you'll be able to tell Braddock the truth about his brother. And I'll be able to convince Lion that Lady Alice never purposely betrayed him. Don't you want me to be your sister-in-law?"

Olivia perked up slightly at that. "This is the first I've heard of that. Have you had a change of mind? Are you willing to marry Lion? Have you told him you will?''

''Yes. Yes. And I can't. Not yet. Not until I've figured out the mystery surrounding Lady Alice. Which is why I need you to come with me tonight. I need you to distract Lion long enough for me to sneak away to the Lover's Walk.''

''I don't know, Charlie. Meeting a strange man on a dark walkway does not sound like such a good idea to me.''

''Trust me, Livy. I know what I'm doing.''

''Very well, Charlie. I will go.''

''And you will help me distract Lion?''

''It is against my better judgment.''

''Please, Livy,'' Charlotte cajoled.

''Very well. I will distract Lion. Now go away and let me rest.''

Having been successful in convincing Olivia that they should still attend the masquerade, Charlotte set out to find Lion and accomplish the same task—using different arguments, of course.

He was nowhere to be found in the three-story town house.

Charlotte finally went to the butler and asked, ''Harvey, has the earl left the house? I've looked everywhere for him, but I can't find him.''

''I have not seen the earl since luncheon, Lady—Charlie,'' he replied.

It had taken her longer to get the ancient Trent

butler to use her first name than any of the other servants. But she had told him she would consider it a discourtesy if he did not. That had allowed him to accede to her wishes.

Charlotte watched Stiles check to see if anyone had caught her using his first name. He had explained once that he did not mind if *she* called him Harvey, but he did not want any of the other servants thinking *they* could do the same.

Charlotte had given Harvey a lecture on equality that had fallen on deaf ears. Harvey could hear just fine, he simply did not choose to embrace her point of view.

"A butler is to the servants as a duke is to the nobility," he had explained. "It is the way of the world. There are those who give orders and those who take them. Where would we be if the maid-of-all-work considered herself the equal of the housekeeper?" he asked.

"In a better world," Charlotte said.

Stiles was not impressed. Despite all her arguments, he remained convinced that chaos would result if England abandoned the class structure that was all he knew. Charlotte had to be satisfied with crumbling one tiny corner of the class structure through Stiles's willingness to address her, and to be addressed, in familiar terms.

"Do you have any idea where the earl might be hiding?" she asked the dignified butler.

"Did you check the third floor gallery?"

"Nothing but paintings of moldy ancestors," Charlotte said, wrinkling her nose.

"The kitchen?"

"The earl knows where the kitchen is? He goes there?" Charlotte asked in mocking amazement.

The butler chuckled. "Oh, yes. When he was a boy . . . But that was long ago and before he lost his parents. I remember when . . ."

Charlotte had listened to more than a few reminiscences by Stiles, but daylight was fading, and she had to ensure that her plans for the evening remained intact. "I am sorry to interrupt you, Harvey, but it's urgent that I find the earl. Do you have any other suggestions where I might look?"

"Perhaps he has gone to the attic."

"I didn't know there was one."

"Oh, yes. A great deal of furniture and clothing is stored there. In the gables, above the third floor. A steep stairway behind the maids' quarters leads up to it."

"Why would he go there?" Charlotte asked curiously.

"It was a place he went as a boy, when he wanted to be alone."

"Thank you, Harvey. I'll look for him there."

The attic was laced with cobwebs, and the only light sifted in through two small, dirty windows at either end of the sloping roof. "Lion?" Charlotte called. "Are you up here?"

"How did you find me?"

Charlotte nearly jumped out of her skin when he appeared behind her, stepping out from behind several stacked wooden crates. "You did that on purpose," she accused.

He grinned. "It was always fun to scare the maids when they came looking for me. It helped that there was a family of dormouses—dormice?—living up here, at least one of whom could always be counted on to scurry across the floor at just the right moment."

"What's a dormouse?"

"Similar to a mouse, but a little larger, about the size of a small squirrel. I used to feed them when I was a child. I looked where their nest used to be. It's gone."

"You came up here looking for a family of dormice?" Charlotte asked.

"Actually, I came up here to be alone."

"Oh." Charlotte realized, suddenly, how alone they were. It was as though no one else existed. The sounds of hackneys and carriages and curricles rattling over the cobblestones, or the clattering of coal heading down a chute into someone's basement, or fishmongers and flower girls hawking their wares, could not be heard all the way up here. It was almost like being in the country.

"Oh," she said again. This time it was a sound of wonder. "It's so quiet up here."

"Yes."

They stood in silence. Staring at each other.

He had cobwebs in his hair. And dust on the knees of his breeches. And desire in his eyes.

"Go back downstairs, Charlotte."

She shook her head. "I need to speak with you."

"It's dangerous up here," he said, taking a step toward her.

Charlotte held her ground. "You can't scare me off with the threat of dormice," she scoffed.

"What about lions?" he said. "Do they scare you?"

This one did. Especially when he was stalking her, about to pounce. No one was likely to knock at the attic door. No one but Stiles knew they were up here. If she gave in to Lion here, there would be nothing and no one to stop him.

"Charlie."

He made the detested nickname sound like a lover's caress. She was so mesmerized by his intense, silvery gaze, that it was not until his hands tightened on either side of her waist that she realized he had caught his prey.

She swallowed hard. "Lion, this is wrong."

His lips curled. "I have been telling myself that ever since you walked through that door. I have been saying to myself, 'Lion, you are the chit's guardian. It's your duty to protect her from importuning gentlemen.' And do you know what I have been answering myself?'' he asked.

She shook her head slowly.

'' 'Have you ever seen anything as beautiful as her eyes? Or as charming as her freckles? Or as willful as her chin? Have you ever wanted anything in your life more than you want to kiss her lips right now, this instant?'

''Do you know what I answered myself, Charlie?''

''No.''

''Exactly right,'' he said with a gentle, teasing smile. ''I said, 'No, Lion, you have never wanted anything, or anyone, more than you want her right now.' ''

''Lion, we can't—you can't—we mustn't—''

He cut her off by capturing her mouth with his, by devouring her with his lips and teeth and tongue. She was consumed by his passion, and it fed hers. She had never felt such hunger, such a craving for something . . . something . . .

To be closer to him. To be inside him. To have him inside her.

She did not stop him when his hands curved around her breasts, nor when one found its way inside her bodice to touch her flesh, nor even when he unbuttoned the back of her dress and shoved it off one shoulder, so his mouth could close on her nipple through her thin muslin chemise.

She cried out as he suckled and held his head close, afraid he would stop. Afraid it would be over before the craving would be satisfied.

She could not get enough. She could not feel enough.

His mouth returned to hers, and he murmured, "Put your tongue in my mouth, Charlie. Taste me."

A gently bred lady should have been—would have been—shocked or appalled or revolted by such a request. Husbands had mistresses for such depravities. Copulation was for procreation. Wives did not enjoy themselves in bed.

Charlotte never had a mother to tell her to lie still and do her duty. She had died too soon. Her father had said what happened between a man and a woman in the bedroom was a joy and a wonder. No more. No less.

Charlotte did what Lion asked willingly, excitedly, eager to please him and herself. She felt shivery, quivery all over, as she searched the inside of his mouth with her tongue, finding rich textures and sensuous tastes, and discovering secrets only a lover would know.

He liked it when she nibbled on his upper lip. Or sucked his lower lip into her mouth. Or traced the inside of his upper lip with her tongue. He was impatient. He wanted more. He wanted everything at once.

There was no telling where things would have ended, if the dormouse had not run over her foot.

Charlotte shrieked and jerked herself from Lion's embrace, hopping up and down as though she were on fire.

"What's the matter?" Lion said, trying to grasp her shoulders, trying to hold her still while she struggled to be free.

"A mouse!" she cried, grabbing his neck to get her feet off the floor. "A mouse ran over my foot!"

He picked her up and set her on one of the crates off the floor and looked around for the offending rodent.

Sure enough, a dormouse scurried from behind the crate Charlotte was sitting on, through a hole in the floor, and was gone.

"You *are* afraid of dormice!" he said, turning to her with a laugh. She watched the laugh get caught in his throat when he looked at her.

She was suddenly aware of her dress hanging off of one shoulder. Of the cold, damp spot on the front of her chemise. Of her swollen lips. And her tangled hair.

He had not fared much better in their loving encounter. His neck cloth had come undone, and his hair stood on end.

"Oh, God," he said. "I almost . . . Charlotte, I . . ."

He came to her and took her hand and said, "Please marry me, Charlotte."

For a moment she felt euphoric. That feeling lasted only as long as it took her to identify the look in his eyes as guilt. Not love. There was no love.

She pulled her hand free of his and used it to pull her dress back up over her shoulder. "No, Lion. I won't."

"You must," he said fiercely. "I have . . . I have taken unconscionable advantage of you."

"You did not hear me complaining," she said. "I enjoyed myself as much as you did."

"Enjoyed? Charlotte!" he roared. "A lady does not *enjoy* a tryst with a man who is not her husband."

"I did."

"Charlotte—"

She put her fingertips against his lips to cut him off. "Please, Lion. Let's not argue about it. I want a husband who will love me. Because of what happened with Lady Alice your heart is not whole. When it is . . . if it ever is . . . I would like to have it."

Making certain there were no dormouses in the vicinity, she hopped down from the crate and turned her back to him. "Will you please button my dress for me?"

For a moment she thought he would refuse. She looked at him over her shoulder and said, "Would you like me to go downstairs to the maids' quarters and ask one of them to button me up?"

He flushed. And took a step closer so he could reach the buttons. She was amused that he seemed much less adept at buttoning her dress up, than he had been at unbuttoning it.

While she had his attention, she made the plea she had come to make in the first place. "Lion," she said, "We're still going to the masquerade tonight, aren't we?"

"You still want to go?" he asked.

She turned to face him, so he had to button the top button with his hands over her shoulders. She looked up at him with her most earnest expression and said, "The reason I wanted to go to the masquerade—that Livy needed something to cheer her up—is still true. In fact, after what happened this morning with Braddock, she is more Friday-faced than ever."

"If she is so melancholy," Lion said dryly, "maybe she would rather be by herself."

"Oh, that is the very worst thing for a sad person to do. Livy needs company. She needs to dance and talk and enjoy herself. Will you take us?"

"Very well, Charlotte," he said. "If it would please you."

"Oh, Lion, it would." She stood on her toes

and gave him a quick kiss on the lips and then turned and ran for the door. She didn't trust herself, otherwise, not to stay and ask him to unbutton her dress again. He was so very good at it.

At the door she turned and said, "Lady Alice did not betray you, Lion. Nor would I."

Then she opened the door and hurried down the stairs, leaving him to enjoy the dormouse and his solitude.

12

 CHARLOTTE WAS FACED WITH YET AN-
other argument when she tried to get
Olivia to put on the shepherdess's costume she had commissioned to be made
for her.

"The skirt doesn't even cover my limbs," she
protested in shocked tones. "It stops halfway
down."

"That's the whole idea," Charlotte said. "You
will be wearing white stockings with pretty red ribbons crisscrossed around them."

"My limbs—"

"I have seen your legs, Livy," Charlotte said,
"and aside from one being longer than the other,
they look the same as mine. Besides, it will be so
dark, no one will even notice."

"How are you going to get this costume past Lion's scrutiny?" Olivia said.

"Oh, he'll be so busy yelling at me, he won't even notice what you're wearing," Charlotte reassured her with a grin.

"What *are* you wearing?" Olivia asked.

"Wait and see."

Actually, once Charlotte saw herself in the mirror, she thought this time she might have gone too far. She looked like she was wearing a sheet she had grabbed after rising naked from a bed with her lover. Maybe that was an exaggeration, but not by much. The togas worn by the Elgin Marbles had not looked nearly so revealing.

Of course, this actually was a sheet, a white silk one she had found in the cupboards where linens were kept. A ruby brooch she had begged from Olivia held the costume together at one shoulder. The other shoulder was bare.

She had stolen a bit of tasseled gold drapery cord from the library, crisscrossed it under her breasts, and tied it in a knot around her waist to secure the sheet in place. But if there was much of a breeze at Vauxhall, she was in trouble.

Denbigh would not be focused on Olivia's stocking-covered legs, because he would be staring at her bare ones. She was practically naked under the toga and barefoot except for a pair of fragile white satin sandals that tied with pretty bows at the backs of her ankles. She had seen them in a shop window one day, after she had been to visit the Elgin Marbles, and had bought them on a whim. She had never had occasion to wear them until now.

Maybe it was the kisses—among other things—she had shared with Lion in the attic that made her eyes look so exotic and mysterious.

Or maybe it was the lining of kohl she had induced Sally to apply.

"He will never let you leave the house," Sally said as she stared, wide-eyed, at the image of her mistress in the mirror.

Charlotte was inclined to agree.

If there had been more time, she would have tried to come up with another costume. But it was already nine o'clock in the evening, and she did not want to take the chance of missing her assignation at Lover's Walk.

"It is not so bad," she hedged.

"As what? A Cyprian would think twice about venturing forth dressed like that," Sally said.

"It will be dark," Charlotte said.

"Lady Alice said that Vauxhall—except for the walkways where no proper young lady would allow herself to be caught dead—is lit by hundreds of lanterns."

"Damn and blast! There's no help for it now, Sally. I'll have to brazen it out."

"Brazen is the right word," Sally muttered under her breath, "as a Covent Garden abbess."

"Thank you, Sally," Charlotte said, working to keep the edge from her voice. "I have taken your point."

She readjusted the slippery fabric across her breasts and belly and left the room. She figured it was best if she and Olivia went downstairs together. That way, Denbigh would not be able to make up his mind which of them provided the worst offense to his eyes and his consequence, and he would thus be rendered speechless.

She hoped.

She knocked on Olivia's bedroom door, and when it opened and she saw Olivia's expression said, "Don't say a word. Lion will say it for you."

Olivia's hazel eyes crinkled at the corners with laughter. "I understand now what you meant earlier this afternoon. I feel positively overdressed in comparison."

"Stubble it," Charlotte said. But she was glad to see Olivia smiling again.

When they arrived at the drawing room door, where Stiles had told them the earl was waiting, Charlotte got cold feet.

"You go in first, Livy."

"I think your first idea was the best one. I think we had better go in together," Olivia said.

Charlotte took a deep breath and stepped inside.

To her horror, the Duke and Duchess of Trent were sitting in the two chairs before the fire. She had already whirled in retreat when the duke called out, "Come here, Charlie, and let me see you. And can that really be Livy? You look charming, dear girl."

Charlotte kept her head high and her eyes straight ahead. She could hardly believe she was walking around practically naked in front of Denbigh's grandparents. The thought of Lion seeing her like this had not been so bad. To be honest, there was a devilish imp inside her that had *wanted* Denbigh to see her as daring and decadent.

She was barely aware that Olivia took her hand and led her, like a lost sheep, over to stand in front of the duke and duchess.

"What do you think of my two girls, Lizzie?" the duke asked his wife.

"Why, Livy," the duchess said. "Arthur is right. You do look charming as a shepherdess. That crooked staff is the perfect touch. And Charlotte . . ."

Charlotte waited for the *coup de grace*. It was almost better to be cut down by the duchess, she thought, than have Denbigh do it.

"You are Diana, the Huntress, come to life!" the duchess exclaimed.

"What?" Charlotte turned her head to meet the duchess's gaze and was startled to realize the old woman had the same silvery gray eyes as Lion. Hers were a little darker perhaps, than his, as though they had tarnished with age.

"Don't you agree, Lion?" the duchess said.

Bolstered by the words of support from the duchess, Charlotte turned to look at him. She had never expected Denbigh to approve the costume. What she saw in his eyes was frightening to behold.

Not rebuke. Naked desire.

"She is Diana," he said. "As she was meant to be."

Charlotte felt her nipples peak. Her own desire, an answer to his, was impossible to hide.

"It's time to go," Denbigh said. "We cannot delay, or we will miss the fireworks."

"Fireworks?" Charlotte said stupidly. Who needed to leave home for fireworks? There were plenty of them right here.

To Charlotte's surprise and relief, Denbigh settled his domino over her shoulders to hide her arousal, and in the process, revealed his own. Charlotte had never approved of staring, but some things were too interesting to let pass by.

"I could see you were chilled," he murmured in her ear.

That might have been the reason her nipples had peaked. But it wasn't. And he knew it.

But she blessed him for protecting her from the too-knowing eyes of the duke and duchess.

Denbigh spirited the three of them into the carriage without more ado, merely substituting her cloak for his own at the door. Once they were in Denbigh's town carriage on their way to Vauxhall, he gave her the tongue-lashing that had not been possible in front of his grandparents.

"What were you thinking of, Charlotte? No lady reveals so much in public."

"It is a costume, Lion. I'm Diana, the Huntress."

"You're Attila the Hun," he said. "Running roughshod over every feeling of delicacy."

"You're being unfair, Lion," Olivia protested. "The purpose of a masquerade is to dress up and pretend you are someone else. Masks are worn so that no one will be recognized and faulted in any way for how they are dressed. I promise you, no one will know it is Charlotte behind the mask."

"I will know!"

The air within the carriage was electrified. With those few words, Denbigh had admitted his real objection to Charlotte's costume. It was sexually provocative . . . to him.

None of them said anything else during the ride to Vauxhall, but Charlotte's mind was racing with plans for when and how she could make her escape from Denbigh. She wanted the information Sir Fenton had offered her. She needed it to have any hope of a future with Denbigh.

"I asked Lord Burton to join us in our supper box," Denbigh said when they reached the entrance to Vauxhall, north of Kensington Lane. "I thought it would even the numbers."

Charlotte exchanged a dismayed look with Olivia. Now she had two sets of watching eyes to escape.

Percy was already there waiting for them at the supper box.

"Good evening, old man," he said, as he greeted Lion. "Ladies, ladies, you are exquisite," he complimented them.

Denbigh scowled.

Percy ignored him, helping a masked Charlotte and Olivia into the box one at a time and setting their cloaks aside.

"You're Henry the Eighth!" Charlotte exclaimed in delight, when she finally got a good look at him.

"Have the girth for it, my dear Lady Charlotte, don't you think?" Percy chortled, patting a girth that was slightly larger than his own, thanks to a very little padding.

"I have taken the liberty of ordering a light snack," Percy said. "Thinly sliced ham. Chickens as delicate as a sparrow. An assortment of biscuits and cheesecakes. And a quart or two of arrack to wash it all down.''

''What Percy means to say is that the portions are skimpy, and you will need the arrack to keep the biscuits from sticking in your throat,'' Lion interjected.

Percy laughed. ''I'm afraid Lion is right. There are other compensations to Vauxhall. The view is delightful,'' he said, wiggling a pair of false bushy eyebrows at Charlotte and Olivia.

Denbigh growled.

Charlotte laughed. Percy's comment made her costume sound lovely and enticing, rather than unrefined and indecent. She thanked him with her eyes.

She had first met Percy at Almack's, where Lady Jersey had introduced him to her as an old friend of Denbigh's. She would not have picked Percival Porter from a crowd as a person Denbigh would choose to confide in, but the more she saw of Percy, the more she liked him.

He was always in a cheerful mood and did not seem to care that his clothing choices were unfortunate. Despite the fact he was a viscount, he possessed none of the pretensions common to his class. She would have been quite happy to see him here, if she did not perceive him as a complication to her sensitive plans.

Their box was located in the center of the

Grove, in the Cross Walk that ran crosswise through the center of the grounds between the South Walk and the Grand Walk. Unfortunately, the Lover's Walk was the furthermost promenade from where they were situated. She would be lucky if she did not find herself accosted by some lurking rakehell before she got there.

"You're chewing on your lip, Charlotte. What has you worried, I wonder? Planning some mischief?"

Lion's question brought a flush to her cheeks. She immediately let go of her lip and said, "You're sitting right beside me, Lion. What trouble can I get into?"

"I will feel safer if I have you in my grasp," he said. "Come. We will walk."

Not "May I have the honor of walking in the Gardens with you?" or "Will you allow me the pleasure of walking in the Gardens with you?" but "We will walk."

Charlotte wondered what had happened to her strong American backbone as she followed Denbigh out of the supper box without a peep of complaint.

It occurred to her only after he put her arm on his and began to stroll, that if she were clever, she could arrange for Denbigh to escort her almost the entire way to Lover's Walk. Then, all she had to do was figure out some way to send him away for long enough to meet with Sir Fenton.

All in all, Charlotte was feeling quite satisfied with herself as she began her walk with Denbigh through the famous darkened, tree-lined walkways of Vauxhall.

Olivia could not believe she had allowed herself to be manipulated into coming to Vauxhall with Charlotte, only to be abandoned in the supper box with Lord Burton. Not that she did not like Percy. They simply had nothing in common upon which to converse.

After several aborted attempts at discourse, Olivia said, "Do you think, Lord Burton, it might be possible for you to get me some strawberries?"

Percy jumped on her request like a duck on a June bug. "I'm sure I could manage it, Lady Olivia. If you will be comfortable alone for a few minutes."

"I'm sure I will be fine."

Olivia did not expect to be importuned while sitting in the enclosed supper box, even though it was situated among what must have been a hundred boxes, each containing other parties of boisterous revelers. She certainly had no intention of leaving the box by herself.

But not more than a minute after Percy left her alone, a tall, masked figure, dressed all in black like a highwayman, appeared at the entrance to the box and said, "May I join you?"

The blood drained from her head, and she felt faint. "Braddock," she whispered.

He made a sweeping bow and said, "At your service, Lady Olivia."

"How did you find me? What are you doing here? Lord Burton will—"

"Will be regrettably detained by my man."

"My brother will—"

"Will no doubt be gone long enough for me to accomplish my purpose," Braddock said.

"Which is?"

"To take you away with me."

She did not try to run. She could not outrun him. She did not scream. Who would hear her amid all the shrieking laughter?

"Where can we go, that the past will not haunt us?" she said bleakly. "Where the future does not end in tragedy?"

"I am determined to have you," he said in a steely voice.

"What price are you willing to pay?" she asked. "Will you give up your revenge?"

"I cannot."

"Then I cannot come with you, Your Grace."

"I will take you by force, if necessary."

Her eyes went wide. "You cannot mean to abduct me!"

"Why not?" he said, his eyes glittering through the black mask, his mouth taut and harsh beneath it.

"I will hate you for it."

He hesitated. "That is the last thing I want, Lady Olivia."

"Then give me another choice!" she cried.

"Very well. I will spare your brother, if you will come with me now."

"As your doxy? As a kept woman?" she said angrily. "That will only provoke the duel you tell me you are willing to forego!"

"As my wife."

He had shocked her into silence. He was giving her what she had wanted earlier that day. A way she could say yes to his proposal. But oh, the way was fraught with danger! What if he did not keep his word? What if he took her to wife, and he and her brother later came to blows?

Even more to the point, would Lion accept her decision to go with Braddock? Would he feel honor bound to challenge the duke because she had been stolen in the middle of the night from under her brother's nose?

Surely she could assuage Lion's anger. Surely she could make peace between the two people she loved most in the world. And she still had not even told Braddock the truth about his brother. When she did, he would understand why her brother had done what he had. It would ease the tension between them.

"Time is short, Lady Olivia. You must decide."

She glanced at Braddock from beneath lowered lashes. In his fitted black shirt and breeches, his black boots and black cloak and black hat, he had come dressed for an abduction. He was going to take her whether she accepted his offer or not. He said he was giving her a choice, but she did not see it. There was only one answer she could give him.

"I accept your offer of marriage, Your Grace."

Her heart skipped a beat when she saw the roguish smile that split his face the moment she agreed to have him.

"My name is Reeve," he said.

He had not touched her, or even taken a step toward her, since he had entered the box. But there was a feeling of expectation, now that she was his, a tension between them that had not existed before.

She was sitting at the table where Percy had left her, the crooked staff lying at her feet. He crossed to her and drew her to her feet and circled her waist with his arm to support her weight.

Her hands settled on his forearms, and she was surprised at how hard his muscles were.

"Look at me, Olivia," he said.

"It is Livy. To my friends."

She felt him relax into her body, as though a wall had come down between them.

"I am your friend, Livy. And I will be your lover soon," he murmured in her ear.

"And my husband," she said tartly.

"And your husband," he agreed with a tender smile. "Will you say my name, Livy?"

"Reeve," she said, and felt him hiss in a breath. "Reeve," she said again. "Reeve."

It sounded so right, so perfect, like their life together would be. Children! She would have children!

Their lips met and merged. All her hopes and dreams were bound up in him. It was more than a meeting of bodies to her. It was a joining of souls. She was his. Now and forever. For better or worse.

Worse.

She forced the specter of disaster from her mind. He had promised to marry her. He had promised to forego his vengeance. She would not borrow trouble where it did not exist.

But it would be better if Lion did not return and find them together here. It would be better to send her brother a letter explaining everything and give him time to calm down before he could reach Braddock to express his anger and, oh, God, his feelings of betrayal at her decision to marry Braddock.

Please understand, Lion. I love him. I had no choice about whom I loved. Any more than you did. He is the other half of me.

She pulled her mouth free of Braddock's and leaned her head against his chest, where she heard his heart beating fast. "We must go," she said.

"Anxious to be a bride, Livy?"

"Anxious to avoid my brother," she replied.

He stiffened, then relaxed. "As am I. Let us go, then." He stepped back and put his arm out for her to take.

As they left the box, he said, "Have I told you how beautiful you look tonight, Livy?"

She kept her lashes lowered to hide the dismay in her eyes. "False compliments are not necessary, Your Grace."

He stopped abruptly and lifted her chin with his hand. "There is nothing false about my feelings," he said. "To me you are beautiful, Livy. I don't know how I could ever have thought otherwise. And I would be Reeve to you."

She forced herself to raise her eyes and look into his. She might as well know now if he was lying. She could not change what was going to happen, but at least she would not have jumped over the cliff without looking first into the abyss to see how quickly she was going to hit bottom.

His blue eyes looked down at her frankly, openly. And without deceit.

How was it possible he did not see her as plain, when every other man had? How was it possible he did not notice her crippling injury, when it forced her to lean upon his hand?

It was true, then. Love *was* blind.

"Thank you, Reeve," she said softly.

"For what?" he asked.

"For loving me."

There, where anyone passing could see them, the Duke of Braddock pulled Lady Olivia Morgan into his arms and kissed her silly. So silly Olivia was laughing with pleasure and embarrassment and delight when he was done.

"We have a long way to go tonight, Livy," he said, treating her once more to his roguish grin. "It is time we were on our way."

"I am ready, Reeve." *For whatever the future holds.*

She was sitting in the duke's opulent carriage, waiting for him to join her inside, when she saw Lion running toward them. Braddock saw him at the same time. Reeve pulled the carriage door closed behind him, thumped the roof with his fist and yelled, "Drive, Bailey. Drive!"

Olivia watched out the window as Lion's angry face disappeared from sight.

13

 "HAVE YOU BEEN TO VAUXHALL OF-
ten?" Charlotte asked, as Denbigh led
her along one of the tree-lined walkways. It was quiet except for the barest
breeze rustling the leaves overhead, the
crunch of gravel underfoot, and the occasional giggle of a nervous female out of the darkness.

"I used to come here a lot when I was
younger," Denbigh said.

"Why did you stop?"

He smiled down at her. "I outgrew hide and
seek. At least the grown-up version of it that is
played in the darkened walkways here," he said,
gesturing toward a kissing couple half-hidden in the
shadows.

Charlotte realized she had let the earl walk her

277

down one of the less used byways. That it was quite dark. And she was wearing very little.

"Where are we?" she asked.

"Does it matter?"

His voice was low and husky and made her feel jittery inside.

She could not think of a subtle way to ask if this was the Lover's Walk. She did not want to give away her eventual destination. And she would rather not give him any ideas.

"Who were you planning to meet here tonight, Charlotte?" he asked.

The question caught her by surprise, and she made the mistake of stopping. Mistake, because once they were no longer moving, he turned her to face him and put his hands on her shoulders. Her almost bare shoulders.

She had never felt anything quite like it.

The grazing touch of his fingertips was enough to tickle her and make her giggle. She stuck a hand over her mouth, because the giggle sounded too much like those they had heard in the shadows along the walkway. She and Denbigh were not even off the beaten path!

Denbigh must have read her mind.

He backed her up one step, and another, until she ran into a lilac bush behind her.

"Ouch!" she said. "There's a limb stabbing me in the back."

Her gallant savior reached around her to find the offending limb and break it off. Of course, once his arms were around her, it took only a small effort to pull her close.

Charlotte managed to squeeze her arms and elbows in between them at the last second. "Lion, I don't think—"

"Don't think," he said, lowering his head to kiss her.

Charlotte knew now why Vauxhall Gardens was so popular. It had nothing to do with the food, or even the entertainment. She had yet to witness a single explosion of fireworks. Except within her own body.

It was these damned darkened walkways.

Not that Charlotte minded kissing Lion. He was quite good at it, actually. Her knees turned to jelly in two seconds flat. Her nipples became twin buds against her forearms, which were bunched against Denbigh's chest. Her breathing became erratic. And what he was doing to her mouth was causing an embarrassing dampness between her thighs.

"Lion," she said against his mouth, as he nibbled on her lips.

"What is it, Charlotte?"

"Are we near the Lover's Walk?"

"Why do you ask?" he asked, sounding amused.

"I . . . I just wondered."

"We're *on* the Lover's Walk," he said, as he kissed her beneath her ear.

"Oh." She shivered. Like a child rooting for the source of sustenance, she rose on tiptoes, found the same spot beneath his ear, and returned his kiss.

And felt him shiver.

The sound of gravel crunching underfoot warned them of someone's approach. Lion pulled her close, hiding her face against his chest. She shoved her head out from under his arm to see who was passing, on the chance that it was Sir Fenton looking for her.

And saw a checkered domino like the one Lion was wearing. Like Sir Fenton had said he would wear.

"Lion," she whispered.

"Shh."

"Lion," she whispered.

"Shhhhhh."

Sir Fenton was getting away. He might think she had forgotten her appointment. He might not come back.

"Sir Fenton," she called. "I am here."

Lion groaned.

Sir Fenton stopped in his tracks and whispered in the direction of the bushes where they were hidden, "Lady Charlotte? Is that you?"

"It's her, you old fool," Denbigh replied, his voice laced with menace. "And she's with me."

Sir Fenton had already reversed his course when Charlotte called after him, "Sir Fenton! Don't leave! I must speak with you!" She struggled to be free of Denbigh's hold on her. "Let me go, Lion. I have to speak with him!"

"He's too old for you, Charlotte," Lion said.

"I don't want to marry him, you idiot! I just want to interview him."

At the word "idiot," Denbigh's hold loosened, and Charlotte slipped out of his grasp and followed the disappearing figure.

"Wait, Sir Fenton. Please, wait for me!"

For some reason, Fenton wasn't slowing down, and he even made several turns, so that once she almost lost track of him. Charlotte could hear Denbigh's bootsteps crunching in the gravel behind her, which lent her feet wings.

"Sir Fenton," she called, "I'm alone. Wait for me."

Sir Fenton abruptly stopped and turned to wait for her.

She was breathless by the time she finally reached him. "Why—did you—run?" she asked between pants.

"I distinctly heard Denbigh's voice, Lady Charlotte. I did not wish to intrude between you and your guardian."

"We were only walking together until it was

time for me to meet with you," Charlotte reassured him.

He peered beyond her shoulder. "Denbigh did not follow you?"

Charlotte listened for the crunch of gravel and realized she did not hear anything. She did not know what had happened to Denbigh, but she did not doubt he was looking for her even now. She needed to get the information she had come to get before Denbigh caught up to her.

"I guess he got lost," Charlotte said brightly to Sir Fenton. "We're alone."

"Well, well, Lady Charlotte," Sir Fenton said with a crooked smile that appeared like magic out of the darkness. "This is much better."

Charlotte did not like the insinuating tone of his voice. She stated her business quickly. "I came to find out what you can tell me about Lord James Somers."

"Somers?" Sir Fenton mused. "I have not discoursed with anyone by that name lately."

"Probably because he's dead," Charlotte said with asperity.

"Well, that explains it."

"Explains what?"

"Why I don't know him."

Charlotte felt like tearing her hair in frustration. "Sir Fenton, I came here because at Lady Hornby's ball you suggested you might be able to tell me where a couple could go to be alone together.''

"And so I have,'' Sir Fenton said with a satisfied smirk. "For here we are! Just as you desired.''

When Sir Fenton lunged for her, Charlotte leaped backward. Unfortunately, he managed to grab the sheet where it crossed her shoulder and pulled hard enough to break the clasp of Olivia's ruby brooch.

As the brooch came free, and he reined in the fabric, the pin stuck him in the hand. He cried out in surprise and pain. "What was that?''

Charlotte was too busy clutching at loose silk to have much sympathy for him. "You scoundrel!'' she hissed. "You libertine! You rakeshame! You— You—'' she searched her vocabulary for another word to describe Fenton.

"Try lecher,'' a deadly voice behind her said.

Charlotte whirled. "Lion!'' She threw herself toward him, and he caught her in his arms. She felt his fingers move across her bare shoulder where her costume should have been and find a scratch where blood had welled in tiny beads.

"You're hurt,'' he said in a tight voice.

"He's got Livy's ruby brooch, Lion. He tore it off of me. Make him give it back.''

"The chit came here looking for me, Denbigh,'' Sir Fenton blustered. "She only got what she deserved.''

"Get behind me, Charlotte," Denbigh said, setting her aside. He took a step toward Fenton.

"I don't care to engage in a bout of fisticuffs with you, Denbigh."

"You don't have a choice," Lion said.

Charlotte heard the sound of metal grating against metal. She didn't recognize it at first. Then she saw the shine of steel in the moonlight and realized Sir Fenton's gold-handled walking stick had carried a concealed blade, which he was now holding in his hand.

"Be careful, Lion!" she cried. "He has a sword."

"Stay where you are, Charlotte," Denbigh said. "I will handle this." As he spoke, Denbigh untied the domino from his throat, slipped it from his shoulders, and flung it several times around one arm to make a protective pad of silk. Then he continued his predatory stalk in Fenton's direction.

"Stay back," Fenton warned. "I know how to use this to good effect." He whipped the blade several times in the air, making a deadly, whistling sound as though to prove his claim.

Charlotte noticed that, at the same time, he was checking his avenues of escape.

There were none. He was backed into a corner, trapped by trees and shrubs. There was no way out except through Denbigh.

Charlotte could have told Denbigh that a

trapped animal will always fight more viciously, because it knows there is no escape. Fenton gave the lesson to Denbigh himself.

The sword struck like lightning, slashing through the darkness. Denbigh's protected arm came up to block the blow.

Fenton struck again, like a cobra, swift and dangerous.

Denbigh's reflexes were quicker, and he parried the second blow, but Charlotte knew from his surprised grunt that a third stab had found flesh.

"Lion!" she cried.

"Stay where you are, Charlotte." His voice was calm, and he did not sound in the least discomposed, though she knew he must be hurt.

Fenton was breathing like a bellows. Moonlight reflected off beads of sweat on his forehead and glistening rivulets ran down the sides of his face into what were quickly wilting white shirt points. His eyes glittered like an animal's in the moonlight.

Fenton had the weapon, but it became clear, as Charlotte watched the two men, that he was the one whose life was in danger.

Denbigh parried Fenton's next desperate thrust with the wad of silk and reached for Fenton's throat. His fingers tightened, and Charlotte watched the older man drop his weapon and claw at Denbigh's tightening grasp with both hands.

Charlotte ran to Denbigh and grabbed at his

arm. "Let him go, Lion. My hurt is but a scratch. It will heal without a mark."

Fenton's eyes bulged. His breath rattled in his throat.

"Please, Lion. You have killed once for the sake of a lady's honor, and it accomplished nothing! Leave be!"

His jaw clamped tight. He did not even look at her, merely said to Fenton, "If one word of what happened here tonight is repeated, and I will know if it is," he warned, "I will seek you out and finish what I have started."

He let go of Fenton, and the man sank to his knees, holding his throat with both hands, gasping for air.

Denbigh bent to retrieve the sword Fenton had dropped, momentarily taking his eyes off the man.

"Lion, look out!" Charlotte cried.

Fenton slammed a fist-sized stone down as hard as he could against Denbigh's temple.

There was no way Lion could avoid the blow. Charlotte saw the startled look in his eyes before he crumpled to the ground.

Charlotte grabbed for the sword at the same time as Fenton, but he had to go over Lion's body to get to it, and she was there first.

Charlotte could not hold on to both her modesty and the surprisingly heavy sword at the same time. She let go of the silk clutched against her breast and extended the sword protectively in front of her with both hands. "Get out of here! Go! Or I'll thrust this through your heart."

"Give that to me, Lady Charlotte. We both know you won't use it," Fenton said confidently, as he leered at her near-nakedness. "Then, because you owe it to me, I will take that kiss you have been teasing me with since you first came running after me."

Charlotte did not waste time threatening him. She simply stabbed with all her strength at the center of his chest.

At the last instant he leaped aside, and the sword caught him in the shoulder instead of the heart. She knew, from her experience with the pitchfork in Denbigh's thigh, the strength it took to pull metal from flesh. She yanked hard to free the blade, in case Fenton had not gotten the point, and she needed to make it again.

She would not be trifled with. And she wanted him gone.

Fenton took the hint. "Leave be, Lady Charlotte. I yield the field of honor to you." He gave her a lopsided bow while stuffing a handkerchief against the wound in his shoulder.

Charlotte followed him with the point of the sword as he circled around her. She stood vigilant until she was certain he was far enough down the path that he wasn't coming back, then dropped to her knees beside Denbigh.

She lifted his head into her lap and brushed the dark hair away from the bruised spot on the side of his head.

"Oh, my darling," she murmured against his face. "Please be well. Please be all right."

"I'm fine, Charlotte," Denbigh mumbled.

Charlotte wondered for a mortified moment if he had heard the endearment she had used. It was bad enough loving him when he did not love her back, without letting him in on the secret.

"Where's Fenton?" he asked in a groggy voice.

If he had heard her words, she thought ruefully, they had not made much of an impression.

"Fenton ran away," she said.

He put a hand to his temple and hissed as he touched the raw skin and the growing lump. "I don't believe I was stupid enough to fall for that trick." He tried to turn his head in her direction, groaned, and lay still. "Are you all right?" he asked. "Fenton did not say or do anything to offend you after he knocked me out, did he?"

"Not after I picked up his sword and stabbed him with it," Charlotte said.

His brow furrowed, as though, with the blow to his head, he thought his ears might be deceiving him, and confirmed, "You *stabbed* him?"

Charlotte nodded. She was expecting praise for

a job well done. Or at least sympathy for the awfulness of having to do something that made her sick to her stomach.

Denbigh heaved a long-suffering sigh and said, "Charlotte, ladies don't—"

"Don't what?" Charlotte demanded, disappointed at his critical response.

"Engage in sword fights with gentlemen," Denbigh finished.

Charlotte remained silent during the lecture that followed, but she was not listening to it—except to note that every word out of Denbigh's mouth made it clear that all these weeks she had spent with him had not made one whit of difference in his understanding of who and what she was. He still refused to accept anything less from her than the behavior of that paragon of English ladyhood he would like her to become.

When she began listening again, she heard him say, "A real lady would have appealed to Sir Fenton's sense of decency. She would have—"

"A *real* lady would have ended up getting mauled!" Charlotte snapped.

Her angry voice brought his head whipping over in her direction with a grunt of pain. He looked twice, as though he did not believe his eyes any better than he had trusted his ears.

"Cover yourself, Charlotte," he said through tight jaws.

Charlotte looked down and realized her naked breast was pressed practically against his cheek. She let the sword fall—she had not even realized she was still holding it—and rearranged the slippery fabric to cover herself.

Denbigh rolled onto his knees and rose to his feet, where he stood wavering, obviously dizzy.

Charlotte moved in his direction, as though to help support him, and he stuck out a hand to keep her away.

"Don't come near me."

Charlotte gripped the fabric tighter against her chest, holding on to the pieces of her broken heart.

"I cannot believe you actually attacked a gentlemen of the *ton* with a sword," Denbigh said. "We will be lucky if the story of this does not ruin you."

"I attacked him because he threatened to attack me," Charlotte said. "Doesn't that count for anything?"

"I was here to protect you."

"You were knocked senseless!"

He ignored that truth and continued, "What did you hope to accomplish by meeting with Fenton in a darkened walkway?"

"I was searching for proof that Lady Alice did not willingly betray you," she said.

"From Sir Fenton?" he asked incredulously. "Of all the cork-brained, buffle-headed—"

"I am not finished!" she said, cutting him off

furiously. "I wanted proof that Alice did not willingly betray you, so you would be able to believe in love again. I entertained the misbegotten hope that if you could ever learn to love again, you might love me."

"Charlotte, I—"

"I no longer care whether you believe in Lady Alice's fidelity or not. You may wallow in self-pity and bitterness for the rest of your life, if you want to. I'm not going to waste any more of my time trying to heal your heart. Because I know now it would make no difference. You will never be able to accept me for who I am."

His face muscles had tightened until the skin was stretched taut over the bones. "It is time we returned to the supper box, Charlotte," he said. "Percy and Olivia will be wondering where we are."

Charlotte was used to Denbigh's disapproval. The look on his face now was more than that. She felt her nose begin to burn and the first sting of tears in her eyes.

He reached out to take her arm, and she jerked free of his grasp. "I was not done speaking," she said in a voice that was sharp because she was fighting hysteria.

"Our false engagement is at an end. I no longer wish even to pretend an alliance with you. I want the world to know I am looking for a husband. I want the world to know I have rejected you."

She did not wait for him to reach for her again. She ran. When she looked back, he was not following her.

14

 LION TRIED RUNNING AFTER CHARlotte but took two steps and nearly blacked out. He grabbed hold of a branch at the edge of the gravel path and held on until the stars disappeared and he could focus again. His head still was not on straight after that blow Fenton had given him. And he was losing blood at a slow drip from the small wound on his arm. He should have killed the man when he had the chance.

Since there was no dead body in the vicinity, he had to assume Charlotte had not finished the job for him. Though she had apparently tried. The girl might be bird-witted, but there was nothing henhearted about her. She had more courage than most men he knew.

If you admired what she did, why didn't you say so,

instead of lecturing her for not acting like a lady? a voice asked.

He did not like the answer he got.

Because I felt a fool for letting Fenton get the better of me. Because I was embarrassed to be rescued by a chit of seventeen.

It was easier to criticize Charlotte than it was to take the blame for something stupid he had done. While it might be a very human reaction, there was no excuse for his behavior.

He could not blame Charlotte for finding fault with him.

He could not blame her for wanting nothing more to do with him.

She had been on the mark about his feelings, as well. He *was* bitter about what had happened with Alice. And, though he would never have admitted it to another living soul, he might even have indulged in a bit of self-pity.

And he would never have let himself fall in love with her. She was right about that, too.

He was glad she had ended their make-believe engagement. Glad she intended to avoid him in the future. He had never wanted her in his life in the first place. Maybe now things could get back to normal.

He felt a queer tightness in his chest. And an unfamiliar tickle in his throat.

Life would not be the same without Charlotte

Edgerton. It would once again be peaceful . . . restful . . . prosaic.

Denbigh snorted derisively. He could as easily substitute dull, boring, and mundane. Or bleak, dreary, and tedious. How about tiresome, insipid, and flat? Or, in a single word, empty.

Before Charlotte, there had been nothing to live for. She had ended his desolation, filled up his barren days, and challenged him to reach out and grab for life, rather than let it pass him by. Without her . . .

He suddenly realized he did not want to contemplate life without her. What he found even more unimaginable was the thought of some other man touching Charlotte. Kissing her. Holding her. *Making love to her.*

His neck hairs rose, and his body went taut. His hands bunched into fists. He would kill him. He would kill the man who touched Charlotte.

Denbigh looked around and realized he was ready to kill a phantom. Sheepishly, he uncurled his fists. Charlotte would have to marry somebody. He could not imagine her without children. Charlotte would love having children.

He could and would protect her from any gentleman without honorable intentions. But he would have to give her up when the right man came along. Surely someone would.

The man who saddled himself with Charlotte

would have to understand that she needed a firm hand. Not too firm. A tight rein would only make Charlotte fight the bit. A gentle, temperate hand would be better. In moments when one was feeling truly daring, one might give Charlotte her head and see dash and sparkle. Radiance and heat. Rapture and joy.

And Charlotte needed a man who loved her. Someone who would think of ways to make her happy. Someone who would put her needs before his own.

Charlotte needed him.

There was no one else, Denbigh realized. No one else would be able to love her the way he could. Or give her the freedom she needed to run full out, with only a guiding hand to keep her from jumping fences without looking first to make sure there was no dangerous hay rake on the other side.

Lion put a hand to his temple. Maybe Fenton had hit him harder than he had thought. What was he thinking?

Charlotte hated his guts. Charlotte wanted nothing more to do with him. He would never get her to marry him now.

Assuming he wanted to get married. And could manage to stand in front of another altar waiting for another bride to make her appearance. Knowing Charlotte, she would stop on the way to church to rescue some carter's horse from too great a load of beer kegs, and he would be left standing alone again.

Such speculation was moot until he could convince Charlotte that he could accept her the way she was without wanting to change her.

It wasn't going to be easy.

But he didn't have any choice. He needed her as much as she needed him. All he had to do was figure out a way to get the stubborn minx back.

He had better return to the supper box before she did something crazy like . . . Charlotte could do anything. He preferred not to imagine the worst. He would simply hope for the best. He tied a handkerchief around his wounded arm, slipped his domino back on, and arranged his mask so he would not appear conspicuous when he arrived back at the supper box.

He had not gone very far when Percy literally ran into him. "Lion, is that you?"

"Who were you expecting?"

"I ran into someone dressed exactly like you, and when I told him Olivia was missing, he said 'Olivia who?' and I could not believe you had forgotten your own sister, so I said 'Lady Olivia Morgan, of course,' and he said 'Oh, Denbigh's plain-faced sister,' and then I knew it was not you, so I planted him a facer for the insult to Olivia and—"

Denbigh grabbed Percy's arms to cut off the

endless recitation, though he was glad he had let Percy get to the part about socking Fenton in the nose. "Did you say Olivia is missing?"

"That's what I came to tell you," he said. "I went to get her some strawberries, but when I got back, she was gone. I thought she might have wandered away, but that doesn't sound like Olivia, does it?"

"No, it doesn't." Denbigh headed back toward the supper box where he had left Olivia with Percy hurrying along beside him. Now he had not one, but two missing women wandering the most notorious rendezvous for lovers in London.

"How long ago did you leave Olivia alone?" he asked Percy.

"Oh, a half hour at least."

Denbigh groaned. "Too long. That is too long for a young lady to be wandering unprotected at Vauxhall."

"Olivia is not wandering," Percy said.

"What makes you say that?"

"Didn't take her staff. Would have taken that if she planned to walk around. Don't you think?"

"Have you any suggestion what might have happened to her?" Denbigh asked.

"Don't like to say," Percy said.

Denbigh stopped and looked at his friend.

Percy lowered his eyes.

"What is it you know and are not telling me?"

"Didn't think about it at first, but the more I looked and didn't find her, the more it worried me."

"What worried you?"

"The gentlemen who stopped me and chatted at length when I went to get Olivia's strawberries—he is a friend of Braddock's."

Denbigh felt his blood run cold. "Do you think Braddock has her?"

Percy met his gaze and said, "Don't think she'd leave the box alone, Lion. Said she'd wait for me. Wasn't there. What do you think?"

"Braddock," he said in a flat, deadly voice. "I'll kill him this time."

Lion's eyes were focused, but his head was pounding. They had nearly reached the area where the long line of carriages were parked for those attending Vauxhall. Denbigh hoped to intercept Braddock there, if he had indeed abducted Olivia.

Percy suddenly looked around and said, "I say, old man. Where have you put Lady Charlotte? Is she lost, too?"

"Charlotte left my company in rather a hurry," Denbigh said. "If I had to guess, I'd say she probably returned to the supper box."

"Wasn't at the box when I last looked," Percy said.

"When was that?" Denbigh asked.

"Ten minutes ago."

Denbigh tried to figure how long ago Charlotte had left him, and how long it would have taken her to return to the supper box. It was possible she and Percy had simply crossed paths without seeing each other. It was also possible she had not returned to the box.

He wanted to reverse course and go look for her. But if he had to choose between searching for his sister and searching for Charlotte—and he did— at the moment Olivia was the one in greater danger. Charlotte, he was learning, could be counted on, in the ordinary course of things, to take care of herself.

Denbigh searched the doors of each carriage looking for the Braddock coat of arms. He never saw it, because the door was open. Instead he saw Olivia sitting in a carriage. And Braddock standing beside her.

Olivia saw him. Yet she made no move to escape from the carriage. What had Braddock told her? How had he coerced her into leaving with him? He must have threatened her. He must have given her no choice.

He started running toward her but forebore shouting her name, unwilling to attract unwanted attention. He felt outraged that Braddock had stolen his innocent sister. Incensed at the man's gall. And terrified for Olivia. What would Braddock do to her? He could hurt her . . . terrorize her.

He ran as fast as he could, till he was gasping for

breath and his side ached. He watched with furious impotence as Braddock entered the carriage, and it took off at a fast clip through the night.

Lion stopped and leaned forward with his hands on his thighs to catch his breath. He was dizzy again, and nauseated enough to fear he was going to cast up his accounts. He took slow, deep breaths to try and settle his stomach and clear his head.

Percy finally caught up to him, huffing and puffing. "I say, Lion," he panted. "Was that Olivia?"

"Yes. Braddock has her. I'm going after her, Percy. As soon as I can get a fast horse under me. You must do something for me first."

"Anything."

"You must find Charlotte and take her safely home for me. Tell my grandmother what has happened to Olivia, and that I have gone after Braddock to bring her home. Ask her to make up some story to tell my grandfather, so he will not worry. His heart is . . . he is not well. Will you do that for me, Percy?"

"Gladly, Lion. Only, what if I cannot find Charlotte?"

"Tell my grandmother. She will know what to do. If Charlotte has disappeared . . ."

Denbigh could not face that possibility. "Send word to me whatever you discover, Percy. I will want to know."

"I will, Lion. Where do you think Braddock will take Olivia?" he asked.

"God, I don't know!" There were a dozen places Braddock could take Olivia. Which one would he choose? "He won't take her to his town house in London, or to his ladybird's house, either. He knows I will go to both of those places."

"He can drive in any direction out of London," Percy said morosely. "How will you know which way to go?"

"A wolf returns to its den, a fox to its hole. He will go to Kent. It is where he was born and raised."

"How do you know so much about him?" Percy marveled.

"I believe in knowing my enemy," Lion said bitterly. "And I knew everything there was to know about James Somers before I killed him. I learned a great deal about his brother as a consequence. Braddock will go to the manor house in Somersville. You can send word to me at the Slaughtered Sheep. It is an inn there."

"What if you've guessed wrong?" Percy asked.

"It will make no difference. Eventually, I will find Braddock. Or he will turn up with Olivia at his side, flaunting her as his mistress. Then, I will kill him."

* * *

Charlotte had not gone directly back to the supper box. For a long time, she walked the dark byways of Vauxhall Gardens feeling numb inside. She had some decisions to make about what she wanted to do with her life, especially now that Lionel Morgan, Earl of Denbigh, was not going to be a part of it.

She came up with plenty of possibilities, but no real solutions. She needed help to escape him. And there were very few sources she thought she could rely on to come to her aid without exposing her to Denbigh. She made up her mind to approach at least one of them tonight before she went to sleep.

Assuming she could sleep.

Charlotte could not stop crying. It was a very unCharlottelike thing for her to be doing. Her nose kept running, and she knew her eyes were swollen and ugly. She was in no hurry to get back to the supper box until she could get her tears under control. She would never let Denbigh know she had cried over him.

The only reason she returned to the supper box as soon as she did was because she didn't want to worry Olivia, who she knew would be frantic when Lion returned to the supper box without her.

She was therefore surprised, when she returned to the box, to find Olivia missing. She didn't think Lion's sister had gone home, because her crooked staff was still lying on the floor of the box. But the box was empty. Where was everybody?

The answer was obvious.

Looking for her.

She stayed at the supper box, knowing they would probably return to check on whether she had come back. While she waited, she thought of all the nasty things she was going to say to Denbigh if he dared to criticize her for putting everyone to so much trouble.

In the end, only Percy returned, and with a tale almost too fantastic to be believed.

"He says I am to take you home, and tell Her Grace, the Duchess of Trent, where he has gone," he finished.

Charlotte could have argued with him, but she wanted to get home so she could think of what to do next. There had to be a way she could help Olivia. Even if it meant helping Denbigh in the process.

"Will he find Braddock?" Charlotte asked Percy, her heart in her throat.

As the carriage drew out of line and began the drive to Grosvenor Square, he shook his head. "I cannot guess whether he will or not, Lady Charlotte. He says Braddock will go to his manor in Somersville in Kent. But what if he does not? Braddock could take Lady Olivia anywhere, even to India. We might never know what happened to her."

"Surely Braddock would not do anything so

drastic as to take Livy across oceans and continents.''

''Why not? Especially if his aim is to punish Denbigh for the death of Lord James.''

''We have to find out where Braddock has gone,'' Charlotte said.

''How are we going to do that?'' Percy said. ''Braddock is not telling.''

''Maybe not. But his servants will know.''

''What?''

''His servants. Servants know everything. You English treat them as though they don't exist, even though they are right there when you say the most personal things. As though they did not have eyes and ears to see and hear and tongues to speak again what was spoken in their presence.''

Percy looked at her goggle-eyed. ''My valet——''

''Knows where you are tonight, where you were last night, and most likely where you are going tomorrow night,'' Charlotte said.

Percy looked sheepish. ''It is true, Lady Charlotte. Maybe there is something to what you say. And we have a way to contact Lion with whatever news we discover. I am to send any messages to him at the Slaughtered Sheep in Somersville.

''When I set you down in Grosvenor Square, I will go directly to Braddock's town house and——''

''I'll go with you,'' Charlotte said.

''Lady Charlotte——''

"Don't try to talk me out of it," Charlotte said. "My mind is made up."

She nearly laughed at the woeful look on Percy's face as he said, "Lion will kill me for allowing it."

"Lion will thank you for saving Olivia," Charlotte countered.

Percy's face brightened. "I will be a hero."

"Yes, you will," Charlotte agreed.

"I have never been a hero. It will be a novel experience. *Percy to the rescue.* I rather like it," he said with a smile.

As they were both soon to discover, although Braddock's servants very likely knew all there was to know about his movements, they very definitely were not talking.

"That butler was almost rude to me," Percy said when they were seated again in Denbigh's carriage.

"It cannot be such a dead end as it looks. There must be some way to get them to tell us what they know," Charlotte mused.

"Draw and quarter them," Percy said. "Put them on the rack. Give them twenty lashes."

"Spoken like a true hero," Charlotte said sardonically.

"I have never been one. And I wanted to be," Percy said, obviously disappointed that they had not succeeded in discovering Braddock's direction.

They arrived at the Duke of Trent's town house

not much later, and Charlotte said, "Don't despair, Percy. You have been something very like a hero tonight."

"What is that?" Percy asked.

"A good friend."

"Thank you, Lady Charlotte. Don't know why Denbigh doesn't marry you. Always a kind word. Pretty. Plump in the pocket." He flushed. "None of my business," he said quickly.

"Good night, Percy," Charlotte said with a kind smile, letting herself out of the carriage without waiting for him to hand her down. "Keep your eyes and ears open. Maybe you will discover some information that may be valuable."

"Wait!" Percy said. "I am supposed to tell Her Grace—"

"I will tell the duchess what has happened. Thank you for bringing me home, Percy," she said. "I know Lion would thank you himself if he were here. And Percy,"

"Yes, Lady Charlotte?"

"If we are going to be friends, you will have to call me Charlie."

"Denbigh would not like it," Percy replied.

In a soft, plaintive voice she said, "I would, Percy. And like the servants, though Denbigh may wish he could ignore me, I am still here, with eyes and ears and a tongue . . . and a will to be your friend."

"I see what you mean," Percy said. "Good night, Charlie."

"Good night, Percy." Charlotte turned and hurried up the stairs.

15

CHARLOTTE KNEW EXACTLY WHERE TO go to find the Duchess of Trent. Lion's grandmother was an unapologetic blue-stocking. Charlotte found her curled up in front of the fire in the library with a copy of the *Life of Nelson* by Robert Southey.

Charlotte had the fleeting thought that when the duchess was finished with the book she would loan it to Percy, so he could vicariously enjoy the exploits of a true British hero.

"Good evening, madam," Charlotte said.

The duchess pulled off her reading spectacles and focused her eyes on Charlotte's face. "You have been crying. What has that scapegrace grandson of mine done now?"

Charlotte dropped onto the footstool at the

duchess's feet and said, "Braddock has stolen Livy."

"Dear God," the duchess said. "And Lion?"

"He has gone after them. He wanted you to know what had happened, and for you to tell the duke what you thought his heart would be able to bear."

The duchess said nothing for a few moments, merely watched her shift uncomfortably on the stool, then asked, "What has you so upset, Charlie? Is it Livy? Or is it something else?"

"Lion and I have parted ways."

"What, exactly, does that mean?" the duchess asked.

"I have cried off our engagement. An announcement will need to be sent to the *Times*."

"Not right away, I hope," the duchess said. "At least not before Livy is safely home."

Charlotte frowned.

"It will draw too much attention in our direction," the duchess explained, "and require uncomfortable answers when callers arrive, and we have no explanation for Livy's absence."

"I see," Charlotte said. "I thought you might be hoping to talk me out of giving him up."

The duchess was quiet again. "You know your own mind, dear. If you no longer love Lion—"

"I never said that!" Charlotte protested. "It is only that *he* does not love *me*."

The duchess sighed and set her spectacles down on her book. She brushed aside a few wispy curls that had fallen onto Charlotte's forehead. "I have never told you why I did not marry your father, have I?"

Charlotte shook her head.

"Perhaps it is time," the duchess said. "Or maybe past time," she murmured. "Your father, Montgomery, and I were once much like you and Lion. I was younger than him, and Monty thought he knew what was best for me. I was a strong-headed chit determined to do things my own way. Monty always insisted on taking the lead and making the decisions."

"Then you know how frustrating it is!" Charlotte said.

"Oh, my, yes," the duchess said. "We brangled and wrangled and fought. What we never did was compromise."

"Compromise?"

"We did not yield a jot to one another. I insisted on my own way. He insisted on his. Then Arthur came along."

"And he let you have your own way?"

"In everything," the duchess said.

"And you liked that better?"

"At the time I did. I broke off with your father and got engaged to Arthur."

"And have lived happily ever after," Charlotte

said, a frown furrowing her brow. "Are you saying I will find someone besides Lion who will make me happy?"

"No, no. You are missing the whole point of the story," the duchess said. "I have learned in the many, many years since I married Arthur, that while it is pleasant to have one's own way without argument, life is not nearly so interesting that way. And while I love Arthur, I was never *in love* with him.

"I have never experienced with Arthur the passion I shared with your father. It remained a passion of the heart, since we never had the opportunity to share our bodies. The one great regret of my life is that I did not know enough to recognize the other half of myself before he took himself halfway around the world and married another woman."

"My mother," Charlotte breathed.

The duchess nodded. "Once Monty was married, I married Arthur. I have been content, my dear. I have been happy. But there is an empty place inside me that was never filled. And now, never will be.

"If you love Lion as I loved your father, if he is the other half of you, then you must find a way to yield to him what you can yield."

"But he wants to change me into someone else entirely. I cannot, madam. I cannot be what he wants me to be!"

"Then I'm sorry, child," the duchess said. "For both of you."

Charlotte stared at the duchess with stark eyes. She felt a sob building in her throat, and fled the room, rather than shed hopeless tears over Lion in the presence of his grandmother.

She ran up the stairs two at a time, not caring who saw her, and several of the servants did. She raced down the hall to her room and shut the door behind her and threw herself on the bed, pressing her face against the coverlet to drown the sounds of despair she was making.

Lion *was* the other half of her. But she could not give up the essence of herself, even to be with him. If he made her into someone else, the two halves that should have fit together, his and hers, no longer would.

"Charlie?"

When Charlotte first heard the female voice, she thought for one brief second it was Olivia. She shoved herself up off the bed and saw—Sally.

"Hello, Sally," she said, turning her face away to hide her tears.

"Stiles had the housekeeper come find me," Sally said. "He's worried about you, Charlie."

"Tell him I'm fine, Sally."

"But you aren't," Sally pointed out.

"There's no help for it," Charlotte said, putting her hand to her mouth to stifle another sob.

Sally sat her six-months' bulk beside Charlotte and put her arm around Charlotte's shoulder. "There, there," she said. "Tell Sally all about it."

Sally's face was so sympathetic, and Charlotte felt so awful, that everything came tumbling out. How she had fallen in love with Lion, but he could not love her because of what had happened with Lady Alice. How she had tried to find out the truth about Alice and failed. How the duchess had said if Denbigh was the other half of her she would never be happy without him. And how their love was doomed because he could not change, and she would not.

"Oh, dear. Oh, my," Sally said.

When Charlotte looked up, having said most of her speech with her face against Sally's ample bosom, she saw that her maid's brown eyes were drenched with tears. "I'm sorry, Sally. I've made you cry, too."

"I don't care if it is a sin," Sally said. "And I cannot believe that God will not understand why I have to tell."

"What are you talking about?" Charlotte said.

"Lady Alice's secret," Sally said. "I have to tell you."

"But, Sally—"

"She was raped," Sally said. "There I've said it. It's too late to take it back."

Charlotte gasped. "How horrible!"

"The earl never knew," Sally continued. "Lady Alice kept it a secret from him. Lord James came into her room one night at a house party they both attended. He was drunk and thought he was in a room with some other lady who had invited him to come to her. When he had used Lady Alice and lay snoring on top of her, she called to me in the next room to come and help remove him.

"She did not say anything to anyone at the time, because she knew it would cause a scandal. She felt guilty about deceiving the earl, but she loved him and wanted to marry him. Then she found out she was carrying Lord James's child."

"That poor girl," Charlotte said.

"She went to Lord James and told him what had happened, but he had no memory of the incident, and he would not marry her. Lady Alice was desperate, but she didn't know what to do. She tried to go through with the marriage, hoping that the earl would understand on their wedding night when she explained everything to him.

"In the end she could not do it. What if the child was a boy? The earl would have to raise Lord James's son as his heir. So she wrote the earl a note, drank a whole bottle of laudanum and waited to die.

"Then she had second thoughts about the note. She read it aloud to me once, when the drugs began to take effect, so I heard the whole of it. She was afraid the earl would challenge Lord James to a duel, and that Denbigh might be shot because of her. She did not want that to happen. So she asked me to burn the note.

"I threw it onto the fire, but it was not entirely burnt, and the earl found the remnants of it. The bottom of the note, where she wrote to him about the rape, was missing."

"Oh, Sally. Lion surely must believe in Alice's love once he hears this story. I can never repay you for risking your immortal soul to tell me such a secret."

"Surely God will understand," Sally said.

Charlotte smiled at her through her tears. "Now all I have to do is figure out a way to get the servants in Braddock's household, who have turned out to be surprisingly loyal and closemouthed, to tell me where the duke has taken Lady Olivia."

"That's easy," Sally said. "I'll ask Rufus, one of the duke's footmen. He'll tell me."

"Why would he do that?"

"We're walking out together. Rufus is willing to marry me even as I am. He says the baby's mine and he loves me, so he'll love the baby, too."

Charlotte gave Sally a hug. "I'm so happy for you, Sally. Are you sure it won't endanger Rufus's position if he tells me where the duke has gone?"

"Oh, I'm not worried. If Rufus is let go, I'm sure you'll find him another place."

Charlotte laughed. "And so I will! Can you

make arrangements to see him first thing tomorrow morning?''

"I'll do even better," Sally said with a twinkle in her eye. "Rufus and I are sneaking out to meet each other later tonight."

Charlotte didn't waste the time while Sally was meeting with Rufus. She sought out Stiles and asked, "Do you know someone who can lend me a pair of breeches that will fit me?"

Stiles kept his face impassive. "Breeches, Charlie? Did I hear you correctly?"

She grinned. "You heard me fine. I thought the underfootman was about my size," she said. "Would you ask him to give them to Clementine, the maid-of-all-work? Have her bring them up to me in fifteen minutes, if you can manage it."

"I will do my best, Charlie," Stiles said.

The breeches were there in ten, and Charlotte was dressed in thirteen, having importuned the earl's valet, Theobald, to loan her a shirt from Denbigh's cupboard.

"A starched shirt?" Theobald inquired.

"Without starch would be more comfortable," she said.

"Very well." Theobald had gone to a different drawer and found a soft, mended shirt that was many sizes too big for her.

"He refuses to throw it away," he said. "But his lordship will not mind if you borrow it."

"Why won't he throw it away?" she asked.

"He was wearing it when he proposed to Lady Alice." Theobald paused and added, "And on the day he dueled with Lord James."

Charlotte fingered the darned spot on one shoulder. "What happened here?" she asked.

"That is where the bullet passed through."

Charlotte started and stared. "But Lord James missed!"

Theobald shook his head. "The earl did not want anyone to know. He went to the country and stayed until the wound was healed. Do you still want to wear it?"

She had taken it and folded up the arms and tucked in the tails and felt closer to Lion because of it. This shirt was going to know one more very special moment in his life. Only this one was going to be happy, if she had anything to say about it.

She paced her bedroom in her riding half-boots, waiting for word from Sally. At last she heard a knock on her door and opened it to let her maid inside.

"What did you find out?" she asked.

"He's taking her to his manor in Somersville," Sally said.

"That's where Denbigh is traveling!" Charlotte said. "He guessed that was where the duke would go. I've got to get there before Denbigh confronts the duke and tell him what I've learned about the reason Alice refused to marry him."

"There's something else you should know."

"What?" Charlotte said, fearing the worst.

Sally grinned. "The duke procured a special license the day before he left."

A special license was necessary for anyone who wished to marry without the banns being read. With a special license, the duke could wed Livy any time he wanted.

"He wants to marry her?" Charlotte marveled. "I can hardly believe it! Then why did he steal her away?"

"Because he didn't think her brother would allow the marriage," Sally said.

"Is there anything you did not find out?" Charlotte asked, shaking her head in disbelief.

"I suppose there must be. But since I did not find it out, I don't know what it was. I guess you will have to discover those things for yourself."

Charlotte laughed at Sally's ridiculous chatter. She felt almost carefree. She knew where Olivia was, and that there was a good chance Braddock had honorable intentions. She had the information she needed to give Denbigh a reason to believe in love again. She had the benefit of the Duchess of Trent's experience with her one true love. And last, but not least, Charlotte had the skill and determination to ride horseback through the night to catch up to

Denbigh, and the fortitude and pluck to make him listen to her when she got there.

"Oh, I did think to ask one more thing of Rufus," Sally said.

"What was that?"

"Directions how to get to Somersville," Sally said.

Charlotte smiled. "Thanks, Sally."

To Charlotte's relief, Somersville was no more than three hours southeast of London. She didn't have a terribly long ride ahead of her. And she would be able to make good speed riding astride. On the other hand, the proximity of the duke's manor to London meant that Denbigh would probably confront Braddock long before she got there.

Unless something happened to delay the duke, or her information was wrong, and Braddock never arrived at his manor in Kent. But that was wishful thinking.

She had better prepare herself for the more grim reality of what was going to happen when Denbigh caught up to the Duke of Braddock and be ready to comfort Olivia.

Or be comforted by her.

Lion was sitting in a private dining room at the Slaughtered Sheep, the expected letter from Percy in hand. He had already been to Somersville Manor and been told the duke was not in residence. Lion had not been satisfied until he checked the stable for the duke's London coach. When he saw it was not there, he believed the servants who had politely, but firmly, turned him away.

Percy had been right. For all Lion knew, the duke could be on his way to the continent with Olivia, while he was on a wild goose chase across England.

He had been perplexed by the last few lines of Percy's letter.

Lady Charlotte was waiting at the box when I returned. She had been crying. I took her home as you requested. I like her, Lion. Why don't you marry her?

A commotion in the main taproom distracted him from his contemplation of Percy's query. The noise seemed to get louder with time, rather than settling down. He had been thinking about taking a room at the inn for the rest of the night—little though there was of it—but if there was a brawl going on, maybe he would do better to stay somewhere else.

He opened the door, took one look and roared, "Charlotte! What are you doing here? And in breeches?"

Charlotte stared at him, a broom extended overhead. His roar so startled the man who had apparently been bothering her that he also froze—long enough for Charlotte to recover from her surprise and complete the arc of the broom.

The man lost his balance and bent over to try and get it back, at which point Charlotte gave him a sideways smack with the broom that sent him hurtling out through an open window. He could be heard screaming as he fell.

Then all was silent.

"Hello, Lion," Charlotte said, setting the broom back beside the fireplace.

Denbigh didn't answer. He was busy staring at her.

She was wearing breeches again, giving him an excellent view of her legs and hips, and he realized suddenly that through all the weeks she had worn a dress, he had always been aware of what she looked like underneath it.

No wonder he had always been so irritable when she was around. He had spent half the time in a state of semi-arousal. And the rest of the time fully aroused.

It took him a moment to recognize the shirt as one of his, and to realize that she had never looked more enticing to him than now.

The proprietor came into the taproom and said, "Begging your pardon, my lord, but will you require a room for the night?"

"Two rooms," Denbigh said. "One for myself and one for the lady."

The innkeeper took a second incredulous look when he realized Charlotte was not a boy. "We don't allow queer goings on," he said eyeing the two of them.

Denbigh handed the man a gold coin. "We require two rooms," he repeated.

"Top of the stairs," the innkeeper said, "and the room next to it. Door connects the two. Locks from both sides, if that's your pleasure. Or leave it open."

"Thank you," Denbigh said in a chilly voice.

"I'll be goin' off to bed now."

"Good night," Denbigh said. He waited until the innkeeper had left, took Charlotte by the arm and hauled her up the stairs. He shoved her inside the first room the innkeeper had offered him and closed the door behind him.

He walked through the open connecting door and checked to make sure the other room was empty. He then walked out to the hall, locked the door from the outside, and stalked back into the other room. He found Charlotte standing exactly where he had left her beside the brass-railed bed.

"What are you doing here?" he demanded. "And why are you dressed like that?"

"I came to keep you from killing Braddock.

And breeches were the only way I could ride astride.''

Denbigh groaned. ''You rode all the way from London dressed like that?''

''It was dark. Nobody saw me.''

''Did you bring any baggage? A change of clothes?''

She shook her head. ''It never occurred to me. Did you?''

He had to admit he was also without the barest necessities. He had known if he went home to pack Theobald would insist on coming with him, and he didn't want to be slowed down by his valet.

Charlotte sat on the bed and bounced up and down on it, testing the softness. It sagged woefully in the middle.

''Charlotte,'' he said in a soft voice.

''What, Lion?''

''Please sit in a chair while I am in the room.'' He was having enough trouble keeping his hands off of her. It was too much temptation seeing her on that bed.

She stared at the ladderback chair in the corner, then stretched out on the bed with her hands behind her head on the pillow and her half-boots crossed. ''I don't know about you, Lion, but I have been riding neck-or-nothing for more than three hours. Lying down is infinitely more comfortable for certain body parts than sitting up would be. If you know what I mean.''

He did.

She turned on her side and rested her head on her hand. ''I took a chance you might be here, but I didn't really expect to find you. I thought you would already have gone to Somersville Manor.''

''I have.''

She crawled down to the foot of the bed and sat back on her heels in front of him. ''Was the duke there? Was Livy?''

He shook his head. ''The servants said no, and I checked the stable and found no carriage.''

A deep V of worry appeared on her brow. ''That's strange. I have it on good authority that the duke is bringing Olivia to his home in Somersville.''

''What authority?'' Denbigh asked.

She gave him a gamine smile. ''The duke's footman, Rufus.''

''By what magic incantation did you persuade him to speak, when Percy said the servants had refused to say a word?''

''Oh, I didn't do it, Sally did.''

''Sally?''

''Alice's maid. My new maid. You know, the one in the family way.''

''*Alice's* maid has been working in my house?'' Denbigh said in a strangled voice.

''And doing a very good job, I might add,''

Charlotte said, ignoring his look of horrified shock. "In fact, it's because of Sally that I'm here tonight. Or rather, this morning, since it is past midnight."

"Nearly dawn," he corrected.

"Hardly worth getting two rooms, if you think about it," Charlotte said. "We won't get a wink of sleep before it is time to get up again."

Denbigh knew she could not know how provocative her speech was, and he could not correct her without telling her so. He shoved the picture of her in bed with him out of his mind and said, "Why is Sally the reason you're here?"

"Because she knew the rest of the information contained in the note you found in Alice's room . . . the part that was burned away."

Denbigh stiffened. "Sally could not know what was on that note. She cannot read."

"Alice read it to her." Charlotte paused and said, "The part where she wrote that Lord James came into her room one night at a house party and mistook her for another woman and raped her."

Denbigh felt the blood leave his face. He had never suspected. Never imagined anything so horrible. Poor Alice!

Charlotte inched up onto her knees and put her hands on his shoulders. "Lady Alice didn't betray you, Lion. She loved you, just as you believed she did. She went to Lord James when she found out she was with child, but he would not marry her.

"She thought of marrying you anyway, but she didn't want you to be forced to raise another man's child as your own."

"I would not have cared!"

"Even if it were a boy? Even if some other man's child were your heir?" she asked with brutal frankness.

"Alice should have told me. She should have given me the choice." He shoved a hand through his hair and paced away toward the window.

"Would you have married her?"

He turned to face her. "I don't know what I would have done. But at least she could have gone away and had the child. She did not have to kill herself."

"Can you forgive her?"

"I don't know. From what you have told me, James Somers was guilty of more than merely seducing my bride. For the past year since I killed him, I have spent a great many hours regretting his death at such a young age. I will do so no more."

Denbigh did not know when his hands had come to rest on Charlotte's waist, but he saw they were. She had scooted closer to him on the bed, so their bodies were a mere inch apart. It would not take much to pull her close. Or to lay her down on the bed beneath him.

"Will you let Livy marry Braddock now?" Charlotte asked.

"That depends on Braddock."

"What do you mean?"

"Maybe I can forgive Alice for killing herself and forgive myself for James Somers's death. The question is whether Braddock can ever overlook the fact his future brother-in-law killed his brother."

"I see," Charlotte mused. "But if he could not, why would he have taken a special license with him when he left town with Livy?"

"Did he?" Denbigh asked, surprised.

"Oh, yes," Charlotte said. "Rufus said when the duke left, he was carrying a special license in his pocket."

"I don't know," Denbigh said. "Maybe he had not yet made up his mind what he wanted to do."

"When will we know?" Charlotte asked.

"When he shows up tomorrow morning," Denbigh said in a hollow voice. "Or when he does not."

She tightened her arms around his neck—how had they gotten there?—and laid her body against his.

"No, Charlotte," he said.

"I . . . I want to."

"To what?" he said in a harsh voice.

"Make love with you."

"Without benefit of marriage? Without any vows of love between us?"

"That can wait."

"Until when?"

"Whenever we get around to it."

Denbigh had never done anything in his life as difficult as pulling Charlotte's arms from around his neck and taking a step back from her. One look at her face, and he knew he had done the wrong thing. Again. There was no way she could understand why he did not want to make love with her here. Like this. Right now.

And though he opened his mouth to try and explain, she never gave him the chance. She clambered off the bed, ran through the connecting door and slammed it shut behind her.

The last thing he heard was the key turning in the lock behind her.

Damn and blast. Why wasn't anything ever easy with Charlotte?

16

BRADDOCK LAY BESIDE OLIVIA IN THE large, comfortable bed at his hunting box in Somersville and watched her sleep. She trusted him implicitly. He had not yet decided whether he would betray that trust.

Had he ever thought her plain? He wondered how that was possible. As they had driven away from London, her hazel eyes had become progressively more bright, until they were almost a tawny gold. Her smile had relaxed until the corners of her lips turned up like a satisfied cat's. She had sat serenely, head bowed, while he had taken the pins from her hair himself. It had cascaded in silken waves all the way to her waist.

It had not been difficult to seduce her. Once she had made the decision to come with him, she had gladly participated in whatever he asked of her in the carriage.

"Lift your arms above your head, Livy," he had said.

She arched her brows in curiosity, but did as he bid her. While she was thus defenseless, he cupped her breasts with both hands, brushing his thumbs across the crests. She closed her eyes and bit her lip to keep from crying out, but even so, she made a sound in her throat that caused his body to draw up tight with pleasure.

"Put your hands on my shoulders, Livy," he whispered in her ear.

And she had.

Of her own accord, one of her hands had sifted up into his hair, while the other traced the shape of his shoulder.

And all the while he had been pressing his lips to hers, testing their softness, and probing the closed seam of her lips with his tongue.

"Open up and let me in, Livy," he had said.

And she did.

Her mouth opened, and he thrust inside, claiming her with his lips and teeth and tongue. She moaned into his mouth, and his body surged with such pleasure that for long moments, he could not form a coherent thought.

"Undress me, Livy," he commanded her.

Her eyes went wide with surprise. Then absorption. And eventually, delight.

"I have wanted to touch you," she admitted shyly, when she had his shirt unbuttoned. She traced his ribs, and the muscles along his belly, and even played with the dark nipples that budded beneath her touch.

Reeve had never been so moved by anything in his life.

She leaned forward and pressed her lips against his skin, and he felt his heart begin to thud. She used her mouth to taste him, to caress him, to revere him.

Reeve had never known a woman could want a man as she wanted him. He should have felt triumphant.

He felt humbled. And ashamed.

He might have stopped his seduction. He might have returned her to London untouched. If she had not sent her hand downward. If she had not traced the male part of him and looked up at him and said, "What does it feel like for you to be inside a woman? I have always wondered. And what will it feel like when you are inside of me?"

He had taken his time making her ready for him. She had been nervous. And frightened. He had settled her on his lap facing him on the seat and played with her under her skirt until she was wet and slick and undulated against him when his fingers slid inside her.

Her eyes were glazed and full of joy.

"Are you sure?" he had asked. "Do you want me?" he had asked.

"Very sure," she had said. "Very much," she had said.

He had explained what he was going to do, and that it might hurt, and that she should be ready for the pain.

He saw the fear in her eyes. And the determination to endure it.

"Am I hurting you?" he asked as he pressed himself inside her slowly.

"No," she said. But she bit her lip, and tears sprang to her eyes.

In the end, it had not been possible to go slow. The membrane was too thick to be easily broken, and he was afraid if he did not do it quickly, he would not do it at all.

She cried out, and he caught the sound with his mouth, as gravity helped her slide down until she was full of him.

He held her close and very still against his body, so close he could hear the frantic, hummingbird wing-beat of her heart. And feel the tenseness of the muscles in her legs.

"Is your leg hurting you?" he asked.

"A little," she admitted.

He lifted her, and moved her knee forward until her hip was in a more comfortable position. "Better?" he asked.

He could tell from the way she relaxed against him that the pain was gone. All the pain.

He moved slowly inside her, taking his time, letting the rocking carriage do some of the work for him. He suckled her breasts, round and beautifully formed, and let her suckle him, something he had allowed no other woman to do.

But she had asked if he would like it. And he had said yes.

And he had.

He had felt her excitement and confusion as her body moved toward its climax. Felt the tension and the delight and the fear all wrapped up together. Seen the wonder in her eyes. And the gratitude.

It was the gratitude that had made him close his eyes and find her mouth with his and ravish it.

She had not minded. She had kissed him right back.

He had held her buttocks in his hands, lifting her, thrusting with his hips, and she had rocked up and down on him, searching for the pleasure he could give her.

Until he had come inside her, and she had trembled with joy and cried out his name.

"Reeve. Reeve," she rasped. "I love you. I love you."

Then she had fallen asleep in his arms.

She had been embarrassed when she woke up and discovered he was completely dressed again, while she was lying in his lap with her bodice bunched at her waist. He had smiled at her pinkened cheeks and dipped his mouth to kiss her pebbled nipples. And soon he had been inside her again.

He'd had her again when they arrived at the hunting box. And again not more than an hour ago. He had been watching her sleep ever since.

She had not demanded that he stop at the church and marry her. She had not asked when they would go see the vicar. She had not even asked where they were, and she must know this was not his home.

She had not asked anything of him, except that he love her. And let her love him.

He had told her what was necessary to get her to come with him. He had told her he wanted to marry her. He might even have said that he loved her. He could not remember. He had been a little foxed.

He had not realized he could sink so low. He had not realized he could hate so much. But he hated Denbigh, and he wanted to hurt him. Seducing Denbigh's sister had seemed the best way of avenging James's death.

But he had not counted on her loving him. Or on falling a little in love with her.

Reeve needed to decide whether he was going to marry her or leave her ruined on her brother's doorstep. And he had better do it before she awakened again.

"Reeve?"

He felt the hairs stand up on his arms in response to the sound of her voice calling his name. He could see her eyes glowing in the light from the candle burning on the nightstand. "You fell asleep," he said.

"I never dreamed it would be like this," she mused. "I dreamed it would be wonderful. But I did not know. How could I know?"

"Know what?" he asked, his voice harsh.

"What it would feel like to have a man inside me. To have you inside me."

Tell her now. Tell her quickly. Before you cannot tell her at all.

"Your brother was right, Olivia," he said.

She looked confused. "About what?"

"About me."

He waited for her to figure it out. She was bright. Smart as a whip. She shook her head slowly from side to side.

"No, Reeve. Don't do this."

"I lied, Olivia. There will be no marriage."

She was clutching the sheet against her breasts. "What are you planning to do with me?"

"We will travel this morning to Somersville

337

Manor. Where I expect your brother will be waiting for us. He will be angry, of course. And I will tell him plainly that I have ruined you and why."

"Because of James," she whispered.

"Because of James," he concurred.

"I will tell him I came to you willingly," Olivia said. "I will tell him it was my choice."

His lips flattened. She was not making it easy. She was making it harder than he could have imagined it would be. She was so courageous. And so fiercely loyal to her brother.

As he had been to his.

"Your   brother . . . James . . . Your brother . . ." She seemed to be debating whether to speak, or maybe only debating what she should say.

"What about James?" he asked.

"Nothing," she said. "It is nothing."

Reeve felt confused. He finally had revenge for James's death within his grasp. Why did he not feel more satisfaction? Why did he, instead, feel almost sick inside?

"Why aren't you more upset?" he asked. "Why aren't you furious with me for deceiving you?"

"Because I don't believe you will go through with it," she said simply. "You do love me, you know. I could not feel the way I do about you unless you had some feeling for me in return.

"And you made love with me last night. Not *to* me. *With* me," she said, emphasizing the difference. "If you had only desired revenge against my brother, you would not have loved me. You would have raped me."

He stiffened as she reached out to caress his chest as she spoke. "I know my brother. Lion would not have challenged your brother to a duel—and shot to kill—unless he had suffered a deadly insult from James. All I ask is that when you see Lion, ask him what happened between him and James. And listen to his answer.

"If you still feel compelled to challenge my brother to a duel, I won't stand in your way." Her hand stopped in the center of his chest. "But I won't stand by your side, either. Revenge is an empty, hollow thing, Reeve. I won't aid you in seeking it. You can have me or vengeance. You cannot have both."

She leaned over and pressed her lips against his in a caress that was both sensuous and loving.

He had been the seducer. But he would swear she seduced him. He had no other explanation for why he found himself making love to her yet again, when his only intention had been to inform her that he had betrayed her and begin the final leg of their journey to his home.

It was noon before they left the hunting lodge

for the one hour trip to Somersville Manor. He kept his arm around her the whole way home.

Charlotte did not know her own mind. Or perhaps it was simply that her mind had two opinions on how to deal with Denbigh. One Charlotte wanted nothing to do with her dictatorial guardian, a man who wanted to change her into someone else instead of appreciating her as she was. The other Charlotte wanted to make love with him——and had just told him so to his face. And been refused.

What had she been thinking? Charlotte sighed. She had always leaped before she looked. Denbigh had simply been smart enough to get out of the way.

She was lying on the lumpy mattress in the room connected to Denbigh's, wishing she were somewhere else. Anywhere Denbigh wasn't.

"Charlotte?" Denbigh called through the door.

"Go away."

"I want to talk to you."

"I don't want to talk to you."

"Please open the door," he said plaintively.

"No."

"Open the door, Charlotte."

That was an order, not a request.

She ignored it. What could he do? The door was locked from her side.

He pounded on the door with his fist. "Open

this door, Charlotte. I'm not going to ask nicely again.''

That was asking nicely? She sat up in bed, gauged the sturdiness of the door, and lay back down again.

A moment later she heard a distinctive thump against the door. *Denbigh's shoulder?* Followed by a muffled groan.

''That does it, Charlotte,'' Denbigh called through the door. ''Now you're in trouble.''

Not until morning, she thought. *That door is staying locked until dawn.*

Unfortunately, she could not sleep. She was worried about Livy. And about what Denbigh would do when he met Braddock. Which is when she came up with her brilliant idea.

She would leave the inn, go to Somersville Manor, and sneak inside to wait for Braddock and Livy to arrive. They might even show up in the middle of the night, and there she would be to greet them!

She went to the hall door and turned the knob, only to discover it was locked—from the outside. A captive again! How dare he lock her in!

She marched over to the connecting door and banged on her side of it with her fist. ''Lion? Are you there?''

''Where else would I be?''

''Why am I a prisoner in this room? Why do

you have the door to the hall locked from the outside?''

''How do you know it's locked?'' Denbigh
asked.

''Because I tried it!'' she shouted.

''Where were you going, Charlotte?''

''That does not concern you.''

''If you were trying to leave in the middle of the
night, I think that is my concern. A young woman of
seventeen should not be gallivanting around the
countryside by herself.''

''Stubble it!'' Charlotte said.

Someone banged a shoe on the opposite wall
and shouted in a drunken voice, ''Stop the racket.
I'm tryin' to sleep.''

She went over to the wall and pounded it with
her fist and said, ''It's not polite to yell at ladies!''
She crossed back to the connecting door and said,
''Unlock the door, Lion.''

''The key is on your side,'' he replied.

''I'm not letting you in.''

''Then you're not getting out,'' he said implacably.

A knock came on the outside of Charlotte's
door. ''Who is it?'' she asked.

''The body next door, who can't sleep 'cause of
all your bangin' and clatterin','' an angry voice said.

''Oh, sir, it isn't me,'' Charlotte said in her

littlest girl voice. "It's my guardian in the next room. He's threatening to *beat* me!"

Charlotte heard Denbigh's door being pounded on.

"Open up," a voice said.

She heard the sound of irate voices and then a thump. If she was not mistaken, that was Denbigh hitting the floor!

She quickly turned the key in the lock and opened the connecting door—and came face to face with a furious man.

Beyond him, stretched out on the floor with only his stocking feet showing through the doorway, lay a big brute dressed in his smalls. Denbigh was shaking his fist painfully in front of him, and the knuckles looked scraped and raw. He closed the door on the man, locked it from the inside, and headed for Charlotte.

"What happened?" Charlotte asked.

"Someone tried to interfere between me and my ward," he said in a dangerous voice.

"Oh." Charlotte tried to slam the door between their rooms closed again, but Denbigh stuck his foot in it.

"We need to talk, Charlotte."

"I'm not speaking to you," Charlotte said, leaning her entire weight against the door to keep it closed.

Of course, it was no contest. Denbigh straightened up and the door opened wide. She retreated to the other side of the bed, her arms crossed defiantly—protectively—across her chest. "All right, say what you have to say and get out."

"It isn't that I'm not attracted to you, I am. I think that has been obvious. But you have to remember what my role is in this relationship. I'm the guardian. I'm supposed to be watching over you and protecting you from rakes and rogues and roués.

"When you tempt me like you did just now . . . it isn't as easy for me to say no as you might think."

"It isn't?" Charlotte crawled onto the bed and stopped halfway across it to sit Indian fashion and stare up into Denbigh's face. "What is it about me you find hard to resist?"

"Your freckles, for one thing," he said, reaching out a tentative finger to brush it across her nose.

She swiped it away. "Children have freckles," she said disdainfully. "What else?"

"Your hair." He sifted his fingers through the short curls, brushing them back from her forehead in what was almost a caress.

"It's too short," Charlotte said. And then, in case he hadn't noticed, "but it's growing back."

"It's soft and sleek and . . ." His hand slid into her hair to make his point, and she felt tingles down her spine.

She bobbed out of his way like a boxer in the ring and said, "What else?"

"You. In my shirt."

She looked down at the shirt. It hung on her almost like a nightshirt, it was so big. She had folded the arms up and tied the tails in a knot at her waist so her breasts created two delicate mounds in front.

He captured the long, wilted shirt points with his hands and tugged her toward him. "It makes me feel like you're wearing my skin, like you're somehow inside a part of me."

Charlotte gulped. "It's only a shirt."

One hand slipped down and he undid a button. And another. He placed his palms flat on the bed on either side of her knees, leaned forward and nudged the shirt aside with his nose, then latched on to her breast through her chemise, sucking on her nipple through the cloth.

Charlotte grabbed at his head and held him where he was. But as he bumped against her, she slid backwards. He straightened her legs out and laid himself over her on the bed, nudging her legs apart with his knees, something she realized would have been virtually impossible if she were wearing a dress. Like most girls.

But she wasn't the least bit sorry when he pressed himself against her, with only a few layers of cloth between them. Her body naturally arched upward toward his, and moments after that, she wrapped her legs around him.

He sucked on the flesh at her neck, sending a frisson of feeling scattering across her shoulders, then kissed her chin and her nose and her eyes and her cheeks, before finally finding her mouth.

Charlotte groaned.

She had not even known she wanted this. Or needed it. She loved the weight of him, the feel of his hard body next to her soft one, and his tongue inside her, mimicking the natural thrust of her hips.

"Charlie, Charlie," he murmured. "I can't stop. Make me stop. I don't want to stop," he said, his lips nibbling hungrily at hers, his hands roving voraciously over her body.

"Lion," she murmured. "Love me. Love me, please."

It must have been that word, *love,* that brought him to his senses. He came off of her as though she was a bucking horse and he had lost his seat in the saddle, his feet had come completely out of the stirrups, and he had lost his hold on the reins. He was gone.

When she opened her dazed eyes and sat up to search for him, she found him using the connecting door as a shield between them. He cleared his throat and said, "We will need what rest we can get before we confront the duke tomorrow. Good night, Charlotte."

He closed the door before she could answer him.

Charlotte was furious. She clambered off the bed and ran to the door and kicked it with her boots and hit it with her fists. "Coward!" she called through the door. "You're a coward, Lion. I'm not afraid of love, but you are. Keep running," she said angrily. "See if I care. I'll find some man who isn't afraid to love me, and you'll be sorry."

She ran for a pillow and pressed it against her mouth to keep him from hearing her sobs. She had to get out of here. She couldn't stand to be locked up in this room one more second!

Charlotte looked for another way out and spied the window. A large oak grew right outside, with a convenient limb to climb on. She quickly stuck her leg out onto the sill and began shimmying down the tree. She was grateful for the trousers that made her work easier. She supposed Denbigh would say ladies never climbed trees.

Too bad, Charlotte thought as she swung from a limb like a monkey. They didn't know what they were missing!

She went directly to the stable, saddled the large bay gelding Denbigh had provided as her mount in London, and headed down the road to Somersville Manor, which was clearly visible in the moonlight. She would be there waiting for Livy and His Grace, the Duke of Braddock, when they arrived.

Charlotte was long gone when Denbigh said through the door, "I've been thinking, Charlotte. I . . . I wanted you to know that despite the things I say, I do admire you. More than you know.

"And I admit that although I've asked you to change, I've been unwilling to try any changes myself. But I'm willing to try, Charlotte. If you are. Maybe we could . . . maybe we could each give a little.

"Charlotte? Are you hearing a word I've said? Or are you too stubborn to give an inch!"

He paced in front of the door, listening for any sound on the other side. But she wasn't budging. She was as stubborn, as mule-headed, as intransigent as she had ever accused him of being!

"Fine, Charlotte," Lion said at last. "You have it your way. And I'll have it mine. But never the twain shall meet, Charlotte. Do you hear me? Never the twain shall meet!"

It was only when he had finished his tirade that it dawned on him it was *too* quiet in the next room.

"Charlotte? Are you in there?"

Nothing.

He tried the connecting door and discovered she hadn't bothered to lock it. He did a quick search of the room with his eyes, but he didn't need a second look to tell him she was gone.

The curtains blew in through the open window. He hurried over to it and peered out.

"Charlotte!" he roared. But there was no answer.

Charlotte was long gone.

From the room next door came a thump on the wall, a raucous shout, and the plea, "I'm tryin' to sleep!"

It was hard to feel sorry for the man. Lion doubted he would ever get a full night's sleep again. Not with Charlotte around.

It was then Lion realized the truth. He was going to marry her. Oh, Lord. His life was never going to be peaceful again. That thought should have worried him more than it did.

Denbigh headed down the stairs to search for his future bride. Heaven only knew what trouble she was up to now.

17

THE SUN WAS SLIPPING OVER THE HILL-side on its way to the sky when Charlotte knocked on the door and introduced herself to the Somersville Manor servants as a friend of the future bride of His Grace, the Duke of Braddock.

"I didn't know His Grace was getting married," the butler, Grimes, said.

"Oh, yes," Charlotte replied. "To Lady Olivia Morgan, the Earl of Denbigh's sister."

The butler's bushy eyebrows met with his hairline. "Did you say Denbigh? The same Denbigh that murdered the earl's brother?"

"The same who killed him, but it wasn't murder," Charlotte corrected him as she invited herself inside.

Grimes gave her breeches and man's shirt a

once over and said, "Does the bride bear any resemblance to you?"

Charlotte laughed. "Oh, my, no. She's as prim and proper as can be. Though she does have a slight limp. It does not keep her from most activities, and it will not keep her from bearing the duke an heir."

The butler nodded approvingly. The housekeeper, Mrs. Wilson, appeared, wiping her hands on her apron and said, "I hear you're a friend of the duke's bride. I'm glad to meet you, my lady."

Mrs. Wilson began a curtsy, and Charlotte stopped her. "Oh, no, you mustn't bow to me. I'm plain Charlotte Edgerton, from America." Charlotte held out her hand to be clasped. "It's good to meet you, Mrs. Wilson."

Thus it was that, by the time Denbigh arrived at the duke's front door, Charlotte and most of the staff of Somersville Manor—except for the underfootman, who was home with the measles, and the cook's helper, who had gone to take care of her sick mother—were fast friends.

"Good day, milord," Grimes said as he greeted the Earl of Denbigh with a stoic face. He reached out to take the earl's hat and gloves, but there were none.

"Traveling light," the earl explained. "Has Braddock arrived?"

"Not yet," Grimes said. Then, under his

breath, "But stab me if the fat doesn't fall in the fire when he gets here."

Because the servants did not know what to do with them, and there was no other family in the house to entertain them, Charlotte and Denbigh ended up alone together in the drawing room. For a while Charlotte managed to keep herself busy by picking up each item of bric-a-brac and examining it before setting it back down again.

Denbigh sat in a chair before a cold, ash-blackened fireplace, his crossed leg swinging, watching her like a hawk eyeing a tasty morsel it plans for dinner.

"You have already examined that ormolu clock once, Charlotte," Denbigh said.

"I want to see how it is wound," Charlotte replied.

"And that figurine has not gotten any uglier," Denbigh said, when, for the second time, she picked up a blue china shepherd playing his flute. "Come sit down beside me, Charlotte. It is time we had a talk."

Charlotte eyed him askance. "You did not have to follow me here."

"I am here to meet Braddock and Olivia," Denbigh said, as though Charlotte were not the reason he had arrived at the ungodly, not to mention unfashionably early, hour of eight for a lengthy morning call. Which, as he watched the hands move round on the ormolu clock Charlotte had been handling, was fast turning into an afternoon call, as well.

"Would you let Braddock marry Olivia if he asked you for her hand?" Charlotte asked, settling onto the stool at his feet.

"Yesterday, I would have said no. Today, I will insist upon it."

"What if Livy does not want to marry him?"

"She has no choice. Her reputation has been compromised. Braddock must make it right. Or answer to me."

"You mean you will demand satisfaction?" Charlotte said.

"I mean exactly that."

"There is an easier way to solve this coil."

"Suppose you enlighten me," Denbigh suggested.

"Tell Braddock the truth."

"Tell me what truth?"

Charlotte whirled so fast she nearly fell off the tiny stool and, in fact, Denbigh had to steady her. It was a good thing, she realized, that Denbigh had to hold on to her, because she felt an immediate and violent animosity arc between the two men. Without someone blocking their direct path to each other, there was a distinct possibility they would simply have attacked like two wolves, going for each other's throats.

"Get up, Charlotte," Denbigh said, giving her a push to get her out of his way so he could stand.

She stood, but she did not move six inches from where she was. She kept herself firmly between the two powerful adversaries. She met Olivia's gaze when she entered the drawing room and saw the other woman recognized the danger the same as she did.

"Here is your sister, Denbigh," Braddock said, thrusting Olivia in front of him. "You may have her back."

"She is your affianced wife now, Braddock. Or she will shortly be a grieving widow."

"Stop it! Both of you!" Charlotte said. "Can't you see you're upsetting Livy?"

Both men looked at Olivia, whose head hung down, and whose hands were gripped so tightly before her that her knuckles were white.

"Hold your head up, Livy," Charlotte said. "You have nothing to be ashamed of. It is these two dunderheads who ought to be hung out to dry."

"Be still, Charlotte," Denbigh warned.

"I will not!" Charlotte said. "I am as much involved in this as any of you. I am a victim, as well. Because both of you were wounded by what happened. And Livy and I will be the ones to suffer.

"Tell Braddock the truth, Lion. He deserves to

know. Otherwise, he will be killing you now and regretting it later," Charlotte said.

"What is she talking about?" Braddock asked.

Denbigh hesitated, made eye contact with a madly gesturing Charlotte, and said, "I challenged your brother to a duel to satisfy my honor, not for the frivolous reason you may have heard."

"James was a cub. What could he have done to offend you that could not be satisfied some other, less lethal way?" Braddock demanded.

"He seduced . . ." Denbigh paused, corrected himself, and continued, "He raped the woman who would have been my wife. When she found she was carrying James's child, he would not marry her. So she killed herself."

Braddock's eyes were filled with horror. "James? James could not—He would not—"

"Lady Alice left a note for me, naming the father of her child," Denbigh said. He lowered his eyes and admitted, "I did not know about the rape when I killed him. It was enough that he had seduced the woman I loved and then abandoned her."

"What proof have you of such a . . . a disturbing accusation?" Braddock asked. "Rape is . . . a heinous crime."

"You say that," Denbigh snarled, "And yet you show up with my sister after a night spent in God knows what debauchery!"

The two men surged toward each other, and

only the physical interference of the two women kept them from laying hands on each other.

"Stop it, Lion!" Charlotte cried.

"I was willing!" Olivia said. "Listen to me, Lion. Listen! *I was willing.*"

Olivia's words apparently penetrated Denbigh's consciousness, because he froze and stared at her.

Charlotte could see that Olivia spoke the truth. There was a softness about her, a glow that had not been there before her night with Braddock. And Braddock's hand on her shoulder was gentle and supportive. He had not forced her.

Whether Olivia had known when she gave herself to Braddock what he intended to say to Denbigh the next morning was another matter.

"I need proof," Braddock said. "I cannot believe what you say about James without proof."

"There is none," Denbigh said flatly. "Only a dead woman and a charred note written in her hand. Only she knows if she was telling the truth. I confess I did not challenge the truth of what she wrote. I was too enraged, too inflamed to do other than what I did.

"I can tell you this, if it is any comfort," Denbigh said. "When I confronted your brother with the truth as he lay dying, he did not deny it."

"Did he . . . did he say aught else?" Braddock asked.

Denbigh shook his head. "There was not time."

Braddock turned to Olivia, took her hands in his and gripped them tightly. To Charlotte's surprise, Olivia lifted her head and looked Braddock right in the eye.

"Did you listen, Reeve?"

"I listened, Livy. And I understand better what happened. But I do not see how I can forgive your brother."

"What if it were me, Reeve. And someone had violated me. What would you do to him?"

Charlotte watched, and saw Denbigh watching too, as the duke's neck hairs hackled. His jaw grew taut, and his arm muscles flexed.

"I would kill him," Braddock said without hesitation.

Charlotte exchanged a triumphant look with Denbigh. There was proof and more that Braddock loved Olivia. But instead of relief on Denbigh's face, she saw a stark look for which she could find no explanation.

She took a step closer to him and said, "What is wrong?"

"I am as blind as Braddock," Denbigh said.

"What do you mean?"

He looked down at her, his silvery gray eyes feral as he admitted, "If any man touched you, I would do the same as Braddock. I would kill him."

Charlotte stared at Lion wide-eyed. It was the closest he had ever come to a declaration of love. Maybe he had to grow a little more accustomed to the fact before he would be able to accept it.

She was having a little trouble accepting it herself. Not the love. She was ready for that. But Denbigh's willingness to share it with her was exciting to contemplate.

"I cannot change the past," Denbigh said to Braddock. "God knows I wish I could. For the sake of my sister's happiness, I am willing to leave it in the past, where it belongs, and go on with life. Can you do the same?" he asked Braddock.

Charlotte watched Olivia closely. Her face looked calm, almost confident. She looked up at Braddock and said, "Reeve, the choice is yours. But if I am carrying your heir—"

Braddock clamped his hand over Olivia's mouth. "I am asking for your sister's hand in marriage, Denbigh. What say you?"

"She is yours. May you have a long and fruitful life together."

The two men reached out to each other for the first time, but it was to clasp hands in peace, rather than level weapons of death.

"Have I any say in this matter?" Olivia asked archly.

"Only if what you have to say is yes," Braddock said as he turned back to her.

Olivia smiled radiantly up at him and said, "Yes, Reeve. I will be your wife."

To Charlotte's amazement, shy Livy stood on tiptoe and kissed the fearsome duke square on the lips.

The fearsome duke did not seem to mind. He smiled, wrapped his arms around her, and kissed her back.

Charlotte felt a little awkward around all that sensual celebration, because it was blatantly apparent that she and Denbigh were not joining in the fun.

"Come, Charlotte, let's take a walk in the rose garden and leave the newly affianced couple alone for a few minutes." Lion called back over his shoulder, "A few minutes only, Braddock."

Braddock grinned and said, "If you are going to be such a strict chaperon I will have to make Olivia my wife all the sooner."

"Use that special license in your pocket," Denbigh said.

Olivia pursed her lips and put her balled fists on her hips. "Why, you faker!"

Braddock flushed. "I could not make up my mind what I wanted to do with you," he admitted.

Denbigh could appreciate the feeling. When he turned to say as much to Charlotte, Charlotte was gone.

Damn and blast, could she never stay put for one moment?

He was out the French doors and headed for the rose garden a moment later, since that was where they had talked about going. Besides, it was the perfect place for Charlotte, because it looked pretty and smelled sweet . . . and had thorns.

She was standing among the red roses, trying to pick one without much success.

"Let me help you with that," he said.

She turned to him, startled, and cried out when she pricked her finger on one of the thorns.

He took her hand, tenderly kissed the scratch, and felt her shiver. "Is that better?"

"Don't be nice to me, Lion. I won't be able to stand it if you're nice to me."

"Stand what, Charlotte?"

"Going away."

"Are you going away?" he asked.

She nodded. "Back to America."

"When were you planning to make this journey?" he asked, feeling a knot of tension in his gut.

"I thought I would leave as soon as I say goodbye to Olivia and Braddock and your grandmother and grandfather and Percy, and of course Stiles and Theobald and Sally and—"

"Aren't you forgetting someone, Charlotte?"

"Who?" she asked.

"Me."

"Oh, no. You see, you're going with me."

Denbigh stood stunned for a moment, then roared, "Charlotte!"

"I thought we could go for a visit so you could meet some of my friends," she cajoled him.

"Charlotte," he said, gesturing her toward him with his finger. "Come here."

"You can't keep me here in England forever, Lion. You'll have to let me go back to America sometime. It might as well be now, before we have children to bring along. Children tend to get seasick, you know."

"Charlotte," Denbigh warned.

"I've been as patient as I can be, Lion. But you are moving too slow. You might as well face it. You are never going to be free of me. You'll be wearing a pair of leg-shackles before Christmas, so you might as well give in graciously and say you will marry me."

"Charlie," he said against her lips. "I do."

"Do what?"

"Intend to marry you, baggage."

Charlotte threw herself into his arms. "I knew it!" she said. "I told Livy and Sally and Grimes and Theobald—"

"Is there anyone you did not tell?" he asked.

"Only you," she said. "I decided to let you figure it out for yourself."

"Thank you for that," he said with a wry twist of his mouth. He would gladly accept a pair of leg-shackles if Charlotte came along with them.

"There is something you have forgotten, Lion," Charlotte said as she nuzzled his neck. "Three words."

"What are they?" he asked.

"Those are not the words," she said, exasperated.

"Oh," he said. "You mean, I want you."

"Lion!"

He smiled at her and took her hands in his. "Will you marry me, Charlotte? I want you to be the mother of my children. I want to spend the rest of my life with you as my wife."

She searched his face, and he knew she was waiting for him to say those three words. He did love her. But keeping it to himself seemed safer. At least until they were securely wed.

He watched the struggle going on in her face, while she decided whether what he had said was enough.

Finally she said, "I will marry you, Lion. And I promise to do everything I can to make sure our life stays exciting and interesting and wonderful."

Lion smiled and shook his head. He believed she meant every word of what she said. He was afraid she did.

Lion could not wait for what the future had in store. Being held captive for the rest of his life by one impossibly unpredictable woman might not be such a bad thing after all.

Epilogue

 THE BRIDE WAS LATE. THE GUESTS WERE starting to whisper. Lionel Morgan, Earl of Denbigh, stood waiting near the altar of the small country church in Sussex with his best friend and groomsman, Percival Porter, Viscount Burton.

"Where is she, Percy?" Denbigh asked. "What do you suppose is causing the delay?"

"You know Charlie, Lion. She is probably headed to the church neck-or-nothing as we speak."

Lion raised a brow. "Not in breeches, I hope."

"Olivia assured me a bridal gown was delivered to Denbigh Castle yesterday," Percy said.

"That does not mean the chit will wear it."

"Be patient," Percy said. "It cannot be long now."

"I hope not," Denbigh muttered. He reached a

finger between his neck and the immaculate Waterfall his valet had created with his neck cloth that morning.

"May I be the first to wish you happy," Theobald had said, as he gave the stiffly starched material one last tuck.

"How is your sister?" Denbigh asked.

"She cannot believe her good fortune, my lord," Theobald said as he brushed a nonexistent piece of lint from Lion's shoulder. "A cottage of her own. It is more than she ever dreamed."

"Thank Charlotte," Denbigh said. "It was her idea."

Mrs. Tinsworthy had been in tears, her apron covering her face when he passed her in the hall. "It is a happy day, milord. I cannot wait to hear the patter of little feet."

Denbigh had felt a shiver of expectation run through him. With Charlotte as their mother, who knew what imps and minxes might soon be galloping up and down the halls of Denbigh Castle.

He could not wait, either.

A commotion in the church vestry attracted Denbigh's attention. Heads swiveled in the congregation to see what was amiss. Charlotte had invited everyone. Lords and ladies sat beside footmen and cook's helpers.

When Denbigh had pointed out that English nobility and their servants did not usually mingle socially, Charlotte had replied, "I want my friends around me, Lion. And Galbraith is as much my friend as Lady Hornby."

Since Denbigh liked Galbraith a great deal more than Lady Hornby, he did not argue further.

It took Denbigh only a moment to recognize his grandfather and grandmother, the Duke and Duchess of Trent, entering the church.

Charlotte was not with them.

The duke stomped his way down the aisle to Denbigh, using the duchess's arm and his hickory cane to support him.

Denbigh's heart was pounding. "Where is she?" he asked the moment they reached him.

"The silly chit is out in front of the church. She says she will not marry you until she can speak with you privately."

Denbigh had heard *she will not marry you* and only barely caught the last of the duke's message. "What? She wants to talk? About what?"

"I think you had better speak with her, Lion," his grandmother said.

Denbigh ignored the interested, curious looks from those in the congregation as he marched down the aisle. Everyone in attendance knew enough about Charlotte to understand that nothing was ever certain when she was involved. His heart was in his throat as he stepped out the front door of the church into the summer sunshine.

Charlotte was not there.

He felt an instant of panic, followed by irritation and relief when he saw her standing in the shadows of a nearby oak. At least she was wearing a dress, he thought, as he strode toward her. And a very pretty one at that—a light shade of green, with small capped sleeves, a square neck, and a delicate ribbon tied under her breasts.

There was no question in his mind of whether the wedding was going to take place. Charlotte must wed him.

Last night they had anticipated the honeymoon.

He had not intended for it to happen. He had been careful not to be alone with Charlotte, because he knew how much he wanted her. Every time he looked at her his body got hard. He had been re- duced to walking behind the furniture every time he entered a room where she was, to hide the physical change that inevitably occurred.

Very late last night she had come knocking at his door. She had entered before he bid her to do so, closed the door behind her, and whispered, "Lion, are you awake?"

"I am now," he had said. "What are you doing in here, Charlotte?"

The chit had crossed the room in the dark and climbed right up onto the bed and crawled across it until she ran right into him. He had sat up in alarm and grabbed her arms. "What is going on, Charlotte?"

She had grabbed him around the neck and pressed her body against his and said, "Hold me, Lion. I'm scared."

His arms had gone tight around her. He slept naked, and the feel of her with only her sheer nightgown between them was exquisite. "I have you, Charlotte," he said. "Don't be afraid. I will protect you. Nothing can hurt you now."

She had clutched him tighter. "I love you, Lion," she said. "I love you more than life itself."

"I know, Charlotte," he said. "I know you do."

"Love me, Lion," she pleaded. "Love me."

She had not given him any choice. Her mouth had sought his in the darkness and her tongue had slipped into his mouth and he had been lost.

He had thought nothing Charlotte did could surprise him. But she had. Where he expected her to take the lead, she was shy. Where he expected her to hold back, she was far ahead of him.

He kissed her, he caressed her, he could not get enough of touching her. The feel of her small hands on him, on every part of him, had driven him wild.

He learned something else about her. Charlotte was a noisy lover. Not that he minded the sighs of pleasure or the groans of agonizing delight or her cries of "Do that again," or "More, please, Lion," or "That feels so good!" He was sure Charlotte had no idea a proper English wife was supposed to lie still and quiet beneath her husband. And he was not about to tell her.

He had not wanted to hurt her, and he had gone as slow as he could when he broached her. But he knew there had been pain. She had gripped his arms hard enough to leave crescent imprints of her fingernails on his skin. But when he was fully seated she had said, "I feel so full, Lion. Full of you. Inside of me. Oh, I like it."

He had, too.

She had been a generous lover, and a passionate one and, being Charlotte, a very enthusiastic one. He had been exhausted and sated and satisfied when finally she lay beside him, their bodies sweat-slick, their hearts racing, their breathing labored.

One of the hardest things he had ever done was to kiss her good-bye and escort her to the door and send her away to her own bed. Ever since, he had been looking forward to his wedding day. And his wedding night.

It seemed Charlotte was having second thoughts. Not that he was going to allow such rebellion at this point.

He felt a moment of alarm when he joined her beneath the shady oak and saw she had been crying. "Charlotte?"

When she saw him, she flung herself against

him. Charlotte never did anything halfway. He would say that for her.

His arms closed around her, and he held her tight for a moment, glad that whatever was troubling her was not something to do with him. "What's wrong?" he murmured.

"Everything."

He forced her back and tipped her chin up so he could look into her tear-bright green eyes. "Everything? That encompasses a great deal, Charlotte. Could you narrow that down? We have a whole churchful of people waiting to witness our wedding."

"I can't marry you, Lion."

At first he thought she was simply being melodramatic. As he looked down into her eyes, he realized that something was greatly amiss. "What is troubling you, Charlotte?" he asked.

"Do you love me, Lion?" she asked, searching his face as though the answer were written there.

"What?" The question startled him, coming as it seemed to, from nowhere. "I'm marrying you, brat," he said tenderly.

"Maybe not," she said, lifting her chin stubbornly.

He frowned. "What crochet has taken hold of you now, Charlotte? What is this all about?"

"Do you love me, Lion?" she asked again.

He had not said the words, he realized. He had

avoided saying them when he proposed to her. And she had let him get away with the omission. Apparently, she needed to hear them now. Or there was going to be no wedding.

He caught a tear at the corner of her eye with his knuckle and brushed it away. "I don't know why I have been so clutch-fisted with my feelings," he said. "I think I have not wanted to admit how much I care for you, Charlotte, for fear I will find myself nursing another broken heart.

"But . . ." He lowered his head and kissed her lips. "I cannot imagine life without you, Charlotte. I cannot imagine the sun shining or the birds singing or life being fun to live unless you are there to live it with me.

"I adore you, Charlie," he said, kissing her lips again. "I admire and honor you. I respect your right to be who you are."

He saw her swallow convulsively.

"But do you love me, Lion?" she asked in a whisper.

He knew now why she had come to his room last night. Why she had been so scared. Why she had pleaded, "Love me, Lion." She had not been seeking physical love. She had wanted to know if he was the other half of her, whether his soul cried out for hers, the way hers did for his. She had wanted to know the answer to the question she was asking now.

"Oh, yes, minx," he said, smiling down at her. "I do love you. Very, very much."

"Oh. Well, then we had better get inside," she said matter-of-factly, slipping her arm through his and walking with a light step toward the church. "It's getting late." She flashed him a teasing look from under lowered lashes. "The sooner we finish the wedding, the sooner we can start the honey-moon."

Inside the church, everyone exchanged grins of relief when they heard the familiar roar, "Char-lotte!"

A NOTE TO READERS

Dear Readers,

Hi! I've had a chance to meet many of you over the past ten years at writers' and fan conferences, and I want to take this opportunity to thank you, and all of you I have not yet met, for your enthusiastic support. I love writing, and it's thrilling to know so many of you are enjoying my characters and their stories.

I've written one more in the Hawk's Way series, and those of you who loved the "bride" books should keep an eye out for *The Temporary Groom*, a Man of the Month from Silhouette Desire in June. I've also written a compelling, full-length contemporary novel titled *I Promise* scheduled for publication by Avon Books in June 1996. Ask your bookseller for the exact date it will be available.

As always, I appreciate hearing your opinions and find inspiration from your questions, comments, and suggestions.

If you would like to be on my mailing list, send me a postcard with your address, or you can write to me at P.O. Box 8531, Pembroke Pines, FL 33084 and enclose a self-addressed, stamped envelope so I can reply. I personally read and answer my mail, though as some of you know, a reply might be delayed if I have a writing deadline.

Best always,
Joan Johnston

May 1996